GHOST OF A CHANCE

ERIC WILDER

PublishAmerica
Baltimore

First printing

ISBN: 1-4137-5936-X
PUBLISHED BY PUBLISHAMERICA, LLLP
www.publishamerica.com
Baltimore

Printed in the United States of America

In loving memory of
Anne Hathaway Pittenger

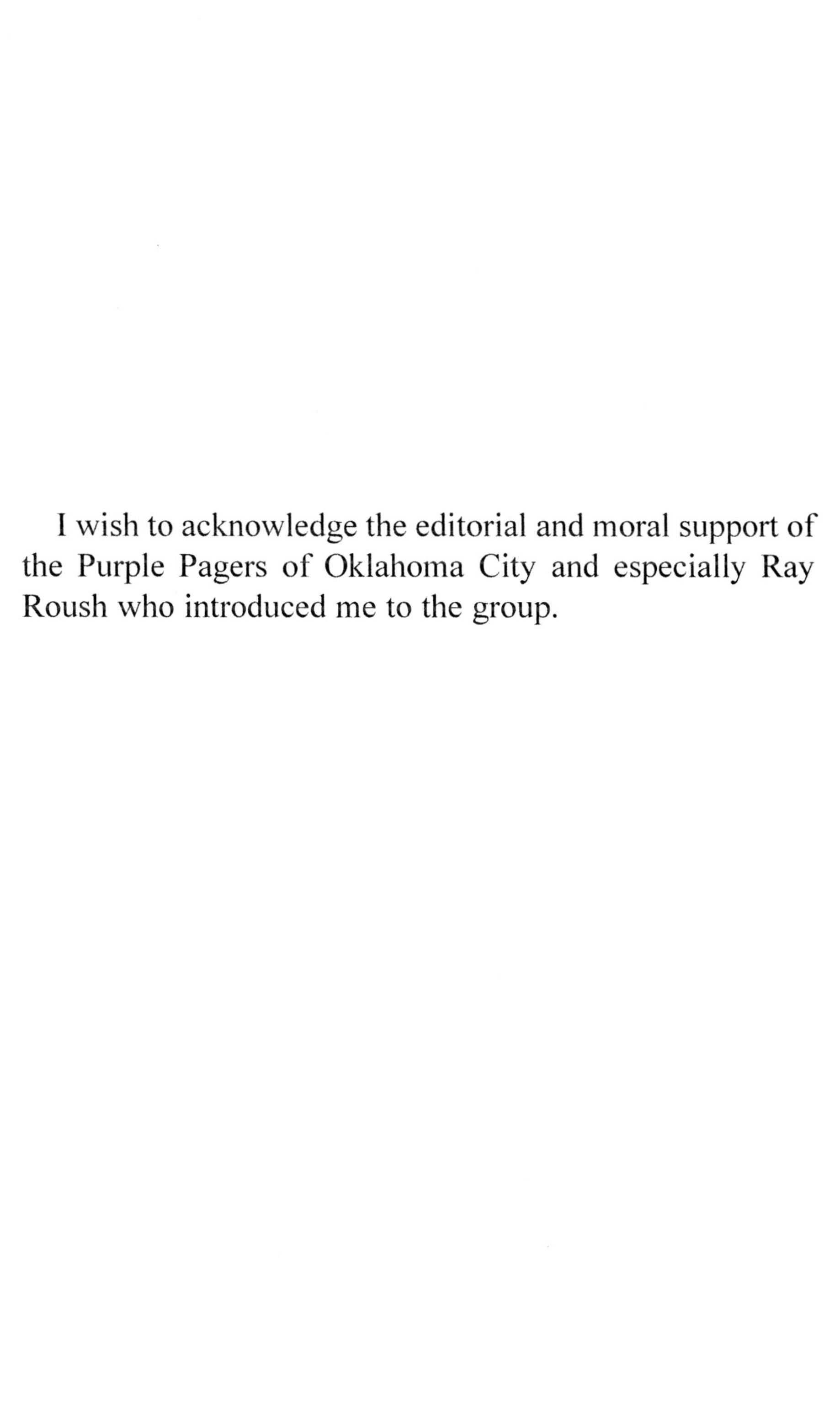

I wish to acknowledge the editorial and moral support of the Purple Pagers of Oklahoma City and especially Ray Roush who introduced me to the group.

CHAPTER ONE

Emma Fitzgerald's rocking chair creaked as she listened to a chorus of crickets holding sway down by the lake. Silent lightning snaked across the sky and angry clouds rolled in behind, toward the island. The approaching storm heightened Emma's senses, imparting a quiet portent of something about to occur.

The storm arrived with thunder booming and lazy raindrops spotting the mosquito netting draping the covered porch. Emma didn't notice, her gaze locked on a point of light far across the lake. Words from behind released her from the spell.

"Miss Emma, you'll catch your death if you don't get in this house. You know it's way past your bedtime."

"It's dry beneath the overhang and I'm not the least bit sleepy. The storm's blowing in and I'm watching that strange light out there."

Pearl Johnson opened the screen door and joined Emma Fitzgerald on the porch. She shivered when thunder rumbled the rafters, causing warm air to surge through the house. With one brown hand she shielded her eyes from some nonexistent glare and stared toward the direction Emma had pointed.

"I don't see nothing, Miss Emma."

"Then I guess you scared it away."

Pearl frowned and shook her big head. "Come on inside. You been brooding out here since dinner and it's getting late."

Emma glanced at her watch's luminous dial. "Then why are you still here?"

"Cause you're distressing me the way you're acting."

Worry lines on Emma's face softened into a smile. She raised up from the rocking chair and wrapped her rangy arms around the big woman.

"Don't fret over me. I'm too old and ornery to let anything get me down very long. Least of all a man. Now you run on home to Raymond before the bottom drops out and drenches that pretty yellow dress of yours."

"You sure?"

Emma pushed Pearl toward the door, waiting until she'd opened the screen and stepped outside. "Sure as this ol' lake's got twelve-foot alligators. Now get on home with you."

Pearl started to say something but shook her head instead and hurried down the stairs. More thunder, closer this time, shook the rafters as the large woman lumbered toward her own house on the far side of the clearing. After Pearl's backside faded into darkness, Emma settled back into the rocking chair and draped a frayed orange afghan over her knees. This time the meow of a striped kitten broke her trance.

"Tiger, you little rascal. Don't you know cats are supposed to hate rain and thunder?"

Tiger didn't seem to mind the rain, curling up in Emma's lap and closing his eyes. Pearl had gone just in time as falling water swelled into a deafening deluge. The pouring rain pooled up on the roof, finally causing a waterfall to stream from the porch overhang. Emma watched the storm as Tiger ignored it with a contented purr. Neither moved until the storm had passed, leaving behind full moonlight cloaked in misty haze. Grabbing Tiger by the scruff of his neck, Emma carried him inside and deposited him on his kitty bed beside the stove.

"Enough attention for one day, you little rascal," she said.

Tiger opened his green eyes long enough to nudge his toy mouse before returning to contented sleep.

Emma started for the stairs but stopped at the window, staring at the lake. Again she saw it. The ephemeral glow of circular light had returned, hanging just over dark water. Forgetting her feather bed, she wrapped the afghan around her shoulders and headed for the door.

The hoot of a distant owl echoed across the clearing as Emma followed the mushy path past the boat dock to the water's edge. Vapor rose off the lake's surface as she stopped beside a pile of brush and stared across the water. Rain had moved north, leaving only dancing shadows to frolic over the lake. An alligator's knotty head appeared ten feet from Emma's muddy slippers but she ignored it. The light floating toward her on a cottony mist had locked her gaze and grew brighter as it approached the bank, the surrounding mist chilling muggy air around her.

Emma's dilated eyes soon recognized the vague outline of a girl's slender body. But something was wrong. It wasn't a live girl but an apparition surrounded by veils of phosphorescence floating through the fog. Consumed by clouds fleeing the lake, Emma's sense of reality dimmed, locking her in place as the spirit girl approached. As she came ever nearer, Emma saw her translucent skin and glowing, colorless hair. Even her eyes were colorless. Emma focused on something clutched in the girl's hand.

"Help me," the spirit girl whispered.

Emma reached for her hand but succeeded only in passing her own gnarled fingers through damp mist as darkness engulfed the spirit's waning image. Emma blinked and when she opened her eyes the girl had vanished. Her hand was damp and cold but no longer empty. The object in her hand emitted an eerie pink glow when she opened her palm.

Sounds of damp earth being shoveled, along with light from a different source liberated Emma's attention away from the spirit girl's gift and the beam of a powerful flashlight overpowered its misty incandescence. Squeezing the newly acquired object still fresh in her hand, Emma decided to investigate. When she reached the slough, following a path through a thick maze of creepers and vines, murky shadows replaced moon-bright sky. She traced the vibrating thread of light through the thicket, locating its origin in a small clearing in the trees. Bracing herself against a cypress trunk, she brushed gray hair from her eyes and caught her breath. Then she saw the large hole in the ground. When a hand touched her shoulder she wheeled around, slipping in the mud as she realized who was with her in the clearing.

"You scared me half to death. I told you to get the hell off my island and never come back."

Instead of an answer, Emma caught the brunt of a shovel across the back of her head. A chorus of bullfrogs began to sing as she toppled into the mire. Miss Emma Fitzgerald never heard them.

CHAPTER TWO

Sheriff Taylor Wright stood knee-deep in shallow water, mopping his forehead with a red bandanna. Remnant humidity from last night's rain sent rivulets of sweat down his neck, providing dive-bombing mosquitoes a tempting target. Something other than mosquitoes occupied his attention as he brushed the swarming creatures away with a subconscious swat. A body, already stiff with rigor.

Sheriff Wright waited as Dave Roberts the assistant medical examiner and Deputy Sam Goodlake pulled the corpse toward shore. Raymond Johnson and his son Ray watched from the bank. When Roberts and Goodlake reached shore with the body, Raymond Johnson fell to his knees and began to sob.

"It's Emma all right," Dave Roberts said. "Been dead a good ten hours, I'd say."

Sheriff Wright pushed Raymond away from the body, turning him toward the lodge. "Ray, take your daddy back to the house. Nothing either of you can do here now. I'll be along directly to ask a few questions."

Raymond resisted the sheriff's advice but Ray took his father's elbow, gently directing him away from the lifeless body of Emma Fitzgerald. Dr. Tom Proctor, the coroner and chief medical examiner, nudged the corpse with the toe of his boot.

"Looks like Emma got herself tangled in a trotline. Maybe drowned. Her nigrahs seem mighty distraught."

"What was she doing out in the lake in the middle of a storm?" asked Sam Goodlake, the lanky deputy.

"Good question," Sheriff Wright said, bending over the body. "Anyone got an answer?"

"She's got something in her hand," Dave Roberts said, ignoring Wright's query as he struggled with Emma's frozen fingers.

Goodlake, Wright, and Proctor watched as Dave Roberts pried open Emma's hand to reveal a crusty piece of jewelry. After palming it once he handed it to the sheriff.

"What is it?" Goodlake asked, craning his long neck for a better view.

"A brooch," Dr. Proctor said. "A cameo brooch."

Sheriff Wright fingered the old brooch, caressing its alabaster edge as Dave Roberts took photos of the body and surrounding area. Something behind Emma's ear caught the sheriff's attention. Using both hands he gently canted the old woman's chin, brushing aside her salt and pepper hair to expose caked blood that had oozed from a swollen contusion on the back of her head. After a careful rotation Wright rested the old woman's head in soft earth then slipped the brooch into his khaki shirt and gave the body one last look.

"Sam, check the lakefront for evidence. I'm taking a little walk down to the lodge and question Pearl and Raymond."

Sam had already begun helping Dave Roberts stuff Emma's body into a rubber bag and didn't bother replying to Wright's request. A two-stroke motorboat engine droned across the lake, causing dozens of turtles to abandon their roosts and splash into the water. The commotion failed to interrupt Sheriff Wright's long stride.

Fitzgerald Lodge loomed in the distance about a hundred yards from the lake's edge. Backed by pine and live oak the rustic abode formed an imposing edifice, dwarfing all other structures and outbuildings on the island. The once active resort had declined in recent years to little more than a worn and neglected fishing camp for locals. Before her untimely demise, Emma Fitzgerald had planned to change all that.

Sheriff Wright recognized the woeful cry of Pearl Johnson as he entered the door and knew before he saw her how distraught she must be. He followed the whimpers to Emma's office at the end of a long hallway. There he found Pearl and Raymond Johnson with Randy Rummels, a local attorney.

"You all right, Pearl?" the sheriff asked.

Pearl wiped her mouth and nose with a paper napkin, blinking away her tears. "No sir, Sheriff, I ain't. I still can't believe Miss Emma's really dead. I should have hung around last night, knowing how blue she was."

Taylor scrawled Pearl's remark in a notebook he carried in the pocket of his western-cut khaki shirt.

"Wasn't your fault she went out in the storm."

Raymond banged the big oak desk with his formidable fist. "Miss Emma wouldn't have gone out in no storm."

"Calm yourself down. She did or she wouldn't have been out there," Sheriff Wright said. "There's one big bump on back of her head. Maybe a limb blew down in the wind and knocked her into the lake. Who saw her alive last?"

"Guess it was me," Pearl said. "I went home last night about ten. About the time the storm hit."

"What were you doing here so late?"

"Miss Emma was brooding and I didn't want to leave her alone."

Taylor Wright turned a chair around, straddled it and rested his arms on the backrest. "Brooding about what?"

"Bones Malone. They had an argument and Miss Emma told him to pack his stuff and move off the island. He left without even bothering to take his things."

Sheriff Wright digested this tidbit of information. "Come to think of it I haven't seen him around lately. Know where he is, or what they were arguing about?"

Raymond and Pearl exchanged perplexed glances. Pearl said, "Whatever it was, Miss Emma took it pretty hard."

"You think Bones is involved in Emma's death?" Wright said, removing his hat to scratch his bald spot.

"Why hell no," Raymond said, turning away from the sheriff's stare and gazing at the hardwood floor. "Maybe they had a little argument but Bones Malone loved that old lady."

"Maybe so, but you said yourself Miss Emma wouldn't have wandered down to the lake in a thunderstorm, no matter how upset she was."

"She was getting along in age," Randy Rummels said.

"Eighty," Raymond said. "And still sharp as any twenty-year-old."

Sheriff Wright tapped the back of the chair twice, reseated his hat atop his head, stood and leaned against one of the floor-to-ceiling bookshelves lining the room.

"What are you doing here, Randy?" he asked. "Smell a healthy legal fee all the way from town?"

Rummels brushed aside Sheriff Wright's professional slur without protest. "How you doing, Sheriff? Guess you know Daddy was Miss Emma's lawyer. I'm discussing her estate with Pearl and Raymond. Emma died intestate."

"You're full of shit," Raymond said. "Miss Emma's had a will for years. I saw it, and so did Pearl. You know it's true because your daddy wrote it."

Randy Rummels shook his head. "I'm Emma Fitzgerald's attorney now and I'm telling you, she never had a will."

"Your father was Miss Emma's lawyer," Pearl said.

"Well, Daddy's dead and nothing ever went on in that firm that I don't know about. Believe me, Sheriff, Emma died intestate."

Raymond's glare left no doubt of his emotional frame of mind or his feelings about Rummels' statement. "You're a liar."

"Who you calling a liar?" Rummels said, jumping to his feet and standing eyeball to eyeball with the larger black man. "You two are just trying to horn in where you don't belong."

"Wait just a minute here," Sheriff Wright said, stepping between the two men. "What difference does it make anyway?"

"Because Miss Emma's will gives us half the marina," Pearl said.

"Miss Emma couldn't run it by herself," Raymond added. "Or afford to pay much in the way of wages. She made up for it by willing us half the marina when she died."

"You're dreaming," Rummels said. "There's no record of any such transaction."

Rummels' declaration was more than Raymond could take. Clenching his hand, he lunged across the desk at the young lawyer. Sheriff Wright interceded again, this time grabbing Raymond's wrist and backing him up with a combination of arm strength and steely eye contact. Rummels sat down, apparently grateful for the sheriff's timely intervention.

"The bank has a mortgage on all Emma's real property. The island, marina and lodge, that is. With no heir and no will," he said, "Everything left in Emma's estate will be used to settle her debt at the bank. I got no ax to grind with the Johnsons here. I'd as soon they got the place as have it go to the bank."

"You're crazy as hell," Raymond said. "Miss Emma never borrowed a penny in her life. She don't owe the bank nothing."

"We have her signature to prove she does," Rummels said.

Sheriff Wright glanced at Pearl and Raymond, not letting his glimpse linger. "So what happens to Raymond and Pearl?"

"Nothing," Rummels said. "They simply vacate the premises."

"We've lived here thirty years," Pearl said. "Miss Emma sold us the house we live in and the yard around it. She filed the deed at the courthouse in Deception and left a copy in her safety deposit box."

Rummels simply shook his head. "No deed, no record of a deed, no way."

Talk of the marina had propelled Raymond into a rapidly disintegrating emotional state. Rocking side to side, he said, "We don't want a damn thing that ain't coming to us, but Miss Emma didn't intend to leave Fitzgerald Island to the Bank of Deception. Check it out at the courthouse and you'll see we ain't lying."

"Never trust a white man," Randy Rummels said with a smirk. "Or in this case, a white woman."

Sheriff Wright frowned at Rummels and pointed toward the door. "Why don't you get the hell out of here? You're just causing trouble."

"Not until I finish my business."

"It's finished," Wright said.

Randy Rummels didn't miss the angry inflection in Sheriff Wright's voice. Realizing he was already pushing his luck, he folded his portfolio and started for the door. "Fine. You straighten it out with these people."

"Watch your tone, Randy," Wright said. "These people took care of Emma for thirty years and deserve a little respect."

"The only thing they deserve is a quick trip off the island. I don't make the rules. I just see they're carried out."

By now Taylor Wright's own adrenaline was pumping. So was young Rummels'. Neither reacted immediately to Pearl's words.

"Maybe Miss Emma's heir can settle the bank debt."

Wright glanced first at Pearl, then at Rummels. "What did you say?"

"I said, Miss Emma has an heir."

"There's no indication of that," Rummels said, slamming his portfolio back on the desk top.

"Yes there is," Pearl said. "Miss Emma has a nephew in Oklahoma."

"Says who?" Rummels said.

Pearl opened the top drawer of the desk, took out an opened letter and handed it to Rummels. After removing the contents slowly, the lawyer made a big production of reading it. When he finished, Sheriff Taylor Wright took it from him.

"What's this all about?" Wright asked after glancing at the letter.

"Miss Emma received it about a week ago and couldn't wait to call the man who sent it. Seem's he's a private investigator in Oklahoma. A young man raised in foster homes."

"Already sounds bogus to me," Rummels said.

"It's the truth," Pearl said. "When Miss Emma talked with the man on the phone he told her he could prove he was her nephew."

"I'll believe it when I see his proof," Rummels said.

"What happens until then?" Wright said.

"Not a damn thing." Rummels turned before reaching the door. Pointing his finger at Raymond, he said, "Until this matter is assessed, don't run off with anything on this island. Sheriff, I'm holding you responsible."

Sheriff Wright waited for the front door to slam before handing the letter to Pearl. "What's this all about? Emma had no family I know of and I've lived here all my life. Where did this long lost nephew come from?"

"Miss Emma's wandering brother," Pearl said. "Seems he had a son while traipsing around the Oklahoma oil fields."

"You think this man is Emma's nephew and can prove it?"

Pearl lowered her eyes. "Don't really know, Sheriff Taylor. I just made that part up because that little weasel Rummels made me so mad. The rest is true, though."

"Could just be a scam artist that sees an opportunity to cut a fat hog. PIs search for lost heirs all the time."

"We don't know nothing about that," Raymond said. "I do know Miss Emma thought he was for real. She was going to call Randy Rummels to change her will."

"Randy says there is no will. Never was one."

"Uh huh," Raymond said as he stalked out of the room.

Wright tapped the desk top twice before following him. Halfway into the hall he turned and scratched his head. "Why would Rummels destroy Emma's will and let the bank take her property instead of letting you two have a shot at it?"

"You're the sheriff," Pearl said. "You tell us."

Sheriff Taylor Wright tipped his hat. "I'll check it out."

"You'll get your chance, Sheriff. Miss Emma's nephew is on his way to Texas. James T. McDivit should be here any minute. When he arrives, you can check him out for yourself."

CHAPTER THREE

James T. "Buck" McDivit had come to Texas for answers. What he found was a giant lake amid a maze of vines, creepers, and lily pads. A place that seemed more like Louisiana than Texas. He quickly realized it was different from both states. Cypress trees grew in abundance, both in the water and out, and Spanish moss, wafting in slow-motion waves, hung from their limbs, caressing the lake's coffee-colored surface. Only the head of a slow-swimming snake disrupted the lake's tranquillity.

East Texas was a place far different from Buck's own home on the flat plains of central Oklahoma. This was a mysterious locale that seemed like a virtual botanical garden replete with subtropical greenery and a climate to match. Buck felt a thousand miles from home.

Interstate highway, replaced by rural Texas blacktop, had long since disappeared in his rearview mirror. Untended hollyhocks, blooming in lavender flower falls that saturated humid air with their cloying fragrances, grew wild beside the road. Damp pathways, none leading anywhere in particular, pierced the tangle of vegetation as a flock of cattle egrets winged high overhead.

Egrets weren't the only wildlife in abundance, nor were oak, cypress and hollyhock the only plants bordering the road. Cascades of blue impatiens, crimson-blossomed rosebushes and clumps of green willow painted the terrain from a diverse palette of color. When a trucker blew his horn, waving an angry fist as he sped past, Buck realized he had slowed to less than twenty miles an hour. Taking the warning to heart, Buck pressed the accelerator and followed after him.

Dense vegetation parted as Buck rounded the next bend. It left him little time to worry about the angry trucker and prevented him from further gawking at the birds and wild flowers. In front of him lay a sleepy Victorian village dwarfed by the mammoth lake. Deception, Texas. Buck quickly realized he was at the literal end of the road.

Deception, once a riverboat stop along the way between New Orleans and Jefferson, was situated many secluded miles from the nearest interstate highway. The old riverboat port had managed to preserve much of its antebellum flavor. Many buildings, some with ornate decks jutting out over the water, still fronted the lake. Tourists wandered the narrow streets, gazing at storefront displays or licking snow cones purchased from vendors vying for space in the town square. Buck parked his Ram Charger and stepped out for a better look.

Near a little park fronting the lake Buck discovered everything wasn't old. Bulldozers and heavy equipment were at work clearing trees and leveling dirt. Someone was building something large and incongruous with the sleepy village and they had already cut a large brown swath across the flourishing sea of green. He completed a quick swing through Deception before returning to his truck and driving to the rear of the Pelican Restaurant. An attorney awaited inside the Pelican to discuss his late aunt's estate. Their recent telephone conversation had left Buck leery about their impending meeting and little doubt that the attorney considered him a money-seeking opportunist.

Afternoon shadows had begun draping the village as gray clouds formed out over the lake. The back of the restaurant seemed unexceptional except for the stacks of fish traps and piles of gill netting strewn across the ground. As Buck scanned the area someone came crashing through the screen door. The disruption ended his thoughts about his meeting with the attorney.

A man that looked big enough to take care of himself came tumbling across the loading dock and slammed headfirst into a packing crate. Lying in a daze, he rubbed his head as two men piled out the door after him.

"Get your black ass out of here," the first attacker said, delivering a vicious kick to the fallen man's ribs.

The big man managed to roll off the dock and crawl on his hands and knees to shelter behind a broken fish trap.

"Next time use the back door," the second attacker said. "Our customers don't want no stinking niggah shuffling past their tables while they're trying to eat."

The two men halted their attack but stood at the door, glaring at the black man on his knees below them. The taller of the two was bone thin with scraggly hair capping his acne-scarred face. His shorter partner whose diminutive height probably resulted from some congenital deformity, was anything but thin. He stood hunched over in a permanent crouch, a large hump crowning his twisted back. Neither man would have had much luck in a beauty contest and Buck could tell by their attitudes they probably liked it that way. He waited until they'd slammed the door behind them before helping the black man to his feet.

"You okay, pard?"

"Take more than those two to get the best of ol' Raymond Johnson," the man said, dusting himself off.

"Looked like they were doing a pretty good job to me."

"They got the drop on me when my back was turned," Raymond Johnson said, rubbing his jaw.

"Take it easy, big fellow, and next time watch your back," Buck said.

Buck quickly forgot the incident and strolled to the front of the restaurant. Daylight was waning but the cobbled parking lot continued radiating heat absorbed from late afternoon sun. He found it cooler inside, frigid air chilling the perspiration on his forehead as he opened the restaurant door. Wiping his forehead with his handkerchief, he greeted the hostess waiting in the entryway.

"I'm meeting a man named Rummels," Buck said. "Know if he's here yet?"

The young woman was dressed in a colorful period costume. Antebellum, he guessed. She had a friendly smile, a pretty red bow in her hair, and made him feel welcome. The woman's warm smile was no accident. Buck McDivit was young, tall and good looking with the body of a trained athlete and piercing blue eyes of a movie star. Dressed in jeans, cowboy boots and western-cut shirt, he could have passed as a young John Wayne.

"Mister Rummels just phoned," she said, quickly flipping through the guest register on the entryway lectern. "I'll seat you and you can wait for him in the dining area."

She led Buck into the main dining room where potted ferns hung in garlands from rough-hewn rafters. Checkerboard tablecloths draped wooden tables and the restaurant's rustic decor blended perfectly with aroma of frying cornmeal floating in from the kitchen. An outside veranda flanked the room on three sides and a damp breeze, moved along by slow-moving ceiling fans, wafted in through the open door.

"Enjoy your dinner," she said, seating him at a corner table overlooking the lake.

Buck barely had time to adjust his chair and stare out at the darkening sky before a waitress appeared and asked him what he wanted to drink. Her red bow went well with a thick thatch of black hair and her own colorful period dress. Buck ordered a Coors and had just finished it when Raymond Rummels arrived. Rummels was wearing dark pinstripes, despite the oppressive outside heat, and a constipated smile. He looked about thirty, trying to pass for fifty.

"You James T. McDivit?"

"One in the same," Buck said, reaching to shake the young lawyer's hand.

Rummels joined him at the table, not bothering to thank their waitress when she brought him a manhattan and Buck another Coors.

"Catfish is the specialty of the house," he said.

"Sounds good to me," Buck said, giving the young woman a thumbs up.

Rummels dismissed her with a dispassionate nod. "I'll come right to the point, McDivit. I'm unaware of any heirs to the Emma Fitzgerald estate. She had no children, adopted or otherwise. Her only brother died years ago in an oil field accident in Oklahoma. To my knowledge, he had no children."

"He had one," Buck said. "Me."

"Then why is there no record of his marriage, or your birth?"

"Because he never married. He carried on for a while with a teenage girl. My mother. I was the result. The family forced her to give me up to the state."

"Why didn't you come forward before now?"

"I didn't know I had any relatives until now. I'm a private investigator in Oklahoma City. While reviewing some public records for a client, I came across a newspaper article that got me thinking about my own roots. Once I decided to track down my parents, the rest was easy. John McDivit was definitely my father."

"Can you prove it?"

Buck handed Rummels a package of information and waited as he pawed through it.

"Birth certificate, eye witness accounts, and a statement from my mother. She had pictures, some belongings and even John McDivit's medical records. There's no doubt I'm his son and that he was the younger brother of Emma Fitzgerald."

"These could be forgeries."

"They're not."

"How do I know that?"

"You'd believe a federal judge wouldn't you?"

The hint of a snicker appeared on Rummels' face but vanished just as quickly. "You bring one with you?"

"No, but I have this affidavit."

Buck handed Rummels a letter his old friend Judge Beamon Dawkins had written for him before leaving Oklahoma. In it, the good judge attested to Buck's good word and the authenticity of the documents already presented the lawyer. Rummels held the letter long enough to read it three times.

"Excuse me a moment," he finally said, hurrying away from the table without explanation.

Remnant daylight had all but disappeared, replaced now by intermittent lightning that veined the sky over the lake. Thunder, shaking roof and windows, soon followed and momentarily caused the lights to dim. Rummels rejoined Buck at the table.

"Assuming your papers are in order and you inherit Emma Fitzgerald's estate, what exactly do you intend to do with it?"

"Don't know," Buck said. "It was never my intention to stake out my aunt's estate. I only wanted to meet the old lady and discuss my father's family with her."

"Then you're denying your inheritance?"

"Didn't say that. What exactly is my inheritance?"

Rummels cleared his throat, finished his manhattan and waved for another. "Emma Fitzgerald's estate consists of an island on Caddo Lake and everything on it. She has some money in the bank, but just enough to pay for the probate."

"What about the island?" Buck asked.

"Emma Fitzgerald operated a lodge and fishing camp, discontinuing lodge service about four years ago. The marina is still operable. But there's a couple of problems, Mr. McDivit."

"Such as?"

"Emma Fitzgerald borrowed money from the bank last year to remodel the lodge and marina and she put up the island as collateral. Emma failed to make a payment on the note for the last six months and the bank had begun foreclosure proceedings prior to her death. The hearing is in ten days. If you want to prevent the foreclosure, you have ten days to repay the bank loan, along with court costs and accumulated attorney fees."

"That's not much notice. You mentioned a second problem."

Rummels rustled his yellow pad, leaning forward in his chair. "They found Emma Fitzgerald floating in the lake. Pearl Johnson, her maid, says she was despondent. The coroner took that into account and ruled her death a suicide. I'm afraid that nullifies Emma's life insurance."

"No one said anything to me about life insurance, or suicide."

"I'm sorry," he said. "When they found her, she had this clasped in her hand," Rummels dropped a crusted cameo brooch into Buck's open palm. "Depression sometimes takes people to the edge. In Emma's case, over the edge."

Nearby thunder shook the rafters followed by slow rain drumming the roof and windows. Distress creased Rummels brow when Buck asked, "What if I pay off the note?"

"Well, of course you have that option. Is that your plan?"

Buck had neither assets nor collateral to satisfy Aunt Emma's note but Rummels didn't know that. Tapping his chin as if he were considering it, Buck said, "Don't know yet. Maybe."

"Pardon me a moment," Rummels said, excusing himself again. He returned shortly with another man. "This is Mr. Hogg Nation. He owns the Pelican."

The distinguished gentleman with the odd name had green eyes and short hair frosting his head white. Despite his hair color, his lineless face proclaimed him no older than forty.

"At your disposal, Mr. McDivit. Hope you're enjoying our hospitality at the Pelican. Your meal and drinks are on the house tonight."

Buck managed a nod and half smile. Raymond Rummels was wringing his hands. His own expression had turned sour.

"Mr. Nation is also my client. He wishes to purchase Fitzgerald Island from you. Two hundred thousand dollars. A generous offer, Mr. McDivit. Enough to pay the bank note and leave twenty-five thousand dollars for your troubles."

Nation's proposal caught Buck by surprise. When he finally managed a reply, he said, "Thanks, but I'd like to visit the island before I decide."

"Take your time and enjoy the catfish," Nation said, moving away toward the kitchen.

Randy Rummels remained standing until his client had departed. During this time, the waitress arrived with a bell-shaped glass filled with an icy-red concoction.

"Mr. Nation would like you to try a hurricane. It's the house specialty." She winked and hurried away.

It was raining harder now, water beading down the picture window in soft sheets. Buck sipped the sugary drink and rain and alcohol had all but hypnotized him when a familiar high-pitched voice returned his attention to the restaurant. Staring across the crowded room, he spotted the two men involved in the incident behind the restaurant. They were drinking and talking loudly, even above the din of the crowd.

"Who are those two men?"

Rummels was chewing on the straw of his manhattan. "Humpback and Deacon John," he said. "They work for Mr. Nation." Before Buck could inquire further, the lawyer glanced at his watch. "I have another appointment. Raymond Johnson, an employee of the marina on Fitzgerald Island, will pick you up shortly and take you there." Handing Buck his business card, he said, "You have a ten days to make up your mind."

Thunder shook the roof as Randy Rummels tapped the back of his chair and started away. Buck wondered, as the lawyer departed, why the man's crooked grin gave him an uneasy feeling in the pit of his gut.

The friendly waitress soon appeared with hush puppies, catfish and another hurricane. Buck handed her his empty glass and took a quick gulp from the fresh drink. The spicy catfish tasted wonderful and whetted Buck's growing thirst. He was feeling light-headed when the waitress appeared for the final time.

"Raymond Johnson is waiting for you on the back porch, Mr. McDivit," she said.

"Call me Buck," he said, stumbling when he tried to get out of the chair. "Which way?"

Buck went out the back door, quite surprised when he realized the man waiting for him was the large black man involved in the scuffle behind the restaurant. Before he could ponder the coincidence, he caught his foot on a net and tumbled into the big man's outstretched arms.

"Little too much of Mr. Nation's hospitality?"

"Afraid so. Was that you that got yourself kicked out the back door a little earlier?"

"Mr. Nation's boys," he said without explanation. "You probably don't remember but I'm Raymond Johnson. You Mr. McDivit?"

"Buck."

Johnson stared at Buck McDivit's extended hand and finally shook it, limply for a man so large. "If you ain't through eating yet, I'll wait out here."

"I'm done," Buck said, unable to stifle a drunken giggle.

"Good. I don't need no more trouble tonight. Let's get out of here," he said.

Concurring with Johnson, Buck followed him off the porch. By now his head was swimming, his vision blurry and tongue thick.

"Where's your car?" Raymond asked.

"Truck's in the back."

The big black man grabbed Buck, supporting his weight and ignoring his helpless giggles. Raymond left him on the steps while he retrieved Buck's suitcase from the truck. The rain had slackened as he herded Buck and his bag down the slope to the lake where a gentle breeze was blowing across the water. It caused the boat and Buck's head on the side of the boat to rock with the waves. Raymond Johnson untied the bowline and pushed away from the dock.

"Couple of miles to the island," he said, maneuvering through a stand of cypress trees surrounding the shadow-dark shoreline. "You okay?"

Buck answered with a giddy laugh. "I think someone spiked my hurricane."

"Sure they did," Johnson said as the high-pitched outboard motor drowned out Buck's slurred words and any further attempt at conversation.

As the boat glided across rain-dimpled water Buck closed his eyes, his mind awash with flickering moonbeams splaying the lake's murky surface. Half an hour later they landed on the island. When they reached a large two-storied house, Raymond Johnson dragged Buck upstairs and dumped him on a feather bed. The suitcase made a hollow thump when it hit the floor, the door shutting behind Raymond as he exited with a damp swoosh. Locked in a drunken stupor, Buck didn't really care.

He lay there for what seemed like hours, mesmerized by slow rain drumming the tin roof as he stared at the ceiling's darkness. Finally he stumbled out of bed, hoping to find an aspirin for his throbbing head. Unable to find the lights or an appropriate pill he embarked instead on a late-night tour of the house.

Moonlight through open windows guided Buck back down the stairs where he found a liquor cabinet amid stormy shadows and resident gloom. What the hell, he thought. A little hair of the dog couldn't make him feel any worse than he already did. He shattered one of the bottles in an eruption of flying glass as he rummaged through the cabinet but the accident didn't deter him. Slugging whiskey straight from an unbroken bottle, he headed down a dark hallway, glassy shards crunching beneath his boots.

Buck stumbled through the house, finally finding a door that led outside. Soft rain continued falling but a few rays of moonlight penetrated the cover of clouds. Reflections off the lake beckoned Buck. Wobbling toward the water's edge, he dribbled whiskey from his open mouth and down his neck then howled at the moon. When he reached the lake he tripped on a cypress knee, tumbling into the mud.

Revived by the dank odor of warm rain and rotting vegetation, Buck watched dull light radiate from a pinpoint across the lake. This time it wasn't the moon. Even after rubbing his eyes he couldn't make it disappear. Instead, it grew larger and drew ever closer.

Sitting in the mud, too stunned to move, he swayed as the vague outline of a veil-shrouded apparition floated toward him. Buck bit his lip and felt the pain but it failed to convince him that he was coherent. When the apparition stopped directly in front of him, he saw it was a girl.

A translucent shawl clung to the girl's thin frame, icy mist drifting around her body, chilling warm night air. Tears flowed down her cheeks. When she reached out to him Buck's neck grew inexplicably warm. Aunt Emma's brooch in his hand began pulsating with pink light as the translucent body of the ghostly vision gleamed brightly.

Buck blinked and when he opened his eyes the girl had disappeared leaving him unsure of what he'd seen. Still very much inebriated, he managed to stumble back to the lodge where he passed out before hitting the sheets.

CHAPTER FOUR

Buck lay moored in a friendly port, swaying ever-so-gently as sleek boats sailed past him. Lying on deck in a tropical hammock he sipped a margarita, watching as naked bathing beauties played volleyball on the beach. An explosion of noise returned him to abrupt reality.

Awakening on a strange bed, Buck found himself still wearing yesterday's clothes, only now plastered with brown sticky mud. A tiger-striped kitten lay shivering on his chest, frightened by the shattering of an emerald vase that had toppled from the night stand. Buck lifted the kitten and stroked its back.

"Made a mess, didn't you, pal?"

Buck only had time for a couple of strokes as a wave of nausea surged from his stomach, forcing him off the bed. Grabbing his mouth, he made a beeline to the bathroom with the kitten following. The kitten rubbed Buck's leg as he hugged the commode. Even though it did his head no good, Buck appreciated the sympathy.

After doffing his muddy clothes and standing under a steamy shower for fifteen minutes, he felt almost human again. As his knotted muscles slowly unwound, he began thinking about exploring the island. But not before swallowing four aspirin and kicking broken glass and his muddy pants under the bed.

The carved oak stairway descended to a wood-paneled room where mounted hunting and fishing trophies and framed newspaper clippings decorated the walls. A leather-bound guest register rested on the rustic check-in counter and the massive stone fireplace in the lobby seemed only for show in these sultry East Texas climes.

One yellow clipping pictured five black men dressed in clothes of a different era encircling a table occupied by a giant, prehistoric-looking fish. A board propped open the creature's mouth revealing barracuda-like teeth and tiny eyes greatly out of proportion to the rest of the creature's monstrous body. The caption read: Giant Alligator Gar Caught in Caddo Lake.

Something heavy thumped against the floor and Buck wheeled around, finding himself staring into the brown eyes of a large black woman. She was sweeping broken glass into a dust tray and looked for all the world like a pre-Civil War slave. In a momentary flush of shame, he remembered breaking the whiskey bottle during his drunken ramble through the house.

The woman's massive girth was surpassed only by the elegant nose distinguishing her face. Not a single wrinkle or blemish marred her almond brown skin and she would have appeared quite regal in another setting. Glancing up from her task, she spoke in a rich baritone voice. "Good morning. Sleep well?"

"Yes, thank you. I'm Buck McDivit."

"I know. My husband Raymond brought you here last night. I'm Pearl Johnson."

Something brushed Buck's leg and he glanced down at the kitten. The animal's back arched as he moved.

"And that's Tiger. Miss Emma's kitten."

"Pleased to meet both of you," he said, stroking the kitten's head. "Tiger and I are already acquainted. Can I help with the mess?"

Pearl's warm smile surprised him. "Thank you, but I'm almost finished. I'm serving breakfast on the veranda. If you're ready to eat, I'll take your order."

"No need. I'll scratch something up in the kitchen."

Anxiety spread over Pearl Johnson's large ebony face. "I don't mind. It's my job."

Feeling insensitive, Buck lowered his voice and said, "Which way is the veranda?"

Pearl's features softened again and she said, "Through the dining room."

Feeling her eyes on his back Buck walked through an open French doorway leading to the lodge's dining room. White tablecloths covered several tables set with antique crystal vases awaiting fresh cut flowers. Forest green carpets graced a polished wood floor and a curving mahogany bar with a smoky, full-length mirror protruded from the back wall. He stopped for a better look.

Indirect light reflecting from the mirror imparted the feel of a bistro open for business, but like a mortuary after dark the room had a finality to it. Ignoring his momentary malaise, Buck hurried beneath a crystal chandelier to the spot where the dining area opened to a canvas-roofed veranda. As Buck chose a table near the door, Tiger wound through his legs.

Screen mesh discouraged bugs from dining on the guests while still affording a magnificent view of the lake. And it was magnificent. Giant cypress trees with water-gorged trunks flanked the shoreline and a watery passage opened into a wide corridor that led to the main part of the lake. Buck jumped when Tiger took a playful swipe at his ankle with a set of very sharp claws.

Mud and hazy mist remained from the past night's rain and wispy clouds curled up from the lake's surface through Spanish moss and gnarly trees. Tiger finally tired of swatting at Buck's sock and jumped into his lap, curling into a ball and closing his eyes. Pearl Johnson interrupted his contemplation, smiling a full-mouthed ivory grin.

"Looks like you made a new friend."

"Guess I did," Buck said, scratching behind Tiger's ears.

"He won't have nothing to do with me but it looks like he decided to let you take Miss Emma's place. What can I get you for breakfast?"

"Please surprise me."

Pearl nodded, filling his coffee cup before returning to the kitchen. When she came back, he said, "Do you believe in ghosts?"

"Why do you ask, Mr. McDivit?"

"Because I think I may have seen one last night. And please just call me Buck."

"Raymond said you'd had a bit to drink. Sure it wasn't a pink elephant?"

Stroking the kitten still asleep in his lap, he ignored her insinuation and said, "I'm serious. I saw something I can't explain."

"Like what?"

Buck didn't immediately answer. Once before, younger and in a similar drunken state, he'd found himself in bed with a woman he'd met in a nightclub. Next morning, dull-headed and alone, only dim memories remained of the incident. So dim, he dismissed the entire episode as a dream. At least until he found a pink undergarment beneath his bed. Like the discovered panties, his own muddy clothes supported the moonlight walk by the lake but he still had trouble believing what he had seen.

"Mr. Buck?"

"Sorry," Buck said, Pearl's voice dimming the memory of his sullied past.

"My mind was somewhere else. I was thinking about the ghost. It was a beautiful young girl." Pearl Johnson simply stared at him. "Ms. Johnson. You all right?"

Pearl nodded. When she served his eggs Benedict it sent him into a further state of disbelief.

"This is my favorite," he said.

The dark lady beamed. "Your Aunt Emma's, too." She turned to leave but stopped and stared at him. "I haven't seen the ghost, but others have. She supposedly haunts the lake."

"Then you do believe in ghosts?"

Pearl Johnson smiled. "I didn't say I do, but others have seen it, too."

Fiddling with his fork, Buck said, "You know someone that has?"

"Raymond saw her. Described her just like you but he'd also had too much to drink that particular night."

"A ghost haunts the lake?" Buck said, overlooking Pearl Johnson's comment concerning his presumed alcoholic indulgence.

"Bessie McKinney's ghost." Mrs. Johnson's big moon face fairly beamed, enjoying herself immensely at the attention he was giving her story. "A girl who died almost a hundred and twenty years ago," she said. "Searchers found her body in a grassy glen. She'd been missing for nearly a week and was petrified when they found her."

"Petrified?"

Pearl nodded, satisfied by the way her explanation affected the young man. "Like a marble statue, every feature preserved as if she were still alive."

"But how?"

Shaking her big head, she said, "No one knows why she was petrified or how she died. Maybe murder."

Buck drummed his fork against the table, disturbed by Pearl's story. "If she had no visible injuries, why would anyone arrive at that conclusion?"

"Because they found a young black man in the grass near the body. He was crying when they discovered him. Searchers hung him before he could tell his story."

"Did he do it?"

Pearl Johnson shook her large head again. "Don't know, nor does anyone else."

The dark lady grew silent, lost in thought as she stared at something out over the lake. Her eyes began to tear.

"Pearl, what's the matter?"

"It's nothing," she said.

Brushing away further questions, she relieved Buck of the sleeping kitten and returned to the kitchen. When he finished eating he took her his dirty dishes. Pearl was peeling an onion by the sink but her tears weren't caused by the onion.

Feeling a sense of family for the first time in his life, Buck touched Pearl's shoulder. "I guess you know about the foreclosure. What's going to happen to you and Raymond?"

Dropping the onion into the sink, she began to sob. "Miss Emma sold Raymond and me our house and the two acres it sits on. She left us half the marina in her will. Now Randy Rummels says there's no record of the sale of the house or the land. He says Miss Emma died without a will. It just seems like there's nothing in the world we can do about it."

Pearl's assessment was Buck's own take on the situation but the emotion raised in him was anger instead of despair. "The lawyer told me Aunt Emma committed suicide. You think that's what happened?"

"Course not," Pearl said. "That lady was the most level-headed person I ever met."

"He also said she was despondent over a man."

"Randy Rummels is a liar and a thief. Miss Emma was upset about her friend Bones Malone leaving the island but losing a man wasn't enough to make her kill herself."

"Sure about that?"

The big woman dabbed her eyes with her apron. "I've known Miss Emma all my life. Worked for her since I was a girl. She even helped deliver Ray Jr."

Grabbing Pearl's elbow, Buck directed her to the kitchen table, refilled her water glass and sat beside her.

"Maybe there's something I can do but I need you to help me sort through what's going on around here. Exactly who is this Bones Malone?"

Pearl closed her eyes, resting her elbows on the table. "Miss Emma's boyfriend. He had a room upstairs for the last year or so."

"And they had a falling out? About what?"

"Don't know the particulars," she said, "but Miss Emma told him to pack his gear and get the hell off the island."

"When did this happen?"

"Two days before Miss Emma died," Pearl said, her tears returning.

Buck waited until she'd sipped more water and had wiped away her tears with the apron. "How does Hogg Nation fit into all this?"

"Don't know that he does," Pearl said.

"Somehow he does. He offered me two hundred thousand dollars for the island. What's his position in Deception?"

"He owns half the county and is building a resort on the lake."

"So he's the one responsible for all the new construction on the outskirts of Deception?" Pearl nodded. As the high-pitch engine noise of a passing motor boat sounded through an open window, Buck touched her shoulder. "I don't have enough money to pay off the bank but maybe we don't need too. I don't believe Aunt Emma killed herself either. If we can prove she didn't, her life insurance will kick in and we can use it to pay off the mortgage."

"How will you prove it?"

"I'll start by talking with the sheriff. I'll do what I can to make things right by you and Raymond. I promise."

Pearl's despair stayed with Buck as he retraced his late-night path to the lake, following his very visible footprints until he reached the spot where he'd fallen. There he found something lying near the impression. It was the antique cameo brooch he'd dropped before stumbling back to the lodge. The discovery only added to his confusion and he decided to take a long walk and sort out his thoughts before going to the marina and talking to Raymond.

Dewy grass quickly soaked his pants as he set out across the island and moisture wafted off a hot stone from the dense mass of surrounding vegetation. He'd heard of sweltering tropics but had no idea they occurred so far north. Flowers, vines, and trees abounded like the interior of an over-fertilized hothouse and giant moss-covered cypress trees grew close to the shoreline, their gnarled roots protruding like bony legs from opaque water. Palmetto, sumac and assorted shrubs gilded the bank with spreading vegetation while towering pines dominated the island's center.

Many creatures matched the prolific vegetation. Minnows swimming in shallow water. Lazy frogs and torpid turtles sunning themselves on half-submerged stumps and branches. Flocks of white cattle egrets soaring overhead and lizards darting after abundant insects. When a large moccasin thicker then Buck's own thigh slipped silently into the water, its appearance caused his heart to perform an unexpected staccato drum roll.

Fallen trees and rotting vegetation lent little comfort to his nervous stride. Even as he kept a nervous eye at the trail before him the paradox of Fitzgerald Island impressed him. The sweet stench of decay in an environment teeming with life. He continued his sweltering trek across the island's sandy loam.

Buck followed a path to the far side of the island where rotting wood and several sunken rowboats protruded from shallow water. Stilt houses reflected sunlight from their tin roofs on the far side of the lake. Deception lay just around the bend.

When Buck finally pushed through high grass to the lake's edge, he found several deep holes in the ground. Freshly dug holes. Shards of pottery littered the ground, along with a flash of something brassy. After plucking the object from the dirt, he saw that it was a brass fitting corroded by age. Glancing at the sun, he gauged the time. Perspiration dripped from Buck's shirt, clinging to his back. It was time to talk to Raymond Johnson. Touching the strange piece of brass, he retraced his path to the lodge.

CHAPTER FIVE

Stress and alcohol had taken a toll on Buck's body and it was later that afternoon before he finally inspected Aunt Emma's marina. He followed a grassy path to the main dock jutting out into shallow water where pier-like walkways led to a frame building coated with fresh white paint. The sign on the roof said FITZGERALD'S LANDING.

Gasoline pumps, minnow bins and an old-fashioned red Coke machine dominated the building's exterior. Business was booming, customers milling about, some fishing, others buying bait or filling gas tanks. Buck found Raymond Johnson behind the cash register of a business that resembled a very bucolic quick-stop service station.

Raymond Johnson sported a Texas-sized grin. "Didn't figure you'd make it out of bed today, Mr. McDivit."

"Can't keep a good man down," Buck said, caught up in Raymond's ebullient mood. "Call me Buck."

This time they shook hands under more pleasant circumstances than the previous night.

"Fine," Johnson said, delivering a hearty slap to Buck's shoulder. "Pearl says you seen a ghost last night."

"Maybe."

Raymond nodded toward a younger man sitting behind the counter. "Wiley will have to take you to Mama Toukee's for a charm to ward off them evil spirits."

Wiley, a younger, trimmer version of Raymond smiled at the mention of his name. He leaned against the wall on the back legs of a cane chair, his dark boots resting on a can of motor oil. His red shirt and khaki pants seemed a size too large for his slender frame.

"How you doing?" he said. "Daddy can get you that charm next time he visits Mama Toukee's. He's about due for a fresh jug of her home brew."

Raymond wagged his finger, shook his big head. "Wiley's my boy, but I swear he must have got his mouth from Pearl's side of the family."

"Don't you believe it," Wiley said. "He can tell a story bigger than Miss Emma's record garfish."

"Keep your eye on him," Raymond said. "I got a customer to wait on."

Wiley and Buck listened to Raymond's booming voice as he returned to the cash register. "Loud, ain't he?" Wiley said as he picked up his magazine and leaned back against the wall.

Wiley's laugh reminded Buck of his father's. "Nice operation you have here."

"You bet it is. Like to take a look around? You can see most everything through that door," Wiley said, pointing.

Buck saluted Wiley and exited through the back door. Outside, board planks protruded like centipede legs from the center walk and red canvas awnings, used to shelter some of the walkways from the weather, added a festive touch to the surroundings. Buck explored the marina, finally reaching the end of the walkway where outboard motor parts lay strewn on old wood. A young black man was working on a motor just inside the open door of a work shed and Buck strolled over to meet him. From the man's muscled frame he could have passed for a running back on a pro football team.

"Afternoon," Buck said.

The man glanced up from his work but didn't bother acknowledging Buck's greeting. Embarrassed by frowning impoliteness Buck turned away, bumping headlong into Raymond Johnson.

"Hey, Buck, you meet Ray, my oldest boy."

"No, but it would be my pleasure."

"Ray, this is Mr. Buck McDivit, Miss Emma's niece and the new owner of Fitzgerald Island."

Buck reached to shake his hand but received the same reaction as before. "Why you wanta be that way?" Raymond said. "Don't know where he gets it from."

"No problem. Ray and I can talk later."

"Sure you can," Raymond said, grabbing Buck's shoulder and steering him back toward the concession. "I closed early for the day. Let's have a cold drink and you can tell me and Wiley all about yourself."

Raymond kept up a lively patois on the way back to the concession, their footsteps echoing against the walkway. Lifting the lid on the old Coke machine he grabbed two cans, handing one to Buck. Taking the other inside, he hoisted his bulky frame to the counter top.

"The letters you wrote Miss Emma said you're from Oklahoma City. A private investigator."

"That's right. I've made a career tracking other people's missing heirs. I thought I might as well find some of my own."

Buck gave him a brief history of his life for the last thirty-one years, then fished inside his pocket for the cameo brooch. He placed it on the counter beside Raymond.

"Aunt Emma had this clutched in her hand when they found her. Any idea what it means?"

Raymond picked it up, turning it in his hand before tossing it to Wiley. "Seen this before?"

Wiley caught the flying object. After giving it a glance he pitched it back to Raymond, his only response being a simple head shake.

From behind, an educated voice said, "It's an antique." It was Ray Jr., a cold drink in his hand. "Lila Richardson can tell you all about it."

Ray disappeared through the door in back of the store before Buck could ask him the next logical question. Raymond responded to the unasked query.

"Miss Lila runs an antique shop in Deception. Her daddy owns half the county."

"I'll look her up," Buck said. "Does Ray work here full time?"

"Teaches at East Texas State. Works here during summer vacation. Finishing his doctorate."

"Impressive. His major?"

"History," Raymond said, the word seeming strangely incongruous as it rolled off his tongue.

"What do you know about Hogg Nation?"

Raymond's big grin disappeared abruptly. "He's a lying, thieving dog who's trying to steal this island from Miss Emma."

Mention of Nation quickly dampened Raymond's friendly manner and caused Buck to recall the events of the previous day. "Your scuffle with those two men yesterday didn't happen just because you walked through Nation's restaurant, did it?"

Johnson slammed his Coke against the counter. "Since I was there to pick you up anyway, I decided to have a little talk with Mr. Hogg Nation."

"About what?"

"About who he paid off to wipe out my recorded deed from the records in the county courthouse. I took my own copy to show him I could still prove who really owns it."

"Daddy really scared him. You can tell by the bump on his hard head."

"Shut up, Wiley," Raymond said.

"Put your copy of the deed in a safe place," Buck said. "That's all the proof of ownership you need."

"That's what I told Nation. Deacon John just laughed in my face and asked me if I'd forgot who the judge is around here. Said niggers were too dumb to own property."

"What judge?"

"Judge Jefferson Travis is Hogg Nation's real close friend," Wiley said. "In this county there's white justice and there's black justice. Deacon John was just telling me how the cow eats the cabbage, as if I didn't already know."

"Cute," Buck said. Because of Raymond's defeated expression, Buck regretted prodding him for answers. Curiosity overcame his reservations. "Why does Nation want this island anyway?"

"Because of his world-class fishing and hunting resort," Wiley said. "He's got a jet airport already built. He needs Fitzgerald Island as part of the package."

"Isn't there some other island more accessible to Deception than this one?"

Wiley shook his head, leaned back against the wall and returned to reading his magazine. By now Raymond's former cheerful demeanor had dissolved into a dark funk. Seeing little use in pumping him for more information, Buck finished his drink and grabbed the brooch from the counter. Flipping it once, he returned it to his pocket as he paused at the door, his hand on the knob.

"I enjoyed our talk. See you around, Wiley. Maybe you can show me the island when you have some free time."

"You bet I can." Wiley said in a friendly voice.

Sounding distinctly concerned, Raymond said, "Say, Buck. What's gonna happen with this place?"

"I'm going to check into things. Poke around here and there."

"Keep us in mind," Johnson said.

With a twinge tugging at Buck's conscience, he returned to the lodge feeling better, despite his growing concern, than he had all morning. The sky was azure and streaked with streamers of milky clouds. High above the marina a turkey buzzard caught in a thermal updraft, looped toward the ground in a slow downward spiral. Before Buck reached full stride, his neck had grown damp from rampant heat and humidity.

Halfway to the lodge the unmuffled engines of a boat racing across the lake caught his attention and he watched as the driver cut the power and let the sleek craft nose into shore. Mired in mud, it halted a few feet before reaching solid ground. The man behind the wheel was Hogg Nation.

"Dammit, DJ," he said. "Jump out and pull us to shore."

Humpback cast a grinning glance at Deacon John and began winding loose rope into a spool on the floor of the boat. It was Buck's closest look at the little humpbacked man. His face was a mess, his flattened nose canting hard left and his ears jutting forward. Oily hair sprayed from beneath his slouch hat and his front teeth were missing. He had the stub of a cigar in his mouth.

"You do it, Hump," Deacon John said." I got my new shoes on."

"Mr. Nation said for you to do it," Humpback countered, not looking up from the rope.

"Somebody do it," Nation shouted over the motor. "Now!"

Deacon John's spindly legs faltered momentarily as he jumped from the boat. Grabbing the bowline, he eased the big runabout into shore then wiped his muddy hands on his red-checked golfing pants. When Humpback followed him to shore, Deacon John kicked mud from the toe of his shoe into the little man's face.

"Ain't no call for that," Humpback said, his grin vanishing.

"Shut up, both of you," Nation said. "Give me a hand out of here."

Humpback and Deacon John ceased bickering and helped Hogg Nation out of the boat as if they were assisting a fine lady. When Humpback stepped on Deacon John's new shoes with his own size eights, he caught a smart slap across the forehead. In retaliation Humpback kicked Deacon John's butt, lost his balance and fell on his own doff into the mud.

"Cut the shit," Nation said. "Now." He forgot the two men's antics when he saw Buck watching from shore. "Hope you enjoyed our hospitality last night."

"The catfish was tasty but whatever you fellows put in your specialty drinks down here left me with a splitting headache this morning."

Humpback and Deacon John snickered, but Nation's glare shut them up. "You considered my offer yet?"

"It's crossed my mind."

"Then let this cross your mind. Here's a cashier's check for two hundred thousand dollars." He held the check in one hand, a contract in the other. "Sign this document and the money is yours. You'll have two days to vacate the premises."

Waving away the check and contract, Buck said, "I can't consider selling the island until you answer a few questions. What about the Johnsons?"

Nation's expression remained unchanged. "What about them?"

"I'd like to know if you intend to continue running the marina and if you'll take care of Raymond and Pearl."

Nation's arm went limp to his side. "Not your concern."

"I'm afraid it is. Anyway, I've decided to stay awhile. Maybe fix up the marina and reopen the lodge."

"Well, you're crazier than that aunt of yours. I'm offering ten times more than this sinkhole is worth."

"I'm not convinced you're doing me a favor. Why do you want the island?"

Nation's already ruddy complexion reddened even further. "None of your business."

"You're wrong," Buck said, turning toward the lodge. "Sorry to waste your time, but I'm not interested."

"You better reconsider, McDivit or the bank and Judge Travis will change your mind for you."

Nation's threat sounded ominous. Before Buck could consider the implication the familiar whop-whop-whop of an approaching helicopter muddled his attention. The little chopper landed in a flurry of swirling dirt and blowing vegetation. After Nation had climbed into the flashy bronze chopper it quickly disappeared over the cypress trees surrounding the island, Spanish moss billowing in the resultant eddy of wind.

Deacon John and Humpback didn't stay for conversation. Climbing back into their boat, they stormed off in the wake of a fan-tail wave that blew water fifteen feet into the air. Buck gazed across the lake for a good five minutes before realizing that sudden and intense silence had hypnotized him into inaction. He felt another sinking spell coming on.

Returning to his room he found Tiger purring and kneading dough against the pillow. Buck joined him, soon falling fast asleep until Pearl knocked on the door later that evening.

CHAPTER SIX

Buck sprang down the stairs feeling rested and alive, his hangover gone and his appetite aroused by the wonderful aroma wafting up from the kitchen. Pearl had arranged a table in the main dining hall and served a Southern meal of beans, ham, and cornbread. Simple fare, but totally delicious. Self-generated electricity dimly lighted the interior of the large room and dancing shadows became a time conveyance, casting the island back into a different century. Tiger broke the spell, jumping into Buck's lap.

Buck stared out the window as late afternoon gold, cast by the setting sun, enveloped the clearing. Blue sky was turning crimson and a lone water bird skimmed the lake's quiet surface as Mrs. Johnson appeared on the porch to refill his coffee cup.

"I met your sons today," Buck said.

"What did you think of my babies?" she said, a smile dominating her expressive face.

"I think your babies have grown into two fine men."

"That they have," she said. "Ray Jr. is working on his doctorate, you know?"

"Raymond told me. You must be very proud."

"I'm proud of both my sons, but they're so different," she said wistfully. "If Ray just didn't have that chip on his shoulder. Raymond's a plain working man, but I sometimes wish Ray was more like him." As if waking from a daydream, she added, "I don't mean to bore you."

"You're not."

Pearl stared at him. "You know, Mr. Buck, in this light you look like your Aunt Emma." Turning away, she hid her face in her hands. "Guess I still haven't got over Miss Emma not being here. You remind me of her and that comforts me. Will you stay with us awhile?"

Pearl's question sent a melancholy wave cresting across Buck's bow. "At least until I resolve the matter with the island."

Pearl took Buck's answer as a statement of positive action and hummed softly to herself as she returned to the kitchen. Buck went out on the porch, basking in darkness awash in moonlight. There he remained until long after Pearly had gone to her own house. When a panther howling across the lake aroused him from his musings, a flickering light down by the dock caught his attention. Remembering the apparition, he decided to investigate.

Night sounds and darkness accompanied his stroll to the lake. Leery of lurking cottonmouths, he stepped lightly until he neared the marina and discovered the source of the light. Instead of Bessie McKinney it was Wiley Johnson, fishing from the dock in the glow of a butane lantern. Disturbed by old wood creaking beneath Buck's feet, Wiley glanced around quickly.

"How you doing?" he said. "Want to wet a hook?"

"Think I'll just watch. Catch many this way?"

"No, but it's peaceful when the sun goes down. Night fishing relaxes me."

"I can see why," Buck said as a gentle breeze rustled cypress leaves.

"What are you doing up so late?" Wiley asked.

"I fell asleep on the veranda. When I awoke I saw your light and thought it was a ghost."

Wiley stifled a laugh. "Bessie McKinney?"

"I know it sounds crazy but I really did see something out on the lake last night. A misty cloud floating across the water toward me that seemed like a girl in distress."

"Like Daddy said. Sounds like you had your snout in Mama Toukee's home brew."

"Maybe, but I know what I saw. At least I think I do."

Wiley pulled his line from the water and laid the cane pole on the dock. Grabbing the handle of a bright red ice chest beside him, he removed its plastic top, fished through the icy contents and extracted two cold bottles of beer. After popping their tops and handing one to Buck, he tossed his line back in the water. Buck noticed there was no bait on the hook.

"You think you saw Bessie McKinney's ghost?"

"Sounds improbable, doesn't it?" Buck said, sipping the cold beer.

A large catfish broke the surface, its splash disturbing a loggerhead resting on a stump. The huge turtle slid into the dark lake with barely a sound, only a single expanding ripple marking his disappearance.

"Maybe not as strange as you think," Wiley said.

"You think I really saw a ghost?"

"Sounds like a paranormal occurrence, at the very least. Give you an example. Crossett is a town in southern Arkansas. Local legend says the railroad track outside town is haunted. Supposedly, a conductor met his demise there. Literally lost his head. The ghost of this headless conductor, they say, haunts the tracks near Crossett."

"And?"

"And I saw it with my own eyes. I worked at a bowling alley part time during college and on a whim I drove to Crossett one night after work with three buddies. We passed through the little town, stopping beside the railroad track. We walked along it, searching for the ghost."

Buoyed by his own recent ghostly vision, Buck listened with rapt attention.

"A dim light appeared in the distance as we walked the track," Wiley said. "Floating just above the railing. When we tried to catch up with it, it moved away. It followed us when we walked back to the car. It would run from us like a child playing tag. Still, we really saw it."

"How much did you have to drink?"

"I won't lie," Wiley said. "We'd all had a few beers that night. But the man in the car, the manager of the bowling alley, didn't drink. He also saw it."

Buck crossed his arms as he thought about the story. "Maybe it was swamp gas."

"Maybe it was a ghost," Wiley said, laughing in a way that reminded Buck of Wiley's father.

Wiley opened two more beers and Buck took a long pull. "What's the deal with Bones Malone?"

"He's lived around these parts all his life. Guess he caught Miss Emma's attention, even if he was quite a bit younger."

"Younger?"

"Wiley chuckled again. "At least twenty years, but If you ask me neither one of them minded a lot."

"What's he do for a living?"

"This and that. Selling fresh-water pearls. Commercial fishing. And he had his hands in other odds and ends."

"Such as?"

"Indian relics, old coins, and the like. Made a little money selling them around."

"Doesn't sound very lucrative."

"No, but he's had a steady job for a year or more, working for the state."

"Doing what?"

"Conducting archeological investigations at proposed building sites. Determining if anything of historic significance is in the ground before allowing construction to begin. Mostly concentrating on Hogg Nation's resort."

Buck remained silent a moment as he considered Wiley's information. "I'm going to look him up and ask him a few questions. Any idea where I might find him?"

"No, but he supposedly has a camp on the lake somewhere."

A bass, breaking the silence as Wiley's words trailed away, slapped the surface with his tail. Heat lightning flashed across the horizon as they finished their beer.

"What's the story on your brother?" Buck finally asked.

Wiley's grin returned. "Different, isn't he?"

"I don't know about that, but he's not very friendly."

"More militant, I'd say."

"You're not that way. Neither is Raymond or Pearl."

"Ray's six years older than me. He played football in college and I played basketball. He's stocky, I'm tall and lean. His skin is coffee-colored. My skin is darker. Maybe Daddy knows something he ain't telling us," he said with a wink.

"You work here full time?"

"Just visiting."

"From where?"

"Here and there."

Buck felt a chill in the conversation and changed the subject. "So Ray's working on a doctorate in history?"

"Not just history. Black history," Wiley said. "And you're a private investigator?" Buck's profession seemed to interest Wiley. Pulling his line from the water, he leaned the pole against the dock. "What exactly does a private investigator do?"

He laughed when Buck said, "This and that."

Wiley had given him more to think about than he could organize in his mind. Beer, night sounds, and a cool breeze blowing up from the south acted as a potent sedative. Along with everything else that had happened since he'd arrived on the island, it left him tired and drowsy. Saying goodbye, he returned through the darkness to the lodge.

Buck awoke to songbirds outside his open bedroom window, a gentle breeze rustling the curtains. Focused light on his face woke him before he was ready. When he rolled out of bed, Tiger moved into the warm spot he'd vacated. After showering, Buck followed his nose to the aroma of bacon and eggs drifting up the stairs. Tiger, managing to rouse himself from his stupor, followed him. When they reached the kitchen, the kitten found a bowl of milk Pearl had left for him, lapping it as Pearl stirred a pan with a long wooden spoon.

"Morning, Mr. Buck. Sleep well?"

"Like a top," he said, stroking Tiger's arched back.

"Ready for breakfast?"

"You bet. I'm starved."

Handing him a cup of coffee, she said, "Find a place on the veranda and I'll bring it out when it's ready."

Humidity choked the hallway as Buck, Tiger dogging his heels, walked outside to the veranda. Morning heat accosted them as they reached the table. Another scorcher, Buck thought as he waited for breakfast. Pearl's breakfast, when it arrived, included her friendly country ambience to enhance the flavor. When Buck finished eating he asked her if someone could give him a ride to Deception.

"Ray will take you. I'll call him now."

Grabbing a notebook off the table, Buck said, "Just how close were Aunt Emma and Bones Malone?"

Pearl would have blushed at his question had her complexion made that particular phenomenon possible. Instead she smiled and said, "Your Aunt Emma would have done anything for that man."

"But they had a falling out and you don't know why?"

She shook her big head. "They got along just fine. Mr. Bones was always doing for Miss Emma."

"Like what?"

"Bringing her pretty flowers, Indian pottery, and things he found down by the lake. Nothing expensive, but she always seemed to appreciate his thoughtfulness."

"They ever argue?"

"Only once," Pearl said, "when she booted him out and told him not to come around again."

"What did he do?"

"Sorry, Mr. Buck. I've racked my brain trying to decide if Mr. Bones might somehow be responsible but for all his faults I believe he really loved your Aunt Emma. In all the time I knew him I never saw him hurt a fly."

Memories of Aunt Emma quickly depressed Pearl. She drifted back into the kitchen. Buck wouldn't let the matter rest. When Pearl returned he said, "Why did Aunt Emma mortgage the island?"

Again Pearl's smile disappeared. "She didn't, Mr. Buck. Sure she wanted to put the lodge and marina back like it was in the old days, but she never borrowed a penny her whole life."

"Then you think Rummels is lying?"

"Like a dog," Pearl said.

Pearl returned to the kitchen and Buck sipped his coffee until Ray arrived. After kissing his mother, Ray frowned at Buck and said, "You ready?"

Ray didn't wait for Buck to answer before hurrying out the door. When Buck reached the dock the boat's motor was already running, Ray waiting at the tiller. He guided them through the maze of cypress trees surrounding Fitzgerald island, increasing speed when he reached open water. Ten minutes passed with neither man speaking.

"Beautiful day," Buck finally said. When Ray refused to even nod, Buck said, "Something about me you don't like?"

"You whites amaze me," Ray said. "You have no regard for anything but your own personal convenience."

"That's a slightly racist remark," Buck said, staring hard into Ray's limpid eyes. "Is everyone around here a bigot?"

Ray laughed, reminding him of Raymond, for the first time since Buck had met him. "So you noticed. Maybe it's a local perversion."

"What is going on here?"

"Why ask me? I think you already know."

"I don't know anything. Please tell me."

Muscles in Ray's big arm flexed and he subconsciously clenched his left hand into a fist. "Same thing that's gone on for a hundred and fifty years around here. Discrimination, racial hatred, bigotry, fear and intimidation."

"I saw black and white children playing together down by the lake."

"Bigotry's taught. You ain't born with it," he said, suddenly adopting the drawl of a Southern field hand.

"Why here?"

Ray slowed the engine and let the boat nose silently through an acre of white-blooming lily pads, their cloying fragrance melding with the sweet fetor of fish and decaying vegetation.

"Mind control," he said. "A powerful shackle."

"Who needs this power?"

"Look around Deception. Go to the bank, grocery store or any of the tourist's shops. See how many blacks you find doing anything other than pushing a broom or polishing some white man's shoes."

Buck hesitated, then said, "You make it sound like a conspiracy."

"More than sounds like it."

"You're joking."

"Am I? Ever heard of the Invisible Empire?"

"You mean —?"

"The Klan, man. Knights of the White Camellia. The Ku Klux Klan."

"The Klan is a force in Deception?"

"Bet your life on it. The Secret Order of Invisible Knights is still viable in East Texas, even after civil war and years of brutal reconstruction. But you knew that already."

"No, I don't. Why do you keep saying that?"

"I saw you down by the lake with Nation and his two thugs. Think I don't know what you intend to do with the island?"

"Not true. If I can find a way to pay off the bank note, I'll keep the island. And I'll see that your mom and dad receive their inheritance. If I discover someone was responsible for Aunt Emma's death, I'll have them put behind bars. That I promise you."

Ray didn't bother commenting. They had cleared the pads and Buck grabbed both sides of the boat as Ray gunned the engine and powered ahead. Draping tentacles of Spanish moss clutched at their faces as they passed beneath a thick grove of water-bound cypress trees. Giving up on conversation, Buck turned his attention to the spectacular scenery and their circuitous path through the hoary water forest.

Off the port bow there were many rotting wood platforms littering the lake, rusted pumping units and oil tanks occupying some of the platforms. Others, abandoned and decaying, had simply become mooring spots for fisherman. Silver fins of a large fish flashed through the lake's coffee-colored surface and overhead a pelican floated against green-cast sky. When they reached Deception, Ray guided the boat into shore and Buck climbed out and started up the hill. Before he'd gone ten paces, he turned and asked one last question.

"Is Nation part of the Klan?"

A smirk was his only answer to Buck's question. "Number for the marina is in the phone book," he said. "When you take care of your business, someone will come for you."

Turning the boat around, Ray headed back to the island. Caught up in the lake's silence and disappearing drone of the boat's tiny engine, Buck watched him disappear into lush subtropical vegetation. Young, attractive and obviously well educated, Ray had a voice as rich as Sidney Poitier's but an attitude that more closely resembled Louis Farrakhon's. Buck wondered why a person with so much going for him could have such a giant grudge against the world. At least the white world.

Now Deception beckoned, and possible answers to questions raised during his first day on the island. Tossing a rock far out into the lake, he watched a circular ripple spread slowly from the point of impact.

CHAPTER SEVEN

Another hot and humid Texas morning, Buck's shirt was already soaked as he climbed the bank to Deception amid crowds of gaping tourists. He would have liked to tour the town himself but he had other things on his mind. A talk with the sheriff topped the list and an old man with a fishing pole on his shoulder directed him to the jail.

The town's municipal complex near the far end of town left Buck immediately impressed. Larger and nicer than similar complexes in many cities, Deception's cut stone and sculptured concrete replaced hand-cut pine slats of the rest of town. Buck located the sheriff's office at the end of a long hallway, Sheriff Taylor Wright at his desk and his gangly deputy standing against the wall. Wright glanced up when Buck opened the door.

"I'm Buck McDivit, Emma Fitzgerald's nephew."

Wright didn't seem impressed. Pointing to the chair in front of his desk, he said, "Have a seat. Been expecting you."

With a red bandanna he wiped his rugged forehead scarred by teenage acne. The air conditioning wasn't working very well and sweat had stained a large ring around the neck of his khaki shirt. He had no discernible drawl and Buck judged from his age he might have lost it while in the Army, possibly Vietnam. Probably along with the bullet-shaped chunk missing from his right ear.

Wright continued staring at the manila folder on the desk and Buck took the opportunity to scope out the room. Framed pictures of Ronald Reagan and George W. Bush hung on the wall and a small rotating fan vibrated on the floor. When the water dispenser burped, Wright shoved the folder out of his way and stared at Buck with unnerving eyes.

Finally he said, "Sorry about your Aunt Emma, McDivit."

"Thanks," Buck said. "Can you tell me what happened?"

A muscle in Wright's cheek twitched and he massaged it until it stopped before reopening the manila folder. "Fisherman found her floating in the middle of the lake, tangled in his trotline."

"She drowned?"

"Looks that way." Sheriff Wright's twitch returned and he said, "Seems unlikely she was fishing because she had her nightgown on." He glanced at the lanky deputy, still propped against the wall. "Sam, get us some coffee."

Sam's bookish appearance, resulting primarily from his unruly hair and thick horn-rimmed glasses, contrasted with his strike khakis, ten-gallon hat and the big .44 at his side.

"Yes, sir," he said, jumping to action at the sheriff's command.

"Sam Goodlake," Sheriff Wright said. "My deputy."

"Pleased to meet you," Buck said.

Goodlake nodded. "Hear you're a P.I. in Oak City."

"Word travels fast in Deception."

"Only thing that does."

Wright and Goodlake both grinned, as if Sam had cracked a private joke. The deputy's sing-song drawl sounded like the twangy riff of a steel guitar but Buck strongly doubted anyone ever kidded him about it, or anything else. He filled two foam cups from a large stainless steel coffee maker as Sheriff Wright, his own amusement quickly fading, drummed his knuckles on the desk top.

"We found Emma floating face down in the water," Wright said. "No boat. No fishing gear. Pearl Johnson said she'd been brooding all day."

A squirrel perched on the window sill cracking pine cones with his teeth. Wright sipped his coffee slowly before continuing his rambling account of Emma Fitzgerald's demise.

"Emma was still awake when Pearl went home for the night. Maybe the storm disoriented her and she wandered down to the lake. Storms around these parts can whip up high winds and waves. Maybe Emma fell in the water and got swept out to the middle of the lake."

Buck sipped his own coffee. "You don't sound convinced."

"That's because I'm not. I just got the coroner's report. Dr. Tom pegs the cause of death as suicide. He thinks Emma just waded into the water and let herself drown."

"Seems a stretch. What's his reasoning?"

"Pearl's testimony, mainly."

"Why rule out accidental death, or foul play?"

The sheriff shot a glance at Sam Goodlake and they both grinned. "Emma could swim like a tadpole and I don't know anyone strong enough to hold that old lady's head under water."

"Mind if I look at the coroner's report?" Buck said.

The file in front of Sheriff Wright was apparently Aunt Emma's and he pushed it across the desk. The folder contained the coroner's report, notes and photos taken at the scene, and Sheriff Wright's account of what he saw. Buck quickly scanned the report.

Dr. Proctor ruled Aunt Emma's death a suicide by drowning, concluded because of Pearl's testimony, the absence of marks of violence on Aunt Emma's body and the water in her lungs. Buck quickly thumbed through the photos until one caught his attention.

"This report says Aunt Emma had no marks of violence on her body. What about this?"

He handed Wright a photo that showed him squatting over Aunt Emma's body, touching the back of her head.

"What about it? We took lots of pictures."

"Looks like blood caked in her hair to me," Buck said.

"Maybe she banged into a stump in the lake. The storm was chopping up the water pretty good out there."

"Then the blood would have washed away before it dried. Looks to me like it caked up in her hair before she ever went in the lake."

"What's your point, McDivit?"

"My point is her death could just as easily be accidental or maybe even murder."

"Emma had no enemies."

"What about Bones Malone?"

"Bones is harmless. If you knew him, you'd know that."

"I'd like to ask him a few questions. Know where I can find him?"

"He's on the lake somewhere. We won't find him till he wants to be found."

Buck shook his head in disbelief. "Can you think of anyone else that might have reason to harm Aunt Emma?"

Wright stretched back in his chair and scratched his chin. "Not many people in Deception agreed with Emma's politics. When I returned to Deception after the War, Emma had a grocery store over in Rambeau. Black town. Some of the folks around here called her a nigger lover."

Buck's neck flushed at Wright's blatant racist remark. He took a deep breath and said, "You think someone might have murdered her because she respected human rights?"

Wright's pasty face colored. "Why hell no. Emma drowned, pure and simple. I don't believe she committed suicide any more than you do, but that's the official finding."

"What about the blood on her head?"

"Maybe a limb fell on her head while she was in the lake. No telling what might have happened during the storm."

Buck kept quiet, waiting to hear the rest of the story. Instead Sheriff Wright closed the file, pushed it to the edge of his desk and began cleaning his nails with an old pocket knife. Buck's interview, it seemed, was over.

At the door, he said, "What about the wound, Sheriff? What did it look like?"

"Better ask Dr. Tom about that. And McDivit," he said. "Watch yourself."

The visit with the Sheriff left Buck with more questions than answers and he somehow doubted Dr. Proctor would rectify the problem. At least not purposely. He set out along the maze of marbled corridors to find his office.

The nameplates Buck found on two adjacent offices surprised him: Hogg Nation, Mayor of Deception and Ben Malone, County Archeologist. It made him wonder how many possible conflicts of interest were at work in Deception. He located the office of the coroner on the second floor.

Municipal employees were leaving for lunch, the coroner's door locked, the hallway empty. No one answered when he knocked. After picking the lock he slipped inside, finding the reception area dark and empty, the door to Dr. Proctor's private office ajar. Pushing it open slowly, Buck peeked inside.

The room was deserted and banks of gray file cabinets on the walls surrounded a stainless steel table used for performing autopsies. Buck searched the file cabinet, soon locating Aunt Emma's autopsy report. An exact copy of the one he'd seen at the sheriff's. The coroner's copy had the notation Emfitz.aut, the name of a computer file, at the bottom of the last page. Aunt Emma's autopsy report was on computer and Buck began searching the office for hardware to access it. He found no computer, not even a dumb terminal.

Backtracking through the reception area he entered Proctor's office and quickly located a computer on his desk. An open window faced the alleyway and someone outside was mowing grass. Focusing on the computer, Buck blocked out the mower's high-pitched whine and concentrated on controlling his elevated heart rate. The computer was active, flying toasters filling the screen. The toasters disappeared, revealing the main menu when he tapped the return key. After calling up Aunt Emma's file on the word processor, he scanned it to satisfy himself it was identical to the hard copy in Proctor's file. A clatter of keys at the door stole his attention from the screen and he glanced around for a place to hide. He froze as a lone woman retrieved a purse from beneath the receptionist's chair then hurried away without noticing Proctor's open door.

Returning the computer to the main menu, Buck scanned the listings for a recovery program to recover files deleted purposely or otherwise. Most computers have one and so did Proctor's. Buck quickly scanned the list of recently deleted files on both drives. And there it was. A baritone voice in the hall halted him again. This time it wasn't the receptionist. Grabbing a loose diskette, Buck hit the return key and restored the deleted file to the diskette. But it was too late to hide. Popping the diskette out of the drive, he slipped over the open second-story windowsill and jumped, twisting his ankle when he hit the ground. As he grimaced in pain, he realized he wasn't alone. Staring down at him was a very startled old man.

CHAPTER EIGHT

Buck stared up into the startled eyes of the man that had been mowing the lawn outside the coroner's office. His ankle refused to support his weight when he attempted to stand. As someone shouted from the window he slumped in pain, waiting for the other shoe to drop.

"What's going on down there?"

"Just me, Dr. Tom," the black man said, shielding Buck from the man's view with the mower's grass bagger.

"That you, Ezra?"

"Yas, sah," the man said in a field hand's drawl. "Big gust a wind about blew your window out just now."

"That what it was?"

"Yas, sah," the man named Ezra said. "Blowed right on over and's gone now."

"All right. You can get back to work now," Dr. Proctor said, slamming his window shut and pulling his blinds.

Buck noticed the old man's deformities for the first time. Polished scar tissue encased his neck and half his face. His right arm lay bent in a permanent crook. When he extended a helping hand, Buck saw the man had three missing fingers. The lumpy appendage remaining at the end of his wrist looked more like a gnarled lobster claw than a hand.

"Are you badly hurt?" he asked, every hint of his former drawl gone.

"My ankle's starting to swell," Buck said. "Must have sprained it."

"Try putting a little weight on it."

Buck's ankle was tender and sensitive to pressure and he didn't think he could run away without answering the old man's questioning stare.

"I'm Buck McDivit. Emma Fitzgerald's nephew. I can explain about what

I was doing in the coroner's office."

"If you're Emma's kin, you don't need to explain anything to me. I'm Ezra Davis."

Ezra Davis put his shoulder under Buck's arm, helping him around the corner to where a strange vehicle awaited. It had bicycle tires in back and smaller front wheels. A simple pipe frame supported a bench seat large enough to carry two adults. An attached wire basket provided baggage room. Leg power, via bicycle chain and two sets of pedals, propelled the contraption. Ezra Davis helped Buck into the vehicle.

"Ol' Betsy," he said. "She doesn't look like much but she gets me where I want to go."

They started down the alleyway at a steady clip, Ezra at the wheel. The grassy path was part of a complex maze of alleys that continued through town. Towering shrubs shrouded both sides of the pathway.

"My own private interstate," Ezra said. "I keep it pruned and mowed. My son and I use it to pick up the garbage behind the buildings twice a week. Long as we're not late picking up the garbage, no one ever bothers us."

"You don't sound like a garbage man."

"What's a garbage man supposed to sound like?" Ezra said.

"Sorry," Buck said, catching the inflection in Ezra's voice. "No offense intended."

"Didn't think there was," Ezra said.

Ezra followed the meandering path through town, finally stopping on its far edge. After parking Ol' Betsy beneath a neatly trimmed shed, he helped Buck through a passageway in the hedge. A complex of about twenty houses lay on the other side. From their shape and size, Buck suspected they were part of a government-subsidized project. Ezra led Buck through the back door of one of the houses and carefully latched the door behind them. He helped Buck to a couch, removed his boot and wrapped his swollen ankle with an ice-filled towel.

"Now you can explain what were you doing in the coroner's office."

"Trying to get a handle on what's going on around here," Buck said.

"I'm an old man. Better tell me what you mean."

Ezra Davis was old and also insistent, but he seemed like someone you could trust. Buck decided to confide in him. "Such as why the coroner thinks Aunt Emma committed suicide, why Hogg Nation wants Fitzgerald Island so badly and how Bones Malone fits into the mix."

Ezra scratched his stubbled chin. "Emma Fitzgerald didn't commit suicide. I can tell you that right now."

"You know that for a fact?"

"I don't know what or who killed Miss Emma but I know she wouldn't have taken her own life."

"My thoughts exactly. What can you tell me about Hogg Nation?"

"He's the kingfish around these parts. Owns most of Deception. What he doesn't own, he either doesn't want or else is well on his way to acquiring." Ezra stepped over to the window and held back the curtain with the back of his hand. "See those men on the hill?"

An old junker Chevy sat parked on the rise overlooking the project. Two men sat on its hood, both in camouflage fatigues that were neatly bloused into highly polished combat boots. One of the men was observing the project through binoculars.

"What are they doing?" Buck asked.

"Watching the project."

"I can see that. What for?"

"Harassment, mostly. They key our cars. Let air out of the tires. Things like that."

"Why don't you call the sheriff?"

"He says there's nothing he can do. They're on public property." As Buck considered this information about the two men, Ezra grinned and said, "You look like you could use a cold glass of water."

"Sounds like heaven," Buck said, glancing around the little house for the first time as Ezra disappeared into the kitchen.

Low ceilings and narrow hallways marked the house as cheaply constructed, but it was neat and tastefully decorated. When Ezra returned from the kitchen with two glasses of ice water, Buck realized there was no air conditioning, only the hum of an attic fan drawing hot air up through the roof.

"So you're Emma's boy," he said. "I see the resemblance."

"You knew her?"

"Worked for her awhile down at her grocery store in Rambeau. Before that I helped her brew the beer she served on her beer boat out in the lake."

"Was she —?"

"One of the nicest woman God ever created. Not a mean bone in her body. A fine lady."

"I wish I had known her."

Ezra Davis stroked the scar tissue on the side of his face and slowly shook his head. Then he spoke in a voice that sounded more like a college professor than garbage man. "Some white people around here called Miss Emma a nigger lover. They're part of a small hard-core element that's full of hate."

"Meaning," Buck said.

"Just that this part of Texas is a throwback to pre-Civil War days. Most whites here have little social interaction with blacks. Integration's the law, but the reality is a strict form of social segregation."

"You sound like someone I know," Buck said. "Your scars?"

Ezra nodded but didn't explain. "People go to extraordinary lengths to justify their bigotry and racism. Here in East Texas time ain't changed a damn thing."

Somewhere down the street a car backfired, causing a dog to yelp. It sounded strangely far away.

"Who are those two men on the hill?"

"Part of the New Southern Right. Cars and boats have replaced their horses, masks, and army fatigues their white sheets. They still practice the same old gospel of terrorism."

"To what purpose?"

Ezra pointed at the wall and said, "This project. Those men or others like them are out there twenty-four hours a day. I haven't told you half of what they've done to us. They've set our houses on fire, strafed us with bullets and intimidated our people. They want us out of here and don't care who they have to harm or kill in order to accomplish their goal."

"The sheriff must be in on what's going on."

Ezra shrugged. "He knows, but what can he do? Arrest one racist around here and another just takes his place."

"What about the Feds?"

"Hogg Nation is well connected, both in Austin and Washington. We've complained but have yet to receive anything more than lip service. Still, we don't intend to give up or leave our homes."

"Good for you," Buck said, probing his sore ankle with his fingers. "The swelling's gone down and I think I can walk. I better go now. Know where I can find Lila Richardson's antique shop?"

"I'll give you a lift in Ol' Betsy. You're white and you must never be seen coming or going from the project."

Buck felt the seriousness in Ezra's voice and took him at his word. Five minutes later they were again traversing the hidden alleyway through town. Ezra stopped Ol' Betsy near a walkway leading to a main street.

"Miss Lila's shop is just around the corner," he said.

Buck stepped down gingerly from the contraption, testing his weight on the sore ankle. It still hurt, but didn't keep him from walking.

"You didn't tell me about your scars," he said.

Ezra Davis rocked forward and nodded, as if he'd waited all along for the inevitable question. "My wife taught at the Negro school in Rambeau. One night someone tossed a Molotov cocktail through the window. Effie was in the building, grading exams. I have these scars to remind me every day of my life how I failed to get her out of that schoolhouse before it became a blazing hell on earth."

CHAPTER NINE

Buck found Lila Richardson's antique shop around the corner, in the heart of the lake front business district. In the park across the street a group of old men played dominoes beneath a giant elm. No one seemed to notice the lone man limp out of the alleyway. Quickly melding into the scenery, Buck entered the realm of brick and wood facades lovingly restored to a semblance of an earlier era.

This portion of Deception had become a tourist's showcase with restaurants, shops and businesses imparting the feel of a historical monument, circa 1850. Heat and humidity permeated late morning as scads of tourists dressed in shorts and tee shirts, shopping storefronts crammed with art, crafts and antiques, strolled on both sides of the street. A big yellow dog with a slow wagging tail had his nose in a trash can and didn't seem to notice the human melee on the street. Lila Richardson's shop was aptly named Lila's Antiques & Collectibles.

Bells sounded as Buck entered the heavy door decorated with cut-glass cherubs prompting a pretty black woman to glance up from her newspaper and flash him a world-class smile.

"Help you?"

After a deep breath and a quick glance around the shop that looked and smelled like concentrated antiquity, he said, "Is Ms. Richardson in?"

Crocheted yellow flowers decorated the woman's floor-length skirt. Her matching yellow ceramic earrings draped almost to her bare shoulders. With a blink of her big brown eyes, she said, "Miss Lila stepped out for a moment. I'm Sara. Maybe I can help you."

Sara slowly leaned over the counter, resting her chin in her palms to reveal more than a glimpse of abundant brown cleavage.

"Maybe so," Buck said, maintaining his composure. "Can you identify an antique for me?"

"Sure that's all you need?" was Sara's suggestive reply.

"Hey, you never know," Buck said, flashing his own best smile.

"Miss Lila will be back shortly. You can browse around until then if you like."

She grinned wickedly when he said, "I already have."

"I better get to work before you get me in trouble," Sara said, grabbing a duster and disappearing behind the cabinet.

The shop was a mass of shelves packed to the ceiling with antiques and Buck barely had time to scan a single object before an attractive woman brushed past him and joined the flirtatious clerk behind the counter. Sara greeted her with a whispered message. After assessing Buck with a discerning stare, the woman joined him. Sara remained behind the counter, grinning as she watched. "I'm Lila Richardson. Sara said you wish to speak with me."

Lila Richardson had memorable hazel eyes that momentarily made him forget Sara's cleavage.

"Buck McDivit," he said. "Someone told me you might know something about this."

Handing her the encrusted brooch, he watched as she turned it slowly in her hand. Without explanation she started away toward the rear of the building. Buck winked at the buxom Sara as he followed the lovely Miss Richardson.

Antiques jammed every inch of the hallway and Lila squeezed down a narrow path to an antique desk where she switched on a lamp, opened a drawer and grabbed a jeweler's loupe. "Have a seat," she said, pointing an elegant finger at the empty chair beside the desk. "This is very crusty and might take a while to clean up."

Lila Richardson placed the loupe against her eye and examined the brooch. Then she began de-scaling it with a stainless steel dental instrument. After ten minutes of silent work, she placed the brooch on the desk top and glanced up at Buck. "Where did you get this?"

"The sheriff found it clutched in my Aunt Emma's hand. Anything you can tell me about it?"

Lila Richardson was a handsome woman and the way she leaned back in her chair and stretched reminded him of Sara. But Lila did have striking hazel eyes. His favorite shade. She exhaled slowly. "The engraved inscription on back of the brooch says 'To My Loving Daughter.' It bears the initials E.M.M. and the date 1870."

"Mean anything to you?"

Again she drew a breath, leaned forward slowly and rested her hands on the desk. "Are you familiar with the story of Bessie McKinney?"

"Somewhat."

"Bessie died in 1872. Her real name was Elizabeth Marie McKinney. Bessie to her friends."

"You think this is Bessie McKinney's brooch?"

Lila Richardson flipped back honey-blonde curls from her face and licked her lips. "Alabaster cameos were quite popular during that era. We could run a check of the courthouse to see who else had those initials, but Bessie naturally comes to mind."

Buck refrained from telling her about the apparition. Instead he said, "You've been a big help, Ms. Richardson."

"No bother. I love old things," she said, relaxing in the chair. "Mind if I ask who gave you my name?" He noticed a puzzling and almost imperceptible change in her expression when he told her. "How do you know Ray Johnson?"

"I inherited Fitzgerald Island from my Aunt Emma. Ray works at the marina." Her cheeks reddened at his answer. "Something the matter?"

"No, nothing. What else can I do for you?"

Lila's question prompted his memory and he fished the brass fitting from his shirt pocket, handing it to her. "One more antiquity. Any ideas?" Lila hefted the heavy rectangular object with both hands. "I found it on the backside of Fitzgerald Island."

"An old piece of brass," she said, scratching the slab with her dental instrument. "This will take more time. Looks like it was buried in the dirt."

"Yes," he said, glancing at his watch. "I really appreciate your help and I'd like to repay you. Have lunch with me?"

Lila's creamy complexion reddened again. "I don't usually accept invitations from gentlemen that I've just met."

"Consider it a business lunch," Buck said. "It'll give me a chance to pick your brain some more and I'll be eternally grateful."

"Well —"

"Please," Buck said. "I promise I'll be a perfect gentleman."

Buck's smile was contagious. "You don't sound Southern, sir, but you're as persuasive as a New Orleans lawyer. I'd be pleased to join you."

"Fantastic. Lead the way."

Before leaving the shop, Lila whispered something to Sara who barely stifled a giggle. Buck and Lila went across the street to a cozy little café where a friendly waiter seated them in a secluded corner near the window. Lila ordered a glass of Chardonnay.

"Thought you Southern girls drank mint juleps," he said.

Lila made a face. "Ever taste one?" Then she said, "I think Sara has a crush on you."

"Oh?"

"Didn't you notice how she was acting at the shop?"

"I just thought she treated everyone that way."

"Hardly," Lila said, stifling her own Southern giggle with a linen napkin.

Caught up in the friendly banter, they laughed aloud until their levity finally abated. When it did Buck said, "I noticed your expression when I mentioned Ray Johnson. Know him?"

Lila sipped her Chardonnay, closing her eyes in an introspective manner. "I've known him all my life. Ray and I grew up together."

Lunch arrived before Buck could probe the topic of Ray Johnson further. Between bites, he said, "East Texas isn't like anything I expected. It has a foreign, exotic flavor."

Lila smiled stopped eating. "I've never thought of it as foreign or exotic, but it does have an interesting history."

"I'd love to hear it."

"I wouldn't want to bore you."

"Not possible."

Buck's comment seemed to please Lila. Her muted accent became more Southern and defined, her words a story teller's chant as she began reciting Deception's history.

"Before the Civil War, a thriving port city grew around Jefferson, a town north of here. River boats steamed up the river from New Orleans following the Mississippi River to the Red River. Near Shreveport, the River intersects Caddo Lake. Boats followed the lake to Big Cypress Bayou, and then Jefferson. Deception was a stop along the way."

"But—"

"I know," Lila interrupted. "Caddo is too shallow for a large boat, but it wasn't then. River boats brought cloth, furniture and finished goods from all over the world, returning with cotton and lumber to mills back east."

The waiter interrupted Lila's story as he wheeled a dessert cart to a halt beside their table.

"Try their lemon meringue pie," Lila goaded. "I promise you it's the best you've ever eaten."

"Uncle," Buck said after finishing his slice of pie. When coffee arrived, he said, "What happened to the water level?"

"A log jam on the river had raised the water level. Engineers called it the Red River Raft. The government destroyed it and river boat traffic halted almost immediately. Deception was dependent on river trade and soon became little more than what you see today."

"A beautiful woman deserted by her cruel lover," Buck said, staring across the table into Lila's bewitching hazel eyes.

"Very poetic, but so very true."

Across the empty restaurant, a waiter dropped a plate, shattering glass releasing them from their trance. Lila stole a peek at her watch.

"I've had a lovely time but I have an appointment in Jefferson this afternoon. Thanks for lunch."

"One more question, please. Do you know Bones Malone?"

"I've done business with Mr. Malone, but I'm not particularly proud of the fact."

"Business?"

"In things he found around the lake. Caddo is a repository of historical objects and Mr. Malone has a knack for ferreting them out."

"You don't approve?"

"My hands aren't lily white. I've bought certain antiquities from Mr. Malone I probably shouldn't have. Pottery and artifacts from Indian mounds."

"But I thought Mr. Malone was an archeologist?"

"Little more than a scavenger, actually. But he does know what's valuable. I'll give him that." Lila started for the door. "I can't remember when I've had a more delightful afternoon but now I have to run."

Halfway to the door she stopped and said, "Would you like to come to my house for dinner tomorrow night?"

"Love to," Buck said.

Lila's exotic eyes sparkled. "My father is hosting a little party. I'd like for you to meet him."

Buck called out to her as she turned for the door. "Wait. Where do you live?"

Realizing her omission, Lila's hand went to her lips in a purely Southern gesture. "The Richardson Mansion. Just outside town. Anyone can tell you where to find it. And Buck, I must confess it's more than just a party. It's black tie and tux."

"Maybe a bit too fancy for a cowboy from Oklahoma City."

"Nonsense," Lila said. "It's a campaign party for my uncle, Jeff Travis. He's running for reelection as judge."

"Judge Travis is your uncle?"

"Yes. Have you two met?"

"Not yet. Is your father in politics, too?"

"President, CEO and primary stockholder of First Deception Bank."

"How many banks does Deception have?"

"Just one, silly."

Lila flashed another pretty smile, exiting the front door before Buck could ask any more questions about Judge Travis or her father. When it dawned on him that this wonderful woman might even be involved in the repossession of Fitzgerald Island, the thought unnerved him.

CHAPTER TEN

Buck decided to pay another visit to Lila's shop. If anyone knew if the lovely Miss Richardson had a dark side, it would surely be Sara. He watched through the restaurant window until Lila hurried out the front door of her shop. He waited another ten minutes to make sure she hadn't forgotten something. With the pie he'd ordered at the restaurant, he started for the door.

It was nearly two when he finally left the restaurant's air-conditioned coolness, outside heat all but forgotten until he opened the restaurant door. A blast of damp air jogged his memory as he stepped off the porch. The obvious discomfort of throngs of sweaty tourists on the street made the temperature seem even more oppressive. He forgot the heat when he entered Lila's shop.

Sara was at the sales counter reading a fashion magazine. She cast a wicked grin when she glanced up and saw him. "Miss Lila's gone," she said. "That means you must be here to see me."

"Good guess."

Leaning on her elbows Sara took a long breath, giving Buck another glimpse of her swelling bosom. "See something you liked?"

"That I did," he said. "I even brought you something."

"For little ol' me? Now what did the handsome white man bring little Sara? Diamonds or pearls?"

"Something twice as sweet. Lemon meringue pie from across the street."

The provocative movement of Sara's hips as she took the slice of pie told Buck she knew he was watching. She retrieved a plastic fork from beneath the counter. After a lingering bite of meringue she licked the sticky tines before forking a bite into Buck's mouth.

"Now just what do I have to do for your little ol' slice of pie?" she asked.

Buck leaned closer. So close their noses almost bumped. "I'm new in town. Fill me in on a few things."

"Like what?"

"Local gossip. Who's doing what to who."

Sara relaxed and said, "Honey, you came to the right place. Not much around here this girl doesn't know."

"What about Lila? You like working for her?"

"I'd stick my arm in an oven if Miss Lila asked me to. She's a real lady. Her daddy's one of the richest men in the county but she don't rub it in anyone's face. She earned everything she has on her own. Everyone's just the same to Miss Lila."

"I thought so."

"Honey, you don't know the half of it. Last summer she was having some work done at the Richardson Mansion. Two workmen were cleaning the chandelier in the hallway. It was priceless, all crystal and silver. Brought over from France before the Civil War.

"Those workmen were clowning and cutting up and somehow broke the chandelier loose from the ceiling. It exploded on the marble floor in a million pieces. Miss Lila cleaned up the glass and the workmen's cuts, never saying a word about the broken chandelier. She's a real Southern lady."

"Is she and Hogg Nation close?"

If my question seemed curious to Sara, she didn't show it.

"Mr. Nation and Miss Lila? They barely know each other."

"What about the rest of the town? What's going on around here?"

"Growing in leaps and bounds. I know you saw the new development down by the lake. Mr. Nation intends to put Deception on the map."

"What part does Lila play in the development?"

"No part at all."

"The development's not a family undertaking?"

"It's Mr. Nation's dream. Something he's worked for all his life."

Sara's pensive tone when speaking of Hogg Nation caught Buck by surprise and he was unable to prevent the sarcastic inflection in his reply. "Maybe Nation's dream is someone else's nightmare."

"Why Mr. Nation has done more good for these parts than any man alive," Sara said defensively. "Surely you can see that?"

All that Buck could see was that he had touched a nerve. Sara obviously didn't care for his attitude and her smile melted away, along with the last crumbs of pie crust which she whisked off the counter. Tossing the plastic fork into the trash she backed against the wall, crossing her arms tightly.

When the bell on the front door rang and a horde of sweaty tourists entered, he used the diversion to depart gracefully.

"See you later, Sara. I'll let you take care of your customers."

Too busy with a potential sale, she didn't notice him limp out the door on his sprained ankle. He'd probably offended Sara but she had told him what he had wanted to hear about Lila. Packing up and returning to Oklahoma had seriously crossed his mind when he first learned Lila was related to Judge Travis. He couldn't remember the last time he'd felt so irrational. The momentary vulnerability bothered him.

A hot breeze blowing up from the lake swept over him as he stepped outside but the roar of an unmuffled boat made him forgot the heat and Lila Richardson. At least for a moment. He watched it race across the lake, rippling open water into a miniature tidal wave and threatening to overturn any moored fishing boat in its path. It was Hogg Nation's boat.

When Buck called the lodge, Pearl informed him Raymond was already waiting for him at the dock. Raymond didn't mention Buck's limp or his silence during the boat trip home. He never shut up long enough to notice.

Shadows were encroaching on the lake when they reached the island. Raymond had run out of stories and bade Buck goodnight with a simple backhand wave. The feather mattress in Buck's room beckoned but the light from Wiley's lantern caught his attention. He was fishing off the dock again and he tossed Buck a cold beer from the ice chest.

"What's up? Hard day at the office?"

"Might say that," Buck said. "I talked with the sheriff, visited the coroner's office, inspected the local housing project and had lunch with the most beautiful woman in East Texas."

"Whewee!" Wiley said. "You did have a busy day."

Pulling off his boot with some difficulty, Buck dangled his swollen foot in the water. It was after nine, the old Coca Cola thermometer on the marina wall still topping eighty-five degrees.

"What happened to your foot?" Wiley asked.

"Sprained it jumping out a window."

Wiley gave Buck a sideways glance but didn't comment on his cryptic reply. The sky signaled rain and flashes of heat lightning, electrifying damp nighttime ozone, laced the horizon. Leaning back against the cypress post, Buck relaxed for the first time in twelve hours.

"What's going on around here?" he finally said.

"A little catfishing and a lot of beer drinking," Wiley said.

"I'm serious. Seems like every time I turn over a rock, another snake crawls out."

"Stay away from rocks." Then, sensing Buck's seriousness, he said, "You all right?"

"Fine, but I have a real problem. No one I've talked to seems to think Aunt Emma committed suicide. Why is suicide the official prognosis of what happened?"

"I'd like to know myself," Wiley said. When Buck told him about his visit to the coroner's office, Wiley's broad grin evaporated. "You broke into the coroner's office? Man, you must be crazy."

"Aunt Emma had a wicked cut on the back of her head. Sheriff Wright has a picture showing caked blood in her hair. The least the blood shows is that Aunt Emma got banged in the head before she went in the lake. Otherwise the water would have washed it away."

"What's the most?" Wiley asked.

"Murder," Buck said, letting the word die away, along with a crooked flash of lightning. Showing Wiley the diskette, he said, "I restored a deleted file off the hard disk in the coroner's office. I believe it's Aunt Emma's original autopsy report."

"You think Proctor doctored the original?"

"That's what I suspect, but I can't pull up the file because I don't have a computer."

"I do. I'll print you a hard copy. You still haven't explained Proctor's motivation."

Buck handed Wiley the diskette. After stowing it in his shirt pocket, Wiley recast his line into the water. "Maybe someone told him to change it. Someone like Hogg Nation, Mayor of Deception."

"To what purpose?" Wiley asked.

"To put a monkey wrench in Aunt Emma's insurance claim. Nation gets the island and we get the shaft. Fitzgerald Island is three miles from Nation's development. I can't figure out why he wants it in the first place."

Wiley pulled his line out of the water and fiddled with the hook a moment before replying. "You're not accusing Nation of murder, are you?"

"I'm accusing him of contriving a wrongful reason for Aunt Emma's death. She didn't commit suicide. Accidental death is more logical but murder is still a possibility."

Distant thunder signaled an approaching storm and cooler temperatures and thoughts of Hogg Nation dissolved away as gentle raindrops began dimpling the lake. Wiley didn't seem to notice.

"Who's this beautiful woman you met today?" he asked.

"Lila Richardson. Know her?"

"Sure do. Her daddy's the one foreclosing on the island."

"Lila has nothing to do with it."

"You sure about that? She's white, ain't she?"

Placing his empty can on the dock, Buck glared at Wiley and shook his head. "So am I, in case you haven't noticed. Is everyone around here a bigot?"

"Just kidding," Wiley said, his grin returning. He tossed Buck another beer. "I'm no bigot, Buck. Promise I'm not."

"I didn't think you were," Buck said. "What's the story on the project in Deception?"

"Government-subsidized housing. Mostly blacks. Built last summer. Some of the white folks around Deception have been up in arms ever since."

"But half the population around here is black."

"And they've lived apart until now. Rambeau is a tar paper and tin roof settlement about ten miles south of here. Blacks may work in Deception but they lived in Rambeau until the government put in the housing project."

"Ezra Davis told me Aunt Emma ran a grocery store in Rambeau."

"Some people around Deception got to thinking maybe she was black herself, but I guess you heard that already."

"What about Nation's men, Humpback and Deacon John? Where do they come from?"

"The Deacon just got sprung from Huntsville Prison. Maximum security. Judge Travis spoke up for him and Nation gave him a job."

"Why was he in Huntsville?"

"Armed robbery, rape, assault with a deadly weapon. He was head of the Aryan Brotherhood at the prison and the warden was mighty happy to see him go."

Buck wondered how Wiley knew so much about Deacon John but decided not to ask. "And Humpback?"

"A recidivist with a record of just about any crime you can name. Child molesting to attempted murder." Wiley tossed his line back in the water. "They both hate blacks and both are suspected of hate crimes committed in the vicinity."

"Such as?"

"Rape, castration, and hanging. Those heinous enough for you?"

"Maybe murder isn't so remote a possibility. Maybe Nation had Aunt Emma killed because of her liberal politics."

"Hogg Nation is a business man. He wouldn't kill anyone unless there was money involved."

Wiley's comment left Buck little to say. By now the sprinkle of rain had turned into a light shower. Wiley acted as if he didn't notice. Dark clouds draped the lake, periodic lightning imparting strobe-like incandescence to the edges of the mottled sky. Pulling his foot out of the water, Buck hoisted himself up.

"Thanks, now let me give you some advice," Buck said, a tone of sternness in his voice.

"What's that?" Wiley said, glancing up from his line.

"You're going to get wet sitting out here in the rain."

Grinning, Wiley rubbed his forearm in a slow, circular motion. "Hey, I got nothing to worry about. My black don't wash off."

Wiley laughed when Buck said, "Neither does my white but I'm not taking any chances."

Buck hurried back to the lodge and stood on the veranda, staring across the lake. Wind, whistling through the cypress brake, had raised whitecaps on the water. Buck didn't notice. He was too busy wondering about Wiley's endless knowledge of Humpback and Deacon John. Between lightning flashes he thought he saw a light way out in the lake and watched until it flickered, disappearing into the night.

CHAPTER ELEVEN

Next morning, Pearl Johnson solved Buck's tuxedo dilemma. "You're about Mr. Malone's size," she said.

Confused, Buck said, "Pardon me?"

"Mr. Malone left most of his belongings in his room upstairs. I'm sure he has a tux in the closet."

As Pearl pointed Buck toward Malone's room he speculated on Aunt Emma's live-in lover. It made him wish he'd known the old woman. Malone's room was different than he'd expected. The name Bones engendered an image of chaos and disarray. Quite the opposite proved true. The bed was neatly made and nothing seemed out of place. Shelves lined every wall and artifacts every shelf. India ink provided labels for broken pottery, old pistols, and photographs. It seemed Bones had collected the entire history of East Texas and stored it in his room.

A piney tobacco odor permeated the room and Buck guessed that Malone was probably a pipe smoker. The room was a veritable museum, history weighing as heavily as the prevailing humidity. Buck opened a window and let the outside breeze whip the blue cotton curtains.

On the wall was a water color painting of a large sidewheeler bearing the name *Mittie Stephens*. Happy black field hands waving from the bank watched as it steamed past. The picture looked so real Buck could almost hear its whistle blowing. Beneath the painting was a yellowed newspaper article. "Gold Ship Sinks!" the headline read. Buck scanned the article with rapt attention.

"— fire erupted on board the *Mittie Stephens*, sidewheeler bound for Jefferson, Texas. One hundred and fifty thousand dollars in gold bullion to pay Reconstruction troops was lost. Many of the more than one hundred passengers die —"

Buck quit reading when something on the floor caught his attention. It was a brass plate bearing the engraved name *Mittie Stephens*. As he fingered the plate, weighing its heft in his palm, he remembered the brass fitting he'd found in the hole on the backside of Fitzgerald Island.

Bones' room also housed a library containing mostly archaeological reference material. The books were arranged in neat, alphabetically correct rows. There was nothing amiss or out of order. Almost nothing. The imposing orderliness of the room drew Buck's attention to a prominent gap on the second shelf. A large book was missing and Buck found it on the small table Malone used for a desk.

The book was really a loose-leaf binder filled with codes and corresponding descriptions. Remembering the India ink labels on Malone's specimens, Buck checked the numbers and letters on an old shotgun against the codes in the book. And there it was. The label said Potpo013. The corresponding description in the loose-leaf binder indicated Malone had found the shotgun at an archeological dig near Potter's Point. It described and classified the gun, detailing its probable age and even postulating on the original owner. Buck returned the book to its place on the shelf.

When Buck finally got around to Malone's closet he quickly found the tuxedo he was looking for. Although old and cut for a different era, the tux was pressed and functional and Buck wondered if Malone had ever worn it.

Tiger followed him to his room. He hung the tux in the closet and changed into shorts and tee shirt. His body needed exercise and his mind craved it. He decided to go for a jog. Several sandy paths behind the lodge led into the pines and he started slowly, wary of heat and humidity. He soon reached a clearing near the top of a gentle rise and stopped to catch his breath. As he did an armadillo, looking like a miniature armor-plated pig, waddled toward him from out of the high grass. He watched it disappear into the underbrush before continuing his run.

Buck's path through the forest soon led to a sandy clearing occupied by little more than patches of saw grass and faded nettle. Several buzzards looped slow circles overhead and the potent odor of decaying flesh assaulted him. He had only to follow his nose to locate the offending smell.

Near the edge of the clearing, mounds of fresh dirt imitated the work of a giant gopher. Someone had dug several closely spaced holes, one quite deep and wide. Face down in the muddy water floated the body of a rabbit that had fallen in the hole and drowned and something shiny flashed up through the shallow water. Buck reached down and fished the shiny object out of the puddle.

The blackened hunk of metal with a leaden feel was an old coin. Something worried Buck as he let a handful of dirt sift through his fingers. The hole was fresh. Someone had dug it the previous night and morning sun had yet to dry the moisture in the dirt. Backing away from the trench, he continued up the sandy path for a mile or more before turning around and returning to the lodge.

Buck was tired but exhilarated when he reached the lodge. After a warm shower, he propped his feet on the bedstead and indulged himself in the comfort of a gentle breeze blowing though the open window. He soon faded into a fitful nap, dreaming of Lila when Pearl woke him for lunch. Buck had a question for Raymond when he joined him on the veranda.

"I'm going to a party across the lake and won't be back until late. Can I use one of the boats?"

Raymond gave Buck a quizzical glance. "Think you can find your way back by yourself?"

"It's not that far."

"No, but you've never done it alone."

"It's due west out of Deception. I'll focus on a western star."

Raymond grinned at Buck's confidence. "If you're sure, I ain't gonna to tell you no. Take the boat with running lights in front," he said, pointing to a bright red boat lapping in the waves against the dock.

"Thanks. What's all the digging about on the backside of the island?"

By the way Raymond scratched his head, Buck surmised he didn't know what he was talking about. "Maybe Wiley's been digging for worms."

"These aren't worm holes. One is big enough to bury someone in."

Raymond's eyes widened. "Nobody's missing round here."

Fingering the lump of gold, Buck said, "Maybe it wasn't bodies they were burying."

"What are you talking about?"

"Doesn't matter. Maybe Wiley or Ray will know about the holes."

They carried their dirty dishes to the kitchen. After pouring coffee from Pearl's bottomless carafe, Raymond sauntered toward the door.

"Got to get back to work," he said. "Buck, you be careful on the lake."

Noon sun had already burned a hole through early morning haze as Buck watched Raymond stroll away toward the marina. Wavelets of light danced between the coffee-colored lake and green-cast sky. This time there were no circling buzzards. Only a crow occupied the clear Texas sky and it voiced a continuous raspy irritation at a passing flock of blackbirds.

Tiger followed Buck to his room, purring and rubbing Buck's leg as he packed a small bag with tux and other necessities. Planning a few hours of research before the party, he included pen and note pad. Hiking the short distance to the marina, he untied the boat Raymond had provided and pushed away from the dock. The engine sputtered, spitting smelly smoke out the back, before finally cranking on the fifth pull of the rope.

Raymond was right. Crossing the lake alone was not the same as crossing it as a passenger but by using the sun as a guide, Buck soon reached open water. He finally saw Deception in the distance and docked the boat some thirty minutes later. Confidence bolstered, he transferred his gear to his truck then walked the streets of Deception until he found the Riverfront Museum. An old lady at the front desk collected his admission and pointed to the brick entryway of the musty old building. Buck was the only person in the place.

He followed the hallway, antiquities covering the walls, until he reached a narrow stairway leading to the building's second floor. A small room served as repository for old newspapers and other documents. Bessie McKinney died in 1872, according to Lila Richardson and Buck began by looking in the file cabinet with the appropriate date. There he found the local newspaper's account of Bessie McKinney. The yellowed newspaper article included a haunting picture.

Searchers had found her sitting on a stump by the lake, eyes open as if she were staring at something in the water. She didn't move when they called her name. The article described her body as unmarked by violence but rock hard and clammy with the feel of death. The picture left Buck with no remaining doubt. Bessie was the girl he'd seen drifting in a mist across the lake. Closing the drawer, he backed out of the room.

The maritime portion of the museum caused Buck to momentarily forget Bessie McKinney. Rows of steamships lay moored for posterity in the pictures lining the walls. Exotic names graced their hulls — *Edinburgh, Thirteenth Era, Lotus No. 3, Fleeta.* Then he came across an old black and white picture of the *Mittie Stephens.* An imposing craft, the *Mittie* was a sidewheeler with two tall smoke stacks and flags on the front and back.

The story accompanying the picture retold the article Buck had read in Malone's room. The *Mittie Stephens*, a three hundred and twelve-ton steamboat built in Madison, Indiana, was carrying more than one-hundred passengers, many kegs of gunpowder and one hundred and fifty thousand dollars in gold to pay the Reconstruction troops in Jefferson. The year was 1869. At midnight the pilot saw smoke rising from hay on board the boat. Within minutes, the boat was run as close to shore as possible and panic quickly overcame the passengers.

As flames advanced, passengers began jumping overboard. The side wheels continued turning since no one had thought to shut down the engines and many of the people in the water were drawn under by the action of the wheels. The catastrophe left only forty-three survivors to recount the tale.

Another article caught Buck's eye. In 1983 a team of researchers had searched for the wreck of the *Mittie Stephens* using sophisticated sounding equipment. Despite their diligence and an accurate description of where the boat went down, the wreck was never located.

"Sir, it's past closing time. I'm afraid you'll have to come back tomorrow."

Startled, Buck wheeled around, staring into the embarrassed eyes of the old woman from the admission desk. "Sorry," she said. "Didn't mean to scare you."

Buck rubbed his chin to prevent her from seeing the flush rising up his neck. "Thought you were a ghost for a minute."

"Wouldn't surprise me," she said. "You couldn't catch me in here after dark by myself."

Buck thanked her and made his way downstairs. Time had passed quickly in the musty old museum. Checking his watch upon reaching the truck, he realized he'd spent nearly three hours reading old newspapers and roaming dusty corridors. Summer sun remained high on the horizon and he stowed his notes in the glove box.

Buck changed into his tux at a service station near the west end of town where a greasy attendant in overalls and welder's cap provided directions to the Richardson Mansion. A few miles down the road he passed a brick wall surrounding what appeared to be a huge estate. The name on the wrought iron gate said Richardson. The main thoroughfare continued into distant pines and Buck followed the landscaped road a half mile before finally reaching the house.

House was a misnomer. What he saw in the distance filled him with visions of Tara at its zenith. Expensive sedans lined the circle driveway and several couples in tuxedos and evening gowns preceded him into a large ensuing party.

Four massive columns fronted the antebellum mansion and a black man in top hat and long-tailed tuxedo greeted Buck at the door. They traversed a marble-walled foyer where a giant gold-framed painting hung from the wall. The elaborate foyer barely prepared him for the ornateness of the rest of the mansion.

A black butler accompanied Buck down a long hallway to a ballroom in the center of the house. Behind the heavy doors, he heard sounds of a party in progress and wasn't disappointed when the butler opened the door. The giant ballroom, its cypress floors highly polished, its lacquered walls decorated with paintings in Greek Revival style, was larger than many small houses. Three magnificent crystal chandeliers hung from the high ceiling but all the ostentatious trappings paled against the ballroom's principal visual attraction: a beautiful winding stairway with lacquered banisters and steps covered by a red velvet rug. Formally attired guests crowded the ballroom and Buck pushed through the throng in search of Lila. He didn't have far to look.

Waves of excitement began pulsating through the ballroom and Buck glanced up the gilded staircase to see what everyone was staring at. It was Lila, posing like a queen at the top of the stairs, radiant in a diamond tiara and ball gown of kelly green. The gown was from a different era, complete with lace, hoops and petticoat and a plunging neckline that revealed more than a generous portion of ivory breasts. Diamonds and emeralds graced Lila's bare neck, a tiara crowning her honey-blonde hair. With everyone's attention focused, she began her floating descent to the ballroom below. When she reached the bottom of the stairs, she twirled like Loretta Young, her performance earning a resounding round of applause.

He watched as Lila began greeting guests, her smile befitting a queen receiving loyal subjects. Finally, she saw Buck and started toward him looking very different than the day they'd met. Lila had attracted him from the first moment but he remembered her as beautiful and businesslike, her ruffled lace collar the only feminine concession to her blue pinstripe dress. Now her golden tresses flowed in synchronous waves, framing her face and highlighting her hazel eyes. And the neckline of her gown left absolutely no doubt of her femininity. Inadvertently, Buck's heart began thumping like a drugged race horse on a very hot day.

CHAPTER TWELVE

Buck marveled at Lila's metamorphosis as she approached him through the crowd. Her smile displayed to good effect the wide mouth and pearly teeth of a cover girl. Some transformation, he thought.

"I'm so happy you came," she said, her Southern accent dripping like honey from a jar.

For some foolish reason Buck could think of nothing else to do except kiss her hand. His inane gesture brought a rosy blush to her cheeks.

"Wouldn't have missed it," he said, holding her hand a moment longer than absolutely necessary. Lila didn't seem to mind.

"I had a wonderful time at lunch yesterday. I feel I've known you all my life."

"Déjà vu?" Buck asked.

"Maybe, but you seem more of a cowboy than anyone I've met here in East Texas.

"I didn't wear my boots or my cowboy hat tonight."

"You look handsome and elegant," she said, leading him through the throng of people in the crowded ballroom. "I want you to meet Daddy."

Stares and whispers caused Buck's neck and ears to burn and he sensed he and Lila were the center of attention. Along the way she introduced him to lawyers, doctors, and politicians. People of wealth and influence. They located Lila's father in a secluded niche behind a large ornamental column. He was smoking a cigar and chatting with two men, one of whom Buck recognized as Hogg Nation. Unmindful of interrupting their conversation, Lila grabbed her father's elbow and turned him around. Buck thought he looked around sixty. About right, as he had guessed Lila's age as somewhere between late twenties and early thirties.

"This is Clayton Richardson III. Daddy, may I present Mr. Buck McDivit."

"Pleased, Mr. McDivit," Richardson said as he palmed Buck's hand in some secret fraternity grip.

Buck nodded at the sire of his beautiful companion. Standing a slender six four, the banker's thinning silver hair highlighted a shining forehead and the hooked bridge of a prominent nose. His sharp eyes fostered the appearance of stern intellect but his persistent smile hinted at a lighter disposition.

"This is my brother, Judge Jefferson Travis and our friend is Mr. Hogg Nation."

As Buck shook hands with Judge Travis and Hogg Nation he noticed the two seemed to know each other very well. Hogg Nation's smile revealed none of the animosity he had shown at their last meeting.

"Mr. McDivit and I have already met," Nation said. "Buck is Emma Fitzgerald's nephew."

Clayton Richardson nodded but didn't acknowledge his bank was in the process of foreclosing on Fitzgerald Island. Judge Travis became animated. "Hogg tells me he's made you a very generous offer for your late Aunt's property."

"Got a minute to talk about it, McDivit?" Nation asked.

Lila, to Buck's surprise, wrapped both her willowy arms around his waist. "Not on your life, Mr. Nation. Buck's my guest and there will be no business talk at this party."

"Sorry, Dauhta," Clayton said, adopting his own rendition of a Southern accent. "We were in the midst of a heated political discussion. We'll just get back to it."

Lila gave her father a playful slap on the cheek. "I know exactly what you were talking about, you old rogue. Probably telling Mr. Nation and Uncle Jeff about some flight attendant you met last week on the plane to Houston."

Clayton Richardson beamed with satisfaction. "You know me too well, Daughta, but don't say it too loudly."

Lila grabbed Buck's elbow, applying gentle but persuasive pressure. "You enjoy yourself, Daddy," she said, standing on her tiptoes and kissing Clayton Richardson's florid cheek. "I'm going to show Buck the garden."

Buck's thoughts returned to Lila's pronounced Southern accent as she pulled him away from the trio. They exited a large French door to a garden bordering one side of the mansion. Peppered with starlight, the sky was bright and dominated by a huge yellow moon.

"Isn't it a beautiful night?" she said.

"Absolutely gorgeous."

Catching Buck's eye, she grinned and said, "What are you looking at?"

A surge of pleasant warmth signaled the redness in his cheeks. He turned away, taking advantage of a shadow.

"Just a lovely Texas rose," he said.

Lila flicked her hand fan and winked at him. "Would you like me to give you a quick tour of the plantation before dinner?" she said.

The garden was landscaped with extensive rows and paths all of which converged beneath a vine-covered arbor. Full time work for a gardener, Buck suspected.

"This was mother's garden. Her pride and joy." Lila smiled, recalling the memory. "I think she cared for it more than she did Daddy."

"Is your mother —"

"Yes, she died when I was ten." Buck's ensuing sympathy brought a gentle touch from Lila's hand. "Thank you for your concern, but I've had many years to reconcile my feelings." Lila broke a blossom from a bush growing beside a gazebo and tossed it to the floor as they passed. "The gazebo was Mother's private place. She came here to meditate."

They soon reached what seemed acres of lush St. Augustine grass. Beyond the white-fenced yard, billowing rows of cotton surrounded the estate like a Christmas tree's snowy base.

"Does the plantation have a name?"

"Of course, silly," Lila said, perky again. "The McKinney Plantation. In constant operation since 1854."

"McKinney. As in Bessie McKinney?"

Lila nodded, an embarrassed grin on her pretty face. "I'm afraid I didn't tell you everything yesterday. Bessie McKinney was my great aunt. Her mother died when she was very young. Bessie's sister, Francine, was the sole heir to the McKinney estate. This estate."

"Francine?"

"Yes. She married Alton Richardson, a returning hero of the Civil War. Alton and Francine are my great-great grandparents."

Buck stared at her a moment, trying to digest what she had just said. "Then you're —"

"Yes. I'm a direct descendent of Bessie McKinney."

"Interesting." After glancing at the field behind the house, he said, "You raise crops?"

"Cotton and maize. And corn, for an occasional home brew."

Her answer raised Buck's eyebrows. "Your father makes moonshine?"

"Just for his own use, silly. And some of his friends."

Buck could only imagine what else the lovely Lila had yet to reveal as they continued along the fence line. When they reached the pecan grove, they stooped beneath the sagging branches. Full summer foliage masked the moonlight, casting pulsating shadows as an evening breeze swayed hoary boughs. At the edge of the grove they encountered several rows of small, wood-framed houses.

"Slave quarters," she said.

"You don't have slaves, do you?"

"We lost the war, Buck. There is no slavery now. Only remnants of a bitter memory."

"Sorry for my stupidity. From the number of empty houses, there must have once been quite a few."

"More than two hundred."

Following the brick pathway, they passed slave quarters and other buildings that included outhouses, smokehouses and the complete gamut of a fully preserved, antebellum plantation.

Lila asked, "Do you know about the *Mittie Stephens*?"

"Were you reading my thoughts just now?"

"I'd like to possess that particular ability. Why do you ask?"

"Because I visited the Riverfront Museum before coming to the party. I was reading about the wreck of the *Mittie Stephens*. It seems strange you would bring up the subject."

"I didn't just bring it up. The brass fitting you left for me to identify bore the serial number from one of the *Mittie Stephens'* engines." Lila's pronouncement didn't surprise Buck as did their ensuing discussion. "Where did you find it?"

"Fitzgerald Island."

Lila massaged her lovely chin and stared up at the moon. "But that's quite impossible. The *Mittie Stephens* sank miles from there."

"Maybe so, but that's where I found it. And I also found this."

He handed her the coin he'd found and watched as she rolled it in her palm. For a long moment she studied it's weathered lines and reflections glimmering off the moon.

"It was minted the same year the *Mittie Stephens* sank."

"Then maybe the reports are wrong. Maybe the remains of the *Mittie*

Stephens are somewhere on Fitzgerald Island"

Lila shook her head and said, "Impossible." The look on her face belied her response.

"I'm sure you're right," Buck said, grabbing her elbow and steering her along the path. "But you promised me a quick tour before dinner and we'd better hurry or we'll be late."

Lila's seductive smile returned. Taking his hand, she pulled him along the cobblestone pathway.

"Judge Travis doesn't look anything like your father," he said. "And they have different last names."

"We're not blood kin," she said. "Granddaddy raised Uncle Jeff as a foster child. You didn't tell me that Mr. Nation wants to buy Fitzgerald Island."

"I thought you knew."

Lila pushed aside a holly bough and it brushed against Buck's face. "Why I had no earthly idea."

"He offered me quite a lot of money."

"Didn't I tell you we weren't discussing business tonight, Mr. McDivit?"

"That you did, Ms. Richardson."

"The night's too beautiful. Don't you agree?"

"A remarkable Southern night for a beautiful Southern woman."

When Lila twirled around, leaned against the trunk of an ancient oak and smiled demurely in the muted moonlight, Buck almost bumped into her. When he did, she wrapped her arms around him, initiating an unexpected kiss that lasted for one burning moment. The kiss sent Buck's head spinning. He'd just begun to trace his fingers down the soft skin of her bare shoulders and breathe deeply of her lilac perfume when she pushed him away. Leaning forward, she slapped his cheek. Not a hard slap, almost a caress.

"Rogue," she said, grinning.

Buck quickly realized she was toying with him. He felt like a real fish, but the taste of bait had him hoping like hell she'd toss it into the water one more time. She glanced at the mansion instead. Their journey had led them in a circle, almost back to the place they had started. Party sounds emanating from the ballroom caused Buck to glance at his watch.

"Maybe we should start back. Your father's probably missing you by now."

"Very observant, Mr. McDivit. I know a shortcut."

Buck followed her through moonlit darkness to the rear of the mansion, past a large detached building. Heavy metal doors on the building barred the entrance to the rectangular edifice constructed totally without windows.

"What's that building?"

"The ice house," she said. "Deception was the first place in the country to make ice."

"Really?"

"They used steam engines powered by gas squeezed from pine knots. It's no longer operable, but Daddy says Larkin McKinney once stored enough ice there to last all summer long. Daddy used to threaten to lock me away in the ice house whenever I was bad. He's since told me Granddaddy used to threaten him the same way."

Buck gave the structure a backwards glance, losing interest as they entered the kitchen. They were surrounded by cooks and helpers, all black. Everyone seemed to know Lila on a first name basis. Unlike the ballroom workers who radiated icy indifference to the people they served, these people treated Lila like a little sister. She responded in kind and Buck decided to forget his confusion and simply enjoy the remainder of the evening.

They climbed a winding flight of stairs to a double doorway leading back to the ballroom. There on the stairway, Buck again found himself with Lila the actress. Everyone watched them descend, Lila playing the Southern belle to the hilt.

"I love making an entrance," she said with a smile.

CHAPTER THIRTEEN

Later, the string quartet stopped playing and Clayton signaled for silence. "It's time we gentlemen retired to the study for cigars and brandy. Lila has something special for you ladies in the sitting room."

On cue, Lila led the women out one door as the men followed Clayton through the other. Buck followed Lila, quickly finding himself the center of attention. Lila took his hand like an errant child. "You'll perturb Daddy if you don't join him and the other gentlemen."

"I'm your guest, not his."

She glanced away and said, "I'm sure he won't see it that way."

"How do you see it?"

"You're a gallant knight and I'm honored by your chivalry but it's misplaced. You should join the other men."

"Am I making you uncomfortable?"

"You know you are," Lila said.

When their hands touched, the same surge of heat raced up his neck as when they kissed in the garden. It didn't stop Lila's flashing hazel eyes from backing Buck toward the door.

"Uncle," he said. "One question before I go."

"If it isn't too insensitive for a lady's ears," she said with a mock pout.

"Why didn't you tell me yesterday that you're related to Bessie McKinney?"

Lila paused, then said, "Because we Southern ladies are very selective about which secrets we keep and which we reveal."

"And which are you keeping?"

Flicking her ornamental fan, Lila answered Buck's question in her thickest Southern accent. "You said one question, Mr. McDivit. That was two."

"Lila, you are a beautiful and mysterious woman."

"Mysterious? Whatever do you mean?"

"Just that you're a puzzle I can't seem to solve. I'll join the men now."

Lila flicked her hand-painted fan in his face. "You do that, you rogue."

Buck waited in the hallway until Lila shut the door behind her, listening to laughter inside the room before going to the study where the men had congregated. Buck wasn't impressed by what he saw. Biting smoke layered the humid study, everyone clutching brandy snifters and half-smoked cigars. Grabbing a snifter from a tray he twirled it in his hand, letting the brandy's poignant aroma waft into his nostrils. He spotted Clayton Richardson and Judge Travis through the smoke and decided to join them.

"Cigar?" Clayton Richardson asked.

"No thanks. I don't smoke."

"Hogg tells me he's made you an attractive offer for the Fitzgerald place," Clayton Richardson said, his Southern accent gone.

"An offer I'm afraid I can't accept," Buck said.

"Why is that?"

"I don't feel Aunt Emma's wanted to sell the island. I'm going to complete the improvements she started and keep the place in the family."

"Then I presume you've arranged financing?"

"I have," Buck said, hoping no one could see through his lie.

When Clayton glanced at the floor, Buck saw a flicker of Lila in his smile. He realized he could never hate this man, even if he were repossessing Fitzgerald Island.

"Jeff," Clayton said. "Please entertain Buck for me. I need to see to something in the kitchen."

Judge Travis nodded and Clayton Richardson disappeared through the cloud of wispy smoke. Richardson's large oak desk resided in an office-like nook at one end of the large study and Travis motioned for Buck to join him. The older man plopped down in the desk's large, overstuffed chair. Alcohol, Buck soon realized, had put the good judge in a foul mood.

"I need another brandy," Judge Travis said. "Samuel, get your lazy black ass over here."

Travis crooked his finger at an old black servant, a man with hair three shades whiter than Hogg Nation's. Samuel quickly responded with a fresh tray of brandy. The judge took a snifter without a word of thanks, and said, "Clayton's nigrahs are very well trained."

"Clayton would appreciate your compliment, Judge," an onlooker said. "It's a long and tiresome process teaching nigrahs anything."

Several men pushed closer in order to join the conversation and Buck listened in disbelief as ugly racial comments began flavoring the conversation.

"God made them that way," one man said.

The judge nodded with a grin. "But it's a boon to us white folk. Otherwise who else would serve our drinks?"

Travis' rhetorical question brought a peal of laughter from the eavesdroppers as Buck suppressed the urge to punch the judge in the nose.

Samuel soon returned with yet another tray of brandy snifters. After placing a glass on the desk for Buck he walked around the big desk, waiting for Judge Travis to take one. When Travis reached for the tray he stumbled, banging his knee into the desk in the process. Everyone was watching but no one smiled. Samuel's jaw was clenched and he bit his lip when the judge's drunken glare landed on him. The old man began backing slowly toward the door.

"I didn't excuse you, Samuel," Travis said. "Put your tray down and turn around here."

Samuel pivoted slowly on one heel until he was facing Travis. Everyone in the room had grown quiet, staring intently in the judge's direction. Samuel's neck was rigid and sweat began beading his forehead. His head cocked slightly backwards as he stared with open eyes at the ceiling. Something was about to happen, likely distasteful, but brandy had left Buck welded in place. He could only watch as Judge Travis pushed aside Samuel's dark jacket, undid his belt buckle and unbuttoned his pants. In one violent motion he yanked down the old man's trousers and boxer shorts.

Samuel never blinked. He just kept gazing at the ceiling, a look of resigned mortification on his face as Judge Jefferson Travis began prodding his private parts with a ruler he'd found on the desk.

"See now, Mr. McDivit, the entire black race's single distinctive attribute."

Buck's face flushed red, his blood molten as it surged downward from his face and neck. But the violent scene had immobilized him and his hands continued to drape his sides. Travis wasn't finished. Grabbing Samuel's bow tie, Judge Travis yanked him forward until the old man's chin banged the desk. Blood spurted from the cut but Travis held him down, not releasing him until he had thumped the old man's head several times with his knuckle.

Samuel winced but did not attempt to pull away.

Still holding the embarrassed and injured man, Travis said, "Nothing up there but a head full of rocks. That right, Samuel?"

"Yes, sah," Samuel said.

"Then pull up your pants and get the hell out of here," he said, shoving Samuel against the bookshelf.

Samuel tripped and dragged down several books on top of his head as he fell. The entire study erupted in laughter as the old man made for the door, still grappling with his pants.

Feeling sick to his stomach, Buck pushed through the crowd and followed Samuel out the door. "You okay?" he said when he caught up with him in the hallway.

"Nothing worse than usual," Samuel said.

"Sorry I didn't do anything to help," Buck said.

Samuel's expression softened. "I know you're Miss Emma's nephew. No kin of hers could be like that herd in there."

"Thanks, but I'm feeling pretty disgusted with myself right now."

The old man grasped Buck's hand. "There's no patented way to react to racism. You watch yourself, son. Bad things happen to good people in this county."

After watching Samuel disappear down the hall, Buck returned to the sitting room to tell Lila he was leaving. She was demonstrating a particularly complicated knitting sequence and apologized to the ladies gathered around her before excusing herself and hurrying Buck back outside. Her touch quelled his heightened emotions and sent him racing from a different stimulus.

"Did Daddy insult you?"

"What makes you think that?"

"Because he insults anyone vying for my attention."

"Is that what I'm doing?"

"Aren't you?"

"Then why do I feel like a fly in a spider web?"

"You think I'm a spider?"

"More like a beautiful leopard stalking its prey."

"And what am I after, Mr. McDivit?"

"You tell me, Miss Richardson."

With her intense gaze riveting his attention, she said, "Someday, maybe I will."

"I look forward to that day." Buck glanced at his watch. "It's been wonderful but I have to go now."

Lila stood on her tiptoes, holding Buck in a lingering embrace, reluctant to release her arms from around his neck. When she did, he turned away and traversed the long hallway to the front porch where an attendant trotted off to retrieve his truck. As he drove beneath the dark row of pecan trees, he opened the truck's sliding roof for a little air.

Whisper-thin clouds draped the full moon's golden lunar glow, one of them reminding him of a young woman dressed in stark white. Feeling a sudden chill, he locked all the doors and started for Deception.

CHAPTER FOURTEEN

The friendliest of country roads can become creepy as a carnival ghost house after dark. The road to Deception proved no exception. Thick fog wisped up from hot blacktop and danced across the roadway as Buck swerved to miss a darting rabbit. The frightened animal scurried into the forest, oblivious to its near demise.

Buck bypassed downtown Deception and found the boat waiting where he'd left it. The motor cranked on the first pull and sent a swirl of vapor curling up from the surface of the lake. Foggy haze continued to thicken as he adjusted the bow light and motored away from shore.

Heavy fog began rolling in as Buck neared the center of the lake. The boat's tiny light provided scant illumination, even on a clear night. Now it was all but useless. He quickly lost sight of land but, thanks to the continued effects of Richardson's brandy, wasn't immediately bothered by the lack of visibility. His blithe oblivion didn't last long.

Within minutes he'd lost all notion of direction and rocked the fuel tank to reassure himself that he had plenty of gas. The heft of a half-empty tank only added to his growing concern. As marauding mosquitos buzzed his head, a distant rumble interrupted the chorus of crickets and frogs. An unmuffled engine. Another boat was on the lake and Buck couldn't tell if it was approaching him or moving away.

"Hello out there," he called, his cry eliciting no response except for silence in the creatures of the lake.

As Buck listened for a reply his boat struck something in the darkness. The collision sent him sprawling. As he pulled himself off the bottom of the boat, he realized he'd rammed one of the old wood-framed drilling platforms. Luckily, he'd struck it at an angle. When he grabbed for a plank, a sharp splinter pierced his hand causing him to recoil and bang his head against the platform. Worse yet, red eyes glared up from the darkness beneath the platform.

When Buck gunned the throttle the motor raced, along with his heart, but the boat remained in place. The impact had thrown the engine out of gear, sticking the boat in brush trapped beneath the musty old platform. Now the boat rocked precariously amid dank odor of stagnate water and dry rot.

As Buck's little craft floated in a circle beneath the platform, it passed through elastic strands of a large spider web. Claustrophobia chilled his neck as the web encircled his face. Forgetting the racing engine, he grabbed the platform and yanked the boat out from under the planking. With hand and head throbbing he slammed the boat into gear, motoring blindly into what he hoped was open water. Again he heard the high-pitched whine of another boat.

Buck threw the engine into neutral, fear of striking a cypress tree or another platform in the thick fog fresh in his mind. After raking the spider web from his face he called for help again and listened for an answer. No help arrived as he felt something crawling down his shirt.

"Hey out there! Can anyone hear me?"

Buck's cry faded as a powerful light penetrated milky fog. It was attached to a fast boat powering straight toward him. Standing, he began waving and yelling.

"Here I am!"

The boat's approaching wail sounded vaguely familiar to Buck but it was too late to worry about it. As it streaked past, it's wake lifted his boat almost out of the water. The little craft remained afloat but rocked dangerously. Then he heard the other boat turning for another pass.

Buck held on, waiting for the swell to subside. The wake had swamped the motor, stalling it. When the boat stopped rocking he yanked the starter cord but the motor only sputtered and died with a sick sounding thump. He had little time to worry about the stalled engine.

The marauding boat's headlight blazed through the fog, powering directly toward him. With little time to react he abandoned ship, diving overboard before the speeding boat plowed into his own craft with a tremendous crash and an ensuing explosion of wood. The wake of the collision sucked him to the bottom of the shallow lake, pinioning him in the murky ooze for a long, terrifying moment. When the wake passed, releasing the suction, he tried to kick toward the surface, his arms flailing against swirling muck and slimy vegetation. But something had his foot in its clammy grasp and refused to let go.

The crooked branch of a submerged tree, part of the rotting mass of vegetation at the bottom of the lake, had trapped Buck's foot. He struggled but his futile attempt served only to deplete what little oxygen was left in his lungs. Despite his efforts, he gained no leverage against the algae-covered stump.

Buck's eyes bulged, his head threatening to explode, his lungs desperate to gasp something, even blood-warm water, into them. Just before losing consciousness he felt icy fingers encircle his ankle. Ephemeral hands freed his ankle from the sunken tree and pushed him toward the lake's surface. Stroking upward in near panic, he belched foul liquid from his lungs as he burst from the black water.

The first cognizant sound Buck recognized was the boat returning at high speed for another pass. Ducking beneath the water, he plunged back to the bottom of the lake just as the boat passed directly overhead. This time no sunken vegetation entrapped him and he bobbed to the surface, coughing up water but in no imminent danger of drowning.

Fog cloaking the lake showed signs of lifting and moonlight illuminated the silky sheath with a pulsating glow. It left Buck with the sensation of being trapped in a giant lava lamp. Having no better plan, he dog-paddled toward what he hoped was the shore. It wasn't. Only rotting vegetation impeded his forward motion, tangling him in scummy tentacles. Tearing loose, he back-stroked into open water.

A dozen or so strokes brought him to the edge of the lake where his feet finally touched shallow bottom. Neck deep in lily pads, he remained in stagnate water until he'd caught his breath, his thoughts turning to poisonous snakes and prehistoric fish with mouths full of razor-sharp teeth swimming around him.

A breeze began blowing fog off the lake and the moon soon poked a small hole in it's gossamer shroud. What he saw frightened him more than the thought of an alligator swimming between his legs. Through the underbrush, not more than twenty feet from where he stood, were Humpback and Deacon John floating silently in their boat. Both carried automatic weapons.

Buck looked for a path of escape as the two men searched the darkness with a powerful spotlight. He found only red eyes glaring back at him from misty darkness near the shore. Suppressing a cough, he almost gagged from the cesspool of stagnate, foul-smelling water surrounding him.

"See anything?" Humpback said.

"Why hell no," the skinny man answered in his distinctive countrified accent. "You think you can do any better?"

Buck didn't hear Humpback's answer and presumed he had ignored Deacon John's angry question.

"Make a loop," Deacon John said. "If he's still alive, he couldn't have gone far."

The engine cranked and the boat moved slowly away. Stepping forward into shallow water, Buck sank into a knee deep mire that sucked his leg into its grasp. Yanking hard enough to dislocate his knee, he managed to pull free but the struggle left his shoe in the muck. Grabbing a quick breath, he swam underwater toward shore, desperately wanting to get out of the water. As Buck crashed out of the lake he ran headlong into a cypress tree, the impact knocking him senseless. When he opened his eyes a hand grabbed the back of his neck, another his mouth, muffling his response.

"Don't have a conniption. It's just me."

Buck recognized the voice of Wiley Johnson.

"Wiley, I—"

"Shhhh," he said, gripping Buck's mouth tighter. "They're still out there."

Wiley released his hold and Buck glanced up into his big face, ebony against the moon. "How did you know I was here?"

"Didn't," he said. "I was fishing."

Buck wanted to ask Wiley what he was fishing for but saved the question for later. Wiley crept into the trees and signaled for Buck to follow. Deacon John and Humpback had docked their boat around the bend and were continuing their search of the shoreline on foot. As they approached Buck and Wiley's position, Buck pressed his face into soft dirt. When Deacon John stepped on a nearby branch, Buck felt the opposite end move beneath his leg.

"I say you're crazy as hell, DJ. I saw him go under when we hit the boat." Waiting for Deacon John's response, Humpback added, "We gonna chase around this shit hole all night?"

Deacon John still didn't answer. Finally, he waded into the lake and back to the boat. Silence gripped the darkness. Buck tried to raise up but Wiley signaled him to remain in place. Harsh engine sound disturbed the silence as Deacon John let the motor idle a minute or two before moving slowly away from shore. Again Wiley shook his head and motioned Buck to remain still.

A shrill whistle sounded from the spot in the lake. A minute later the boat returned, its hull scraping bottom. Water splashed as someone waded from the shore to the boat. When the engine cranked the boat pulled away, this time for good.

Glancing up at Wiley, Buck said, "How did you know someone was still there?"

Wiley didn't answer. Moonlight flooded through parting clouds as he started away through the underbrush, Buck happy to be alive as he followed after him. Wiley led them through the forest and back to the lake where a narrow boat waited, wafting in shallow water.

"Pirogue," Wiley said, replying to Buck's inquisitive stare.

Wiley propelled the sleek little craft through the maze of cypress trees. At the Fitzgerald Island dock, he steadied the pirogue as Buck climbed to shore.

"You have something you want to tell me?" Buck asked.

"Such as?"

"What you were doing on the lake?"

"Night fishing," Wiley said.

With no further explanation, he strolled away to his room in one of the bunkhouses. Still damp from his visit to the bottom of the lake, Buck watched him go.

CHAPTER FIFTEEN

Buck went downstairs next morning still thinking about his dip in the lake and wondering how far Nation was prepared to go to wrestle the island from him. With the incident still fresh in his mind he called to report it to Sheriff Wright. The sheriff's cool attitude left him with a splitting headache. Buck found Pearl slicing tomatoes at the kitchen sink. She looked vivid in a yellow dress printed with red and green flowers that reminded him of a gaudy hot air balloon.

"You okay, Mr. Buck? You look like a tired toad in a tubful of alligators," she said, interrupting his thoughts. "You're worried about losing the island, aren't you?"

"What worries me most is you and Raymond losing your house and the marina."

"Things will work out," Pearl said. She sounded unconvinced. "Maybe what we all need is something to take our minds off the foreclosure. Raymond barbecues the best ribs in three counties. A barbecue might just fit the bill."

Pearl's plan to cheer everyone up with a barbecue seemed perfect to Buck. "Great idea" he said. "We could use a little levity around here and I can repay Lila's hospitality."

"Then I'll send Wiley to town to pick up the ribs and fixins'," Pearl said, grabbing pencil and paper to make a party list.

Buck started to abandon her to her task but had a second thought. "We probably need a case or two of beer and a few bottles of wine."

Glancing up from her list, Pearl pointed to a door in back of the kitchen. "You been in the cellar lately?"

Buck opened the door and fumbled for the light switch just inside the dark stairwell. At the bottom of the limestone stairs he found another switch that flooded the basement with fluorescent lighting. The room was at least twenty degrees cooler than the kitchen and bottles of wine of every vintage and variety lined the walls. Grabbing two bottles, he hurried upstairs.

"Why is the basement so cold?" he asked, handing Pearl the bottles.

"Miss Emma was worried her wine might spoil, even though Raymond assured her the basement stays the same temperature year round."

"It's freezing down there."

Pearl's angry frown told him he'd somehow struck a nerve. She started for the kitchen door and he followed her outside to an industrial-sized breaker box.

"This thing hasn't worked right since the electrician put it in. Guess we need to get him back out here and fix it." Pearl slammed the metal door in disgust. "I'll call Wiley with my list and send him to town right now."

"I'd like to go with him," Buck said, taking the list.

"Fine, Mr. Buck. I'll tell him you're on your way."

Buck found Wiley loading the Coke machine with fresh pop. He grinned when he saw Buck and tossed him a cold can.

"How you feeling?"

"Confused," Buck said. "About why Deacon John and Humpback tried to kill me last night."

"Kill you? You sure about that?"

Wiley's question caught Buck by surprise. "You saw their M-16s. Besides, I heard them talking."

"Maybe they were spotlighting turtles or something. How did they even know you were out there?"

"Hogg Nation must have told them. He was at Lila's party and they work for him."

"So what?"

"So Hogg Nation is determined to get this island, anyway he can."

"Hogg Nation doesn't need to kill you to get the island," Wiley said.

Buck started to reply but checked himself. He had no reason to doubt Wiley's intentions but the young man's placating words and presence on the lake the previous night made him do just that. Still, it didn't make sense and he decided to change the subject before blurting something out he'd regret later.

"Did Pearl call you about the barbecue?"

"Sure did," Wiley said. "I got a boat waiting. You ready to go?"

"Right behind you," Buck said.

It was another hot day and Wiley wiped sweat off his forehead with the back of his hand as he led the way to the boat. Thunder clouds were moving south. Too fast to drop their load, but still elevating the humidity well above the comfort level. A lone egret raised a squawking protest to the heat, taking to the air in a clumsy maneuver of gangly legs and flapping wings.

When they reached the boat, Wiley said, "You just like my company or do you have other business in Deception?"

"Your company's fine but I only have a few days left before the bank forecloses on the island. I need to nose around the courthouse and see if I can dig up a copy of your parent's deed in the records. I also want to stop by and see Lila."

"Sure, but let me do the driving," Wiley said, grinning.

Buck was more than happy to let Wiley guide them across the lake to Deception. Noon sunshine had begun evaporating puddles of water remaining from last night's rain. When they reached Deception, they found the humidity hadn't slowed the hoards of tourists jamming the sidewalks. Sara had apparently forgotten about their discussion concerning Hogg Nation. Now her smile was as warm as the first time they'd met. At least until she spotted Wiley.

"Well, well, well," she said. "Two handsome men to make my day a little brighter."

"You're the one doing the lighting," Wiley said.

Sara latched on to Wiley's hand and he didn't seem to mind. "You're one big man. Bet you have trouble finding gloves and shoes that fit."

"I manage," Wiley said. "Where you from, girl? I know I would have seen you before now if you were from around here."

"Maybe you just didn't notice."

"Oh, I would have noticed."

Wiley and Sara continued holding hands, their banter racy enough to make Buck blush. It had no such effect on the two of them and left Buck with trouble deciding which of them was the boldest. It seemed like a dead heat.

"Is Lila around?" Buck finally asked, interrupting their conversation.

"In back," Sara said, never breaking eye contact with Wiley.

Leaving Wiley and Sara to their flirtatious exchange, Buck wandered down the narrow hallway to Lila's office. He found her studying an old doll with her hand lens.

"Morning," he said.

"Why Mr. McDivit. What a pleasant a surprise."

"I just dropped by to tell you I enjoyed your party last night and to invite you to a barbecue on Fitzgerald Island Friday night."

"Oh how fun," she said. "What time?"

"Whenever you close the shop. Why don't you pack a bag and stay the weekend? There are more rooms in the lodge than I can count." Lila hesitated, thinking about his offer. "Bring Sara along," he added before she had a chance to answer. "We'll have a great time."

"Maybe we'll do just that," she said. "I haven't had a day off in a year and there are other antique shops for the tourists."

"That's the spirit," Buck said.

"You didn't come all the way to Deception just to invite me to a barbecue, did you?"

"I have a few other matters to attend to, but you topped my list."

As Lila encircled his waist and led him down the hallway to the shop, Buck wondered if something in East Texas water caused everyone to become outrageous flirts. If there was, he needed to find out. Someone could bottle it and make millions. To Bucks surprise Lila rushed to hug Wiley when she saw him. Wiley lifted her off the ground, twirling her around twice before setting her down.

"Wiley Johnson, where have you been?"

"Working in Austin," he said.

"Don't you ever call your old friends when you're in for a visit?"

Lila's question seemed to embarrass Wiley. "Haven't been back lately. When I do it's usually just long enough for a short stay with Momma and Daddy."

"Are you here long enough for Buck's barbecue Friday?"

"Wouldn't miss it," he said.

"Good, then we'll get a chance to visit."

"Miss Lila, you never told me about this fine hunk of mankind," Sara said, chiming in.

"He can tell you all about himself Friday. We're closing the shop early and going to Mr. McDivit's barbecue."

Air brakes screeched outside the door and two dozen visitors began pouring out of a tourist bus, many of them directly into Lila's shop. Buck grabbed Wiley's elbow and pulled him to the door.

"See you Friday."

"Call the lodge when you're ready to shut down," Wiley said. "I'll pick you up and take you to the island."

Wiley sported an ear-to-ear grin as they left Lila's shop. It didn't recede until he bumped into a fat man dressed in black socks, tennis shoes, and Bermuda shorts.

"Earth to Wiley," Buck said, fanning his embarrassed companion.

Wiley slowly dragged the back of his hand across his forehead. "Whewee," he said. "How did I miss meeting that gal all these years?"

"Guess it's your lucky day."

"You got that right, and it sounds like we got a date Friday night."

"Whoa, boy" Buck said.

"Who you calling boy?" he said with a grin.

Buck didn't bother replying and Wiley followed him to the parking lot of the Pelican to find his truck.

"Hey, wait a minute. Where you going?"

"To check out the courthouse, then over to Ezra's to invite him to the barbecue."

"Ezra's black."

"So are you. So what?"

"Nothing. I'm going to run over to the grocery store and pick up the things on Mama's list for the barbecue. Need anything?"

"A spare one hundred and fifty thousand dollars or so."

"Can't help you there. The store where I'm going specializes in chitlins and fatback."

"Just my luck," Buck said. "Can you kill a few hours until I run my traps?"

"You bet I can. Maybe Miss Sara can sneak off for a root beer. I'll do Mama's shopping in the meantime but I need a ride to Rambeau"

"What about that nice new supermarket on the edge of town? Don't they even let blacks shop with whites in Deception?"

"They take anyone's money around here, no matter what color they are, but they don't have the gourmet ribs Daddy requires for his famous barbecue. Rambeau ain't much but it does have the best soul food grocery store in this part of the state."

"Jump in," Buck said, unlocking the truck.

Even after days of disuse, Buck's truck started on the first crank. Wiley stroked the leather bucket seat and prodded the padded dash.

"Man, I've never seen a truck like this. You obviously don't poke livestock with it."

"It's a Cowboy Coupe, a special stretched-cab version of your standard Dodge truck."

"I'll say. There's enough room to sack out back there."

"Done it many times. I believe in comfortable stakeouts."

"I thought stakeout vehicles were discreet. Nobody's going to miss this candy-apple red beast."

"Wrong. Almost everyone in Oklahoma has a truck like this."

"And the streets are paved with gold."

"You have my Oklahoma guarantee on it," Buck said.

They reached the outskirts of Rambeau before the two men stopped laughing. After a short drive the pine forest pulled away from Texas blacktop revealing a ramshackle village of slat houses with tin roofs that had never seen a coat of paint. Lazy dogs and naked black children occupied most of the front porches. There were no garages and most of the vehicles were up on blocks. Wiley pointed the way to the grocery store.

"Want me to wait on you?" Buck asked.

"I'll hitch a ride back to the dock when I finish. How long you going to be?"

"Say I meet you at the boat about four."

"You got it," Wiley said, piling out of the truck. "Watch you don't scratch the paint on this cowboy Cadillac."

"No way," Buck said, waving and turning around in the road.

Gunning the engine he hurried back to Deception, hoping to reach the courthouse before it closed for the day.

CHAPTER SIXTEEN

Buck arrived at the court house ten minutes later and ran up the stairs to the land records department. Floor-to-ceiling shelves, all crammed with leather-bound deed books, lined the walls. The clerk, a pink-haired old lady, returned to her People Magazine when Buck indicated his intentions by pointing at the books.

Oklahoma land records are recorded by township and range. Thirty-six sections per township, each section comprised of six hundred and forty acres. Neat and easy. Not so in Texas. Property title is recorded by survey and no two Texas surveys are exactly alike. Luckily, Buck had worked as a oil industry lease broker before becoming a private investigator. His training had come at the end of the oil boom, an era of private jets, high-rollers, rapid ascendancy and even faster declines. The experience had armed him with valuable knowledge concerning chain-of-title.

Courthouse records detail family histories, through good times and bad, life and death. It's all there if you know where to look. Buck started with the Grantor's Book, an index of mortgages, liens and conveyances, subdivided by year and in rough alphabetical order. He went back five years, roughly to the date Aunt Emma sold Pearl and Raymond their property on Fitzgerald Island. As lawyer Rummels had said, no record of the conveyance existed.

Buck continued searching every year for five more years before starting forward, a cloud of dust the only thing he'd managed to raise after an hour's work, a lung full of dust mites rendering his eyes red and his nose running.

It didn't take long to see what had occurred, assuming Raymond and Pearl weren't liars. Since Buck believed the two were scrupulously honest, the likely explanation was that someone had deleted the entry, entering a sham conveyance over the erasure to mask their chicanery. Without knowing book and page number where the deed was originally filed, he had only one remaining courthouse option: search hundreds of books, page by page. Without the luxury of the time it would take to accomplish the task, he borrowed the clerk's yellow pages instead.

Most Texas counties have abstract offices that provide title information for a price. In lieu of accessible county records, it was the only place left to look. The yellow pages listed two abstractors in Deception and their names, Nation's Title and Richardson's Abstract Company, clued him he would likely have no better luck than at the courthouse. Buck decided to check them anyway.

Richardson Abstract Company sounded friendlier so he visited it first. It was down the street from the First Bank of Deception, a stately business housed in an impressive building constructed of Texas Pink Granite. The abstract company shared the same facade.

"Help you?" a man in a neat but dated linen suit asked when Buck entered the door.

"Hope so," Buck said.

The man's bushy white eyebrows twitched. "Come in out of the heat. You're my first customer today."

"Having a slow one, are you?"

"They're all slow around here, except for Mr. Nation's resort and a few new oil wells going down in the lake."

"New wells? I thought they stopped drilling around here fifty years ago."

"Company out of Shreveport found oil in the Petit Lime about two years ago and started drilling shallow wells from here to Vivian."

"Even in the lake?"

"Why not? I grant you we ain't learned a lot in fifty years but I guess we still know how to drill a well in ten foot of water."

Remembering his recent plunge to the bottom of the lake, Buck somehow recalled the bottom depth being at least twice that depth. He stored away the tidbit of information about new oil wells, his land experience signaling him it might be important somewhere down the line.

"Mind if I look at your survey maps?"

"Help yourself," the old man said. "Got the whole county right there on the wall."

The little gray-haired man returned to straightening his desk's nonexistent clutter as Buck studied several large maps tacked to the wall. Unlike anything in the courthouse, they showed all the county surveys. Most Texas surveys are named after the largest landowner and Buck quickly located the Fitzgerald Survey.

"Pardon me, sir. I see there's an oil well on the Fitzgerald Survey. Do you know if it's old or new?"

Cocking his trifocals high on his forehead, the man craned his neck forward to study the oil well symbol on the map.

"Richmond Oil," he said. "Drilled last year."

"Thanks. Can I get an index of every Fitzgerald Survey transaction?"

The little man grinned and massaged his palms. For five dollars a transaction he supplied Buck with an activity index of the Fitzgerald Survey. It provided a citation of book and page number. Something the courthouse couldn't. Armed with the index, Buck returned to the courthouse and began pulling books. He soon learned that Pearl had been wrong about one thing. Aunt Emma had indeed borrowed money from the bank.

Emma purchased the island in 1936 from the Caddo Timber Company, apparently paying cash because no record of a bank mortgage existed in the records. In 1943, she'd mortgaged five acres of lakefront property to the Bank of Deception, repaying the loan in 1944 and extinguishing the mortgage. In 1950 the Bank took a mortgage on the entire island as collateral for a loan to build the marina and lodge. Aunt Emma repaid the loan, paying off the balance she owed in 1970. She'd mortgaged the island again and all her real property, less than two years ago to the bank for money to return the marina and lodge to full service.

That was the entire list. Every transaction that had occurred involving Fitzgerald Island since Aunt Emma had owned it. Every transaction, that is, except the sale of property to Pearl and Raymond Johnson.

The abstractor was computerized and could have deleted and renumbered the entries with ease. Not so the courthouse. The only way to alter a recorded transaction was to ink it out, cover it with correction fluid or remove the page it was on. Either way, some indication should exist suggesting something shady had occurred. Knowing that tidbit of information was the easy part. Finding the alteration proved the problem. Buck continued thumbing the pages, hoping to get lucky.

The courthouse work rewarded Buck with an aching back and distressed sinuses. Despite his efforts he'd managed to locate only one error or omission. But it was a glaring error. Richmond Oil of Shreveport, Louisiana had drilled an oil well on the Fitzgerald Survey the previous year. Even though Aunt Emma had acquired all right and title to Fitzgerald Island from the timber company, including mineral rights, there existed no record of Richmond Oil ever leasing those minerals from Aunt Emma before drilling their well. This was a mistake no oil company was likely to ever make.

A law firm would have checked the title and rendered an opinion of ownership. Such a title opinion would exist for the Richmond Oil #1 Emma Fitzgerald. A competent title attorney would have listed complete chain-of-title in the document. Buck had no doubt that Aunt Emma and the Johnson's appeared in the chain-of-title and he made a note to contact Richmond Oil and arrange to examine the title opinion.

Doubt no longer occupied his mind. Someone had deleted entries from the County record and the person responsible had probably left the original documents in place, thinking no one would ever locate them without a reference in the Grantor's Book. Buck had seven days to prove them wrong. With nothing further to accomplish at the courthouse Buck circled town, parking in front of the project. Ezra answered on his second knock, welcoming him with an angry glare.

"I told you never to come here through the front door."

"There was no one out there but me."

"You're wrong about that. You didn't see them but you can bet they saw you."

"Maybe, but I can take care of myself."

"Uh huh," Ezra said, padding into the kitchen, returning with two glasses of ice water.

"Mighty hot out there today," he said, changing the subject.

Buck winked and drank the water in two gulps. "Didn't notice."

Ezra pointed toward the couch. Resting his head on a cushion, Buck closed his eyes. "I'm screwed, Ezra. I'm going to lose the island and I know it."

The old man's demeanor softened and he chuckled. "You're not here to borrow money from Ol' Ezra and you don't strike me as the type to let a little roadblock get in your way for very long."

"Maybe not. I never owned real estate in my life. What does it matter if I lose it now?"

"Then why do you look like you just been kicked in the head?"

"Pearl and Raymond. I feel responsible for them losing their home."

"Wish I could help," he said.

"Didn't mean to worry you with my problems. Hogg Nation is the root of my predicament and I can deal with him."

Ezra rubbed the stub remaining where his right ear should have been. "Don't be too sure of that. Mr. Nation may be a rattlesnake but Judge Jefferson Travis is a cottonmouth."

"What's that supposed to mean?"

"It means a rattlesnake will at least warn you before it clamps down on your leg."

Shaking the ice in the glass, Buck sipped the water. "Everyone in town probably owes Hogg Nation a favor or two. Seems to me he has more to gain than the judge."

"Maybe," Ezra said. "What else you got going?"

"Barbecue Friday night. Fitzgerald Island. Bring your family along and anyone else you want to invite."

Ezra shook his head slowly, massaging his chin between his thumb and forefinger. "Don't you know by now how things work around here? White people don't socialize with project niggers. You're really itching to get yourself killed."

"Let me worry about that. We'll pick you up Friday afternoon at the dock."

Buck handed Ezra the empty glass.

"Watch your back, Buck," he said.

"I'll do better than that. The best defense is a good offense."

"Yeah, well you watch it anyway. Come on and I'll let you out the back door."

"No way," Buck said. "I came in the front door and that's the way I'm going out. To hell with the Ku Klux Klan."

Buck's impassioned statement earned him a raised eyebrow and head shake as Ezra let him out the front door. Despite Ezra's cynicism, he felt proud of himself as he trotted up the hill toward the truck. The sun had begun tilting to the west.

As he turned the key in the door, someone rammed something hard and cold into the small of his back. The last thing he remembered was a painful blow to the back of his head.

CHAPTER SEVENTEEN

"Afternoon, Okie," someone said.

Through blurry eyes Buck stared at Humpback's ruined face, The man's sour breath almost causing him to heave. Deacon John kicked him in the ribs and this time he did throw up.

"You moron," Humpback said. "Now we gotta clean him up before we take him to the judge.

"Shut up, you little sawed-off shit. You breathed on him, not me."

Humpback glared at his partner but responded to his anger by delivering another boot to Buck's ribs. The attack seemed to momentarily relieve his tension.

"You got your rocks yet?" Deacon John said. "Let's take him down the hall before the judge gets pissed at both of us."

They dragged Buck to a private study at the far end of the large house and shoved him through the door. He landed on his face in the middle of a colorful Persian rug. The ceiling was fully twenty feet above polished oak floors and law books filled massive shelves lining two walls. What hung behind the oak desk in the center of the room was what disturbed Buck. A large swastika, black, white and red, draped the wall for all to see. Judge Jefferson Travis was seated behind the desk.

"Bring him in here," Travis said. Humpback and Deacon John dragged Buck, dropping him into an antique chair, and waited until the judge began shouting. "Now get out. I'll talk to McDivit alone."

Humpback and Deacon John padded out of the study. As Buck gazed around the large room, he quickly saw the Nazi flag wasn't the only right wing epitaph blemishing the walls. There were also framed photos of hanging, torture and castration victims. Horror imprinted their faces. The photos also depicted white-cloaked, cone-headed men. Old photos that had a timely relevance. The images riveted Buck's attention.

"Don't look so surprised, McDivit," Judge Travis said. "It's only a display. Like the museum you visited before Clayton's party."

"I'm out of here," Buck said.

Travis half stood, arms outstretched on the desk, shaking his head. "You got something to learn about our local customs first and I'm here to teach you. Travis sank back into his leather chair and lit his cigar, the acrid odor of burned sulfur remaining long after he blew out the match. "I modeled this room after my father's study. My foster father. As you can see, he had very specific ideas about separation of the races."

"Then he's no different than anyone else around here, far as I can see."

Travis drained his brandy, slapped the empty snifter down on the desk top and rested his head in his palms. "I recognize your type. Bleeding heart liberal. Holier than thou. Look at me straight and tell me you've never once called one of them a nigger."

"You make me want to puke, Travis. You tell me what it is you want before the stench in here causes me to do just that."

The door opened, suppressing Travis' reply. It was Deacon John. "Everything all right, Judge?"

"Don't you think I'd let you know if it wasn't? Get the hell out of here until I call you."

Travis poured another shot of brandy from the decanter on his desk, not bothering to offer one to Buck. "Deak and Hump caught you coming out of the project. What we're you doing over there?"

"I go where I want."

"You didn't answer my question. We have very specific laws here in Deception and whites are not allowed to visit the project."

"You must be in a time warp," Buck said.

"You and everyone else in this county obey me because I represent the law."

"Whose law?"

"The almighty law of the New Southern Right, and by God you'll abide by it or live to regret it."

"You're insane," Buck said, his words hitting a nerve.

Judge Jefferson Travis arose out of his chair, grabbing the brandy carafe and hurling it across the desk. The projectile just missed Buck's head and crashed into the wall behind him. Humpback and Deacon John came hurdling through the door as the broken carafe spilled its last drops of antique liquor on the burnished hardwood floor. Humpback throttled Buck's neck as Deacon John yanked his arms hard enough to wrench them from their sockets. Travis paced around the chair and slapped Buck hard across the mouth.

"You will follow the law," he said, his forehead beading with sweat.

Buck's lower lip felt mushy, his saliva metallic. "Your law, not mine."

The judge regained his composure but continued pacing, his hands clasped tightly behind his neck. "Someday it will be everyone's law," he said. "Right now it's yours. Bring him to the window." Humpback and Deacon John manhandled Buck to the window that overlooked the large backyard. "See for yourself,"

A dozen men in camouflaged uniforms were performing close order drills. "They're looking real good, Judge," Humpback said.

Travis ignored the comment, motioning Humpback and Deacon John to follow him. Deacon John spun Buck toward the hallway, Humpback kicking his backside. The attack sent Buck sprawling across the floor.

"Get off your face, you Okie son-of-a-bitch," Deacon John said, yanking Buck up by the neck.

Travis slammed his fist on the door. "Quit clowning and bring him along."

Deacon John and Humpback herded Buck down the hall to a room where a skinhead instructor was demonstrating how to break down an automatic weapon to a group of men. Camouflage fatigues seemed the common uniform. Travis continued on to two more rooms to show Buck explosives and subversion classes. The tour ended back at Travis' office.

"A glimpse into the future," he said, reseating himself behind his desk. "The army of the New Southern Right."

Buck was hurt but not cowed. "Your army's just a cluster of skin-headed throwbacks."

Whap, went the back of Deacon John's hand. "Shut up, cowpoke. Those men are part of a powerful militia forming all over the country. We're arming and training ourselves to attack and destroy the growing cancer in our society."

"You mean like the women and children murdered in Oklahoma City and those in the Trade Center?"

Buck's remark earned him another vicious slap to the back of the head. The rear window was open and he became aware of troops counting cadence in the backyard.

"Innocents die in war," Travis said. "And we weren't responsible for 9-11."

"Bullshit. It all amounts to terrorism and your so called army is no better than Al Quaida."

Buck's analogy seemed to please Travis rather than anger him and he said, "We both practice a means to an end. Until we're strong enough to confront the government directly, we must satisfy ourselves with cleansing the dregs of society. Ridding ourselves of abortionists, homosexuals and the liberal press that persecutes us. And the black scourge threatening to overrun this country."

"So you're going to kill me for visiting the project?"

"I don't want to kill you, McDivit. Only educate you."

"Sorry," Buck said. "I don't like the curriculum you're offering and I doubt the sheriff will either."

Buck took a chance invoking Wright's name, not knowing the sheriff's political beliefs. Travis didn't seem to know either because he motioned Humpback to deliver another slap to Buck's cheek. Humpback had gripped Buck's neck again as the Judge began to rant. Deacon John pinned Buck's arms behind the back of the chair. His lips were broken, his nose bloody and his splitting headache made him think he might have a concussion. Despite the pain, the Judge's words continued to incite his anger. Lashing forward with his right leg, he smashed Deacon John's shin with the toe of his boot. His attack resulted in a quick reprisal.

"You're a piece of liberal dog shit," the judge said.

"You're wrong," Buck said. "I'm conservative, and a Republican, but there's another word for you, Travis. Nazi."

Buck's words had barely exited his mouth before someone lowered the boom on his fleeting consciousness.

An hour had passed since Wiley finished loading the groceries on the boat. Now he glanced at his watch for the third time in as many minutes. Buck was an hour late and Wiley had started to worry. He let another half hour before heading toward the project and the house of Ezra Johnson.

"Well, look what the cat drug in," Ezra said, seeing Wiley.

Wiley had two large grocery bags in his arm and another on the porch outside the door. "Mind if I stow my groceries in your refrigerator awhile?"

"Bring them in this house," Ezra said, grabbing the bag on the porch.

Once the groceries were stuffed inside the refrigerator, Wiley grabbed

Ezra's hand, pumping it vigorously. "How you doing, Ezra? You seen Buck McDivit?"

"Sure. He left here a few hours ago."

"Did he say where he was headed?"

"Back to the island is what he told me. Something wrong?"

"Don't know," Wiley said. "Buck was supposed to meet me at the boat and he didn't show up. I'm worried."

Ezra went to the window and peered out. "His truck's still in the parking lot."

"Maybe he left it on purpose and decided to walk down to the lake."

"He wouldn't have done that," Ezra said. "I fussed at him for parking there in the first place."

Wiley started for the door. "Better round up some of the boys and look for him. I'm going for the sheriff."

CHAPTER EIGHTEEN

When Wiley returned to the project with Sheriff Taylor Wright and Deputy Sam Goodlake in tow, he found Buck lying on Ezra's couch, an ice bag on his head.

"You okay?" Wiley said, rushing over to see what had happened to him.

"I'll live. I've had more bruises than this lots of times riding rodeo bulls."

"Bull riding my big black butt. Looks like you tangled with a tiger."

"Maybe, but some of the bruises are left over from my dunk in the lake last night."

"What's the problem, McDivit?" Sheriff Wright said, elbowing his way through the group of well-wishers.

Buck spent the next few minutes explaining how Deacon John and Humpback had kidnaped him, taking him to the Judge's house. Eyes grew wide when he related the part about the subversive activity going on at the Judge's mansion. Sheriff Wright wasn't buying any of it.

"I just came from Judge Travis' house. Seems someone broke in and rifled through some of his papers. Wasn't you, was it?"

"Who's accusing who here? Didn't you see the skinheads in the back yard?"

"I only saw the judge. No one else. Sam and I checked the entire house."

"What about Humpback and Deacon John? Did you ask them what they were doing on the lake last night?"

"Yes I did. They called my office this morning. Right after your call. They reported hitting a boat in the lake last night by accident. They searched for victims for more than an hour, finally deciding the boat was empty. Figured it probably floated away from someone's dock in the fog. They were civic minded enough to report the accident and concerned when I told them about you."

"I'll bet."

"No need for sarcasm, McDivit."

"How do you think I should react when I tell you someone beat me to a pulp and all you seem to care about is how civic minded they are? You think I put these bumps and bruises on myself?"

Sheriff Wright reflected on Buck's question before answering. "Judge Travis tells me you got pretty looped at Clayton Richardson's party last night. Maybe your mouth overloaded your brain and someone took offense. Whatever happened to you, I certainly don't believe a county judge from the fine state of Texas is responsible."

"Then you're not going to take my statement?"

"You said your piece and I listened. You've slandered the judge enough already. Wiley, help McDivit over to the clinic and let a doctor look him over."

As Sheriff Wright and Deputy Goodlake headed for the front door, Buck curbed himself from blurting out what he thought about the law keepers loyalties. He managed to refrain himself. Another time, he thought.

It was later that day when Buck and Wiley departed the clinic. His ever-growing number of bruises were painful, his sprained ankle still sore from the plunge from the second-story window. He also felt the effects of the many scrapes he'd incurred during his midnight dip in the lake. After gathering Pearl's groceries he and Wiley started for the lake. This time Wiley drove, parking the truck in a public lot. Buck's muscles were hard knots as they loaded the last bag into the boat, Wiley pushing away from the dock and cranking the engine.

"You okay," Wiley said.

"Back when I was still bull riding, I woke up worse than this lots of times."

"I heard that before, but you ain't woke up yet."

"Thanks for the encouragement," Buck said, ignoring Wiley's newly acquired street accent and big grin.

By now it had grown dark. None of last night's fog remained and a golden moon cast dancing light across the lake's black surface. Wiley guided the boat through an acre of lily pads, the engine idling, letting myriad night sounds surround them. It made Buck think of a primeval slough. He finally asked, "You think I concocted the story about the judge?"

Buck's question made Wiley laugh. "Just be glad you're white and all you got was a beating. If you were black, we'd have been cutting you down from a tree."

"From the trophy photos in the judge's study, I'd say you're right about that. Too bad we can't prove it."

A bobcat growled in the distance, resounding above the engine noise and momentarily quieting the other lake creatures. Their boat glided past a pumping unit on a wooden platform, reminding Buck of his recent experience at the lake's bottom. It also reminded him of his visit to the abstractor's office.

"Say, Wiley, do your parents have an interest in any oil or gas wells?" he asked.

"Sure. Company out of Shreveport drilled a well not far from the island about a year ago. Mom and Dad get about twenty dollars a month in royalties but to hear them tell it, they control an oil company bigger than the Rockefeller'." An owl hooted in the tree above them. When its echo died away, Wiley said, "Why do you ask?"

"Because it proves they own the land they say they do. The oil company will have a record of the transaction and Pearl and Raymond will be able to keep their property."

"What about the rest of the island? Mama says Miss Emma would never have borrowed money from the bank."

"Your mom's wrong about that. Aunt Emma did borrow money. I saw a copy of the document in the courthouse."

Wiley let Buck's information sink in, then said, "But why did she borrow so much? She didn't need anywhere near that amount to fix up the marina and lodge."

"Maybe not," Buck said. "Someone around here has absolutely no qualms about altering legal documents."

"Well, whoever did what, the loan's underwater. The whole island and everything on it isn't worth half what the bank says you owe. You'll play hell finding another bank to lend you that kind of money. Unless you're loaded and you haven't told me."

"I'm not," Buck said. "Our only real hope is Aunt Emma's life insurance. To collect it we have to prove Aunt Emma didn't commit suicide."

"Can you do it before the bank forecloses?"

"It's seven days to the hearing. Foreclosures can take a year or more to complete. We have plenty of time."

"Wrong, white man. In case you forgot, this is Deception, not Oklahoma City. Judge Travis will complete the foreclosure on the island by summary judgement."

Buck knew Wiley was right and stewed in silence until he could take no more. "What can I do? I can't even prove Aunt Emma didn't commit suicide."

"Better start with Hogg Nation. He wants the island in a bad way and maybe that's motive enough for lots of things."

They reached the dock at Fitzgerald Island, Wiley getting his feet wet as he jumped into shallow water and pulled them to shore with the front rope. After helping him unload Pearl's groceries, Buck pushed the boat back into the inlet and cranked the engine.

"Hey," Wiley said. "Where you going?"

"Back to Deception. There's something I need to do there and it won't wait till morning."

"Like what?"

"Like find out why Hogg Nation needs an island ten miles from his development."

Buck turned the boat around and started back toward town. It was dark when he reached Deception. As he jogged up the hill to town he found a different group of tourists replacing the usual day crowd. A rowdy group looking for fun joined throngs of tipsy college kids wandering from one bistro to the next. Music wafted from open doors. Soft jazz and rollicking ragtime. Buck quickly entered the dark alleyway near Lila's shop that led to Ezra's maze.

Scant moonlight penetrated thick shrubs and creeping vines growing in the maze and he realized he would get nowhere without a map and strong light. Aborting his initial plan, he returned to the busy sidewalk of Deception and made a beeline across town toward the county complex.

Buck needn't have worried about Judge Travis or his men spotting his as dark shadows and throngs of tourists masked his progress. When he arrived at the complex, he quickly found a narrow crease between two building and wormed his way back to the maze. Finding light still nonexistent, he felt his way along the building until he reached the first ground floor window. It was locked.

A sophisticated alarm system guarded the building. That he'd determined during his visit to the coroner's office. Using his sense of touch, he searched for an open window, his persistence soon rewarded.

Adrenaline pumping through his veins numbed the pain of his many scrapes and bruises but his sprained ankle collapsed when he slid through the narrow orifice, onto the floor. There he lay a good five minutes, rubbing his ankle and wishing for a double dose of Tylenol. When his brain cleared, he realized he had another problem.

A red light glowed from a keypad on the wall. If he opened the front door, the movement would activate the alarm. And he was in the wrong office. Returning to the window he dropped to the ground, biting his lip to suppress the jolting pain surging through his ankle.

Dragging his throbbing foot, Buck worked his way around the building until he reached the lighted window of Sheriff Wright's office. He entered through a window cracked for ventilation. Wright had apparently gone home for the night but Sam Goodlake was fumbling around in the next room.

Judging by the receiver on the desk, the sheriff's office had at least two phone lines. Taking the chance Goodlake wouldn't notice the second light on the receiver, Buck dialed the number prominently displayed beneath the first button.

"Sheriff's office," Goodlake said, answering the phone on the first ring.

"Deputy Goodlake," Buck said. "Dr. Proctor here."

"How you doing, Dr. Tom?"

"Fine, Sam. Say, the cleaning people called. Said they found my watch in the trash. They left it in the janitor's office. Can you run down and get it for me and hold it until tomorrow?"

"No problem, Doc," Goodlake said.

"Thanks, Sam. See you tomorrow."

Buck hung up the phone. On his initial visit to the county complex, he'd passed the janitor's office just down the hall from the sheriff's. The cleaning crew would need the alarm codes for the large building and the code sheet was probably located in the janitor's office.

Buck didn't have long to wait. Goodlake's keys rattling outside the door informed him he had already acceded to the coroner's request. He watched through a crack in the door as Goodlake strapped on his revolver and carefully fitted the big cowboy hat on his head. He didn't bother turning on the burglar alarm as he went out the door. Hidden in the half-fluorescence of the darkened hallway, Buck shadowed him to the janitor's office.

Goodlake went directly to the back room before turning on the lights, making it easy for Buck to follow behind him. Once in, he scurried under a desk without being seen. Goodlake gave up looking for Dr. Proctor's watch in a few minutes and left him alone in the dark.

The alarm code, a detailed map of the building with the relevant codes for each of the offices, was easy to find. Someone had drawn it by hand and it only took Buck a moment to decipher what it meant. Using an office copier, he duplicated the portion of the code sheet he needed and returned the original to the desk drawer where he'd found it. Then he peeked out the door and glanced down the hall.

Except for a thin beam of light glowing through the cracked doorway at the Sheriff's office, the building showed no sign of occupation. Shutting the door behind him, Buck slipped down the hall to Bones Malone's office. Malone's lock presented no problem. After shutting the door behind him and inputting the code to silence the warning signal, Buck stuffed the code sheet into his pocket for further possible use.

Faint fluorescence from a desk lamp created soft shadows on the walls as Buck gazed around the room. Most of the handwritten notes on Malone's desk related to Hogg Nations' development but everything else indicated his real passion was the wreck of the *Mittie Stephens*. Newspaper articles, old photos and eyewitness accounts of the sinking of the steamboat littered every nook. One bookshelf was devoted to objects evidently collected from the *Mittie Stevens*. All were marked with ascending numbers.

Malone's office filled Buck with strong feelings of déjà vu and he soon realized why. Like Bone's abandoned room at the lodge on Fitzgerald Island, order and impeccable organization ruled the decor. Nothing was out of place. Almost nothing.

A fragment of pottery lay beneath Malone's desk, marked with numbers and letters someone had inscribed in India ink. The label said NATDEV005. Buck wrapped the shard in a sheet of paper and put it in his shirt pocket.

CHAPTER NINETEEN

Buck's visit to Bones Malone's office left him with more questions than answers. It was after ten when he slipped out the window and returned to the street, finding a smaller but no less rambunctious crowd still enjoying Deception's nightlife. Selecting a friendly looking tavern, he earned a relieved smile from an exhausted waitress when he pointed to the bar.

"Just having a drink," he said.

The dimly lit room overlooked the lake and seemed empty except for the bartender. Grabbing a tall stool at the elegantly curved mahogany bar, Buck propped his sore foot up on the brass rail. The stocky bartender, unpacking a box of liquor in the corner, glanced up from his work.

"What'll it be, cowpoke?" he said.

"Coors. Draw if you have it."

"What we got on tap is Lone Star but I can fix you up with a can of Coors"

"How about a bottle?"

"Sorry. Coors in a can or you drink something else."

"Then make it Coors in a can," Buck said.

The burly bartender fished around in the refrigerator behind the bar. He retrieved a can of Coors and a frozen mug and handed them to Buck.

"Keep the mug," Buck said.

Buck noticed he and the bartender weren't alone. A lone man, cradling a tall glass of scotch between his arms, lay slumped over the counter at the end of the bar. When Buck pushed his glass toward the bartender, the man raised his head and glanced around the room.

"Lookee here, Big Sam. We got a bachelor boy in our midst."

"Good guess," Buck said.

"No guess, bub. You don't like to dirty dishes. Marks a bachelor every time."

"Big Sam," Buck said. "Bring my new friend a round of whatever he's drinking and put it on my tab. And I'll buy you one, if you like."

Big Sam, the burly bartender nodded. He handed a fresh scotch to the man in the corner and poured himself a shot of tequila after returning to his spot in back of the bar.

"Thanks, bub," the man at the bar said, hoisting his drink as he nodded at Buck.

Buck raised his own glass. "To Deception. A fine little town."

The man, gray hair and craggy face pinning his age at someplace beyond sixty, moved to the stool beside Buck and introduced himself with a loud voice and slurred accent.

"Otis Spangler's the name. Who might you be, my friend?"

"Buck McDivit."

Spangler clinked his glass against Buck's can of Coors. "And what's your business in Deception, Buck McDivit?"

"I'm Emma Fitzgerald's nephew. I inherited Fitzgerald Island."

"Well, here's to you," Spangler said. "Emma was a fine old friend of mine."

"Then you're drinking free the rest of the night. Just tell me a story or two about Aunt Emma."

Spangler stared at the ceiling. "Finest lady I ever knew."

"You're not just saying that, are you?"

Spangler's eyes twinkled. "I loved that woman with a passion, but unfortunately, I much as I'd like to drink your scotch, I never really met her."

Buck grinned in appreciation. It wasn't his first time to be duped by an old drunk in a bar. "I think I like you anyway, Otis. What's your line of work?"

Shaking his big flat head, Big Sam went to the far corner of the bar on the pretense of straightening some bottles. He'd likely heard Otis' life story more than once. Otis leaned against the bar and made himself comfortable.

"I dust crops for a living."

"Sounds exciting."

Spangler nodded his head in agreement. "Oh, it's that all right. I've crashed a time or two. Still kicking though. What's you're business, Buck?"

"I do odd jobs," Buck said, knowing from experience that announcing his real profession as private investigator often left new acquaintances ill at ease.

Otis didn't buy his duplicity. "Private dick, huh?"

Glancing over his shoulder, Buck said, "Do I have a sign on my back, or something?"

"Your hair's a little long for a cop."

"I was a cop once," Buck said. "How did you know?"

"Your jeans and shirt are freshly pressed and your boots shining like a new penny. That, and the snappy way you walked in the place marks you as a cop or military man. Your hair's too long for soldiering. That don't leave many professions."

"Very observant. What else do you know?"

Otis pivoted slowly on the red bar stool. "I've done enough guessing. Tell me a little bit about yourself."

Buck had finished his first beer and had already started on his second. Unlike Coors beer in Oklahoma, Texas Coors contains more than 3.2 percent alcohol. As he relaxed for the first time all day, the beer's alcohol content began to make him feel like it contained a lot more.

"Before joining the force, I rode bulls awhile in the rodeo. When the oil boom came along, I quit the department and checked land records for one-hundred fifty a day plus expenses. My job went bust like the rest of the industry."

"I can relate," Spangler said. "I used to be an airline pilot."

"Used to be?"

A silly smirk materialized on Otis Spangler's face. Hiccupping, he pointed at his drink. "I couldn't seem to convince the brass that a few little cocktails assisted my flying abilities."

"Narrow-minded bunch," Buck said.

Spangler gave him a high five. "I think I like you, bub. Big Sam, bring me another toddy. And deep six that swill my friend here's drinking. Bring him a man's drink."

"Better not," Buck said, shaking his head and holding up a palm to Big Sam. "Whiskey makes me kind of crazy."

"Exactly what it's supposed to do. Fix Buck up with a straight shot of Kentucky sipping bourbon and a Coors chaser."

Despite Buck's continued protest, Big Sam brought him a shot of bourbon and another Coors. He guessed Otis and Big Sam had pulled the same scam many times but the strong beer had already loosened him to the point that he didn't really care.

"I don't think I'm getting my money's worth. If you can't tell me about Aunt Emma, at least fill me in on what's going on around Deception."

Spangler scratched his graying temple, pursed his lips and glanced around the room. When a fresh thought finally crossed his whiskey-soaked brain, he snapped his fingers and grinned.

"Know what they call this place?" Spangler leaned closer. In a low voice, he said, "Texas Badlands."

"No way. That's West Texas."

Otis tapped the bar with his knuckle. "Nope. Been more murders in this place than anywhere in Texas."

"Aren't you stretching things a bit?"

"No way. There's been boundary disputes in these parts since Thomas Jefferson bought Louisiana from France. Neither country wanted to demand their rights too loud. They were afraid of startin' a war. This kinda became a no-man's land. Claimed by neither Spain or the United States."

By now Buck's rapid consumption of whiskey and beer had thrown his mental state into a confused jumble of sounds and images. Fortunately, his week-long case of nerves was seeping away, along with his clarity.

"No-man's land?"

"That's right. Every drifter and outlaw from ten states moved in here and set up shop. When they'd get drunk they'd smile and ask you what your name was before you came here."

"Doesn't seem like anything has changed," Buck said.

Spangler winked at Big Sam, raising a finger. Without skipping a syllable, he continued his story. "Used to be at least a killing a day back then. The pirate Lafitte had a garrison over at Monterrey. Ambushed riverboats on their way up to Jefferson."

"Lafitte?" Buck said, parroting Spangler's words.

"And Jim Bowie too," Otis said. "Davy Crockett even stopped by on his way to the Alamo."

Buck's words seemed to reverberate and echo against the walls of a distant valley. "Monterrey?"

"A robber town up one of the bayous that drains into Caddo. Long gone now. Only thing left is a graveyard with two bodies, and a buried treasure worth a king's ransom hidden somewhere in those swamps."

Otis Spangler's words were hypnotic, causing time to slow almost to a stop. "Caddo is the largest natural lake in Texas, stretching nearly forty-five miles long and ten miles wide in spots. Problem is half's in Texas, the other half in Louisiana. Further complicating matters the boundary line of two Texas counties splits it right down the middle."

"I know it's big, but —"

Spangler didn't let him finish. "Big ain't the word. Caddo's a maze of swamps, cypress brakes and blind channels. Ain't ten men alive knows half the passageways through that lake. Even the government maps are wrong. So wrong, in fact, they's a joke around here. Far as I'm concerned, this is just a continuation of the Big Thicket."

"Big what?"

"Miles and miles of endless forest," Spangler said. "All the way from north of Beaumont to here. Few towns or villages, and barely any roads."

"Big Thicket," Buck said. "Never heard of it."

"A haven for criminals, killers and ne'er-do-wells. Sure as we're sitting here."

"You're a pilot?"

"Crop duster," Spangler corrected.

"Wish I could see the lake from the air. Sounds interesting."

Otis Spangler shook his head. "You're right about that, bub. Ain't no way you'd find anything from the ground."

"Will you take me up sometime?"

Spangler grinned and downed his drink. "You bet I will. I have a hanger at Deception Airport and you can find me right here most any other time."

Buck glanced at his watch. It was after midnight. Motioning Big Sam for one more drink, he reached for his wallet and pulled
out two twenties.

"Keep the change, Big Sam," he said. "Stay out of the phone lines, Otis."

Otis and Big Sam waved as Buck stumbled out the door. He somehow made it in one piece to the dock as moonlight reflected clearly off the surface of the lake. Water again had a cloaking mist but the memory of his first solo crossing had all but vanquished, along with his sobriety. The trusty motor didn't seem to notice, cranking on the first pull.

Considering his advanced state of insobriety, Buck wouldn't have driven his truck home. The slow-moving boat posed no such dilemma. The only danger he possibly generated was to unsuspecting turtles and frogs sitting on logs and lily pads. That proved a boon because he didn't remember his trip back to the island. After plowing into shore, not bothering to raise the engine, he stumbled to the lodge where Tiger waited at the door for him.

"How you doing, Tiger?" he said, cuddling the purring kitten and scratching behind his ears.

Pearl had gone home earlier that evening leaving Buck and Tiger alone in the lodge. Spangler's booze had left him with a splitting headache and warm night air had sobered him just enough to make the pain noticeable. The headache left him wide awake as Tiger followed him into the kitchen.

Buck started a pot of coffee and located a bottle of aspirin in a cabinet. Two aspirin and four cups of coffee finally knocked a dent in the headache but did nothing to rid his insomnia. Remembering the shard of pottery in his shirt pocket, he started upstairs.

The same piney tobacco odor Buck had noticed during his first visit to Malone's room confronted him when he opened the door. This time more pungent. Probably because of humid night air. Moonlight splaying through the open curtain illuminated the room and Buck didn't bother switching on the overheads. Instead, he went straight to the bookshelf.

The gap in the books he'd found during his first visit to Malone's room had returned and it only took him a moment to realize the loose-leaf notebook was gone. Curtains flapping in a breeze signaled an open window. Buck rested his hands on the sill, peering into darkness.

Malone's room faced the lake and Buck stared at the moon hanging high above dark water. Then another light, a shimmering pinpoint moving slowly toward the island, caught his eye. As he watched, it flickered and disappeared.

CHAPTER TWENTY

It rained sometime during the night and Buck awoke to a damp morning. It was cooler than normal, dark clouds rolling in from the south. Wiley joined him on the veranda and didn't wait long to question him about his return trip to Deception.

"See you made it home okay," he said.

"Never a doubt about that."

Wiley smirked. "How'd things go in town?"

"I payed a little visit to Bones Malone's office."

"Don't want to hear about it," Wiley said, covering his ears and shaking his head.

Buck removed the piece of broken pottery from his pocket and handed it to him. "I found this under his desk. Any ideas?"

Wiley rolled the shard in his palm, stopping when he saw the India ink inscription. "Indian pottery. You find it all over the place around here."

"I didn't know there were Indians in East Texas."

"Caddo Indians. Named the Lake after them. Most were moved to Oklahoma after the Civil War."

"What's your take on the inscription?"

Tiger rubbed against Buck's leg as Wiley studied the mark. Heavy humidity turned into a drizzle of rain that splattered water through the screen and beat a steady timpani against the veranda's tin roof. Buck scooted his chair away from the screen and so did Wiley.

"NATDEV probably refers to Hogg Nation's development," he finally said. "That's what Bones was mostly working on."

"So you think this pottery came from Nation's development?"

"Why not?"

Lightning momentarily illuminated dark storm clouds as Buck pondered the archeological and legal implications. "Maybe Malone found something that impacted Nation's plans."

"Probably not," Wiley said. "If the state shut down construction in East Texas every place they found pottery shards, we'd have to turn out the lights and go someplace else. And what does it have to do with Miss Emma, anyway?"

"Don't know. What I do know is that someone's worried about it."

Wiley's eyes narrowed. "How's that?"

"Malone had a loose-leaf binder in his room upstairs. A key to the artifacts he collected. I came across it the other day when I inspected his room. It's not there anymore. Someone took it."

"You're shittin' me," Wiley said.

"I wish I were. The book is missing and whoever took it went out the upstairs window with it."

"Did you call the sheriff?"

"Why bother?"

Gusting wind blew rain through the screen, backing them even further away from the screen wall. Wiley didn't answer Buck's rhetorical question, Instead, he grabbed a fork and sampled his eggs. Then he said, "When you were in Malone's office did you see his report on the development?"

"If there is one I didn't find it," Buck said. "I suspect the person that took the binder probably got their hands on the report as well. If I could just find Malone, I'd ask him. In lieu of that, I'll have to take a look around the construction site."

"You're not going to find Malone unless he wants you to find him," Wiley said. "And they got a big fence around the construction site and guards at the gate. I doubt Hogg Nation will invite you in for a look-see." Wiley opened the screen door, gazing up at the ever-darkening sky. "Daddy's coming in with a fishing party. Must have got rained out. I better go help him with the customers."

The drizzle of rain became a blinding downpour as Wiley headed out the door. Buck watched him go. Tiger didn't. Not appreciating water splashing in through the screen, he hid between Buck's legs. Buck didn't like the dampness either. Grabbing the kitten he hurried inside to the sofa by the big stone fireplace, waiting nearly an hour until the rain passed over. By then, Tiger lay asleep on his lap. Buck transferred him to a warm spot on the couch, grabbed the phone and called long distance information.

"Richmond Oil Company in Shreveport, please."

When the receptionist answered, Buck requested to speak to someone in the land department. A George Strait ballad played in the receiver until a young woman finally came on the line and said, "Land department."

"Ma'am, I'm calling about the Fitzgerald well your company operates over here in East Texas. Can I speak with the land person that handles this area."

"That would be Brice Culpepper. Hold the line and I'll put him on."

"Thanks," Buck said, again listening to a mournful country tune as the secretary put him on hold. He didn't have long to wait.

"Brice Culpepper. How may I help you?"

"By doing me a big favor before I tell that pretty wife of yours what really happened at your bachelor party."

"Buck T. McDivit. Is that you?"

"You bet it is, Brice buddy. What are you doing in Shreveport? I thought Texaco transferred you to Houston."

"Got caught in a round of big company layoffs. Richmond hired me a year ago to take over their East Texas operations and moved me to Shreveport. Been here ever since."

Buck grinned. For the first time in many days lady luck had finally dealt him a winning hand. He knew Brice Culpepper well. Texaco had hired him during the oil boom and Buck had done brokerage work for the Nevada transplant, checking records and buying leases for him. The U.S. oil industry has contracted in size since the boom days of the eighties and it's fairly common to have a passing acquaintance with almost anyone still employed. That's what Buck had hoped for when he called Richmond Oil. Finding someone he knew as well as Brice was an unexpected bonus.

"Shreveport must be a little confining for the Las Vegas flash."

"No way," Brice said. "We have a race track, the lottery and casino gambling, and Sally and me are hooked on Cajun cooking."

"Glad to hear it. What else is new?"

"Nothing much. What's up with you? You didn't call to talk about old times."

"Your company operates a well in Caddo Lake. The Emma Fitzgerald #1. I was wondering if you have a title opinion on the well."

"If we operate it, we have a title opinion. Want me to put a copy in the mail to you?"

"Why don't you just bring it to me." Buck mentioned the impending barbecue. "The island can't be more than forty miles from Shreveport and the lodge here is huge. You and Sally pack a bag and stay the weekend. It'll be like old times."

"You got a deal, Buck," Brice said. "But on one condition."

"And what might that be?"

"That you don't get drunk and tell Sally what happened at the bachelor party."

Buck agreed with alacrity. After giving Brice directions to the loading dock in Deception, he joined Tiger on the couch and grabbed a needed nap. It was after five when he awoke and went to the kitchen. Pearl was alone, drinking coffee.

"Don't worry about fixing dinner for me," he said. "I'm going into Deception for the rest of the afternoon."

"It's storming outside. lightning will strike you for sure."

"I'll be fine. It's starting to slack off."

"Hard headed, just like Miss Emma," Pearl mumbled as Buck started out the door.

Buck found the boat where he'd left it, tethered to the dock, rocking and rolling in white-capping water. The motor cranked on the first pull. The storm had passed over the island but a steady drizzle continued to fall. Wind had abated and Buck, except for being wet and uncomfortable, had no trouble reaching Deception. Foul weather had caused an early shut-down of construction at the development. A twelve-foot fence surrounded Nation's development but Buck had little trouble finding a loose board and squeezing in between the cracks.

Even though summer darkness comes late in East Texas, black storm clouds cloaked the work site providing all the cover Buck needed. Rain had transformed the site into a muddy mess and he quickly sank up to the ankles of his new boots. Bulldozers and draglines lay deserted. Fresh from moving earth and preparing the foundation, their engines still steamed in the rain. Buck wasn't sure where to begin so he started with the first hole he came to.

Muddy water filled the depression, a ditch trenched by a nearby backhoe that was now mired up to its axle in mud. Deciding it wasn't what he was looking for, Buck avoided the waist-deep water and began looking instead for a hole that someone had dug with a shovel. He quickly found what he was looking for.

Buck recognized the anomalous hole in the ground because it resembled those he'd seen on the backside of Fitzgerald Island. Persistent rain had washed away most of the dirt piled beside the hole. Pottery shards remained. When he picked one up, he realized it wasn't a shard. What he held in his hand as rain poured down the back of his neck was a cup-sized clay pot. A voice behind him almost caused him to tumble into the hole.

"Well, looky here, Hump. I believe we caught us a mud dauber."

Before Buck could react, Deacon John gave him a push and he lurched forward into the shallow hole. As he splashed into muddy water, he somehow managed to hold on to the little pot.

"I knew that boy was a pig," Humpback said. "Now he's found himself a new slop hole to wallow around in."

Thunder clapped down by the lake, joined by an increased downpour of rain. It washed some of the mud from Buck's hair and beaded down his face. As he wiped the grit from his eyes he realized Humpback and Deacon John weren't alone. Humpback held a leash in his hands and was restraining an angry-looking pit bull terrier. Deacon John cradled an equally mean-looking shotgun in his arms.

"What are you doing here, cowpoke?" he said.

"I could ask you the same thing."

Deacon John replied to Buck's remark by kicking mud in his face. The pit bull growled and strained against the leash. Buck realized Humpback was staring at the pot in his hand.

"What's that you're holding?"

"Come down here and I'll show you."

Deacon John pointed the shotgun at Buck's face. "Hand it over. Now."

Buck handed him the pot. "What is it?" Humpback asked.

"Nothing but a damn pot," he said, tossing it back into the hole beside Buck.

Deacon John and Humpback both laughed when Buck said, "Now help me out of here."

"We gotta go now, but we'll leave Cyclone here to help you outta the hole."

They unleashed the pit bull and started away through the storm. Buck called after them. "I could drown in here."

"We'll send the sheriff for you. Tomorrow maybe."

As Humpback's laughter died away in the storm Buck sensed what a fix he was in. Muddy water was gushing into the hole and had already risen to his chest. Several things kept him from crawling out. His elbows sank into soggy earth when he tried to leverage himself over the bank, suction threatening to suck off his boots. And then there was the pit bull, growling at him from the edge of the hole.

The pit bull was angry but unable to get at Buck anymore than Buck was able to get out of the hole. As the water rose to Buck's chin, his boots stuck even deeper in the mud. Branches and debris began sweeping past him in the swirling water. When a large chunk of foam insulation floated by, he grabbed it and held on.

Deception sat on a slight rise overlooking the lake, ground sloping toward the lake like a natural bowl. The construction site was located on the slope of the bowl. Rain had continued all day. Now runoff coming from the rise above the lake flowed like a river, all grass and vegetation that once controlled it long since stripped away by construction. After swallowing a second lung full of water Buck levered himself against a two-by-four and pulled with all his strength.

All his strength was just enough. As his feet popped loose from the new boots, the wildly surging water carried him over the board and out of the hole. But it wasn't over. Upon seeing Buck float free of the muddy pit the guard dog made a charge, lunging through the mud and leaping on his back. The current carried them toward the lake as they struggled. Then an even greater surge of water came over the rise.

The pit bull had locked his fangs into the remnants of Buck's torn western shirt and refused to let go. It didn't matter. The rush of water swept them down the hill, toward the lake and construction workers had even provided a gap in the gate to accommodate such an occurrence.

Buck and the angry dog hit the lake in a tumult of debris and swirling water. Both were swept immediately to the muddy bottom. Buck surfaced quickly but not the stunned pit bull. Reaching beneath the whitecaps, Buck grabbed the sputtering dog's collar and yanked him to the surface. Against the powerful swirl he struggled to shore, dragging the hapless dog behind him.

Cyclone had swallowed lots of water and sprawled on the grass, trying to cough up water from his lungs without a lot of luck. Realizing the dog's dilemma, Buck picked him up by the hindquarters and pounded his back until a half quart of liquid issued from the beast's mouth. When it did, the once angry dog wagged his tail and licked Buck's hand in gratitude.

"It's okay, boy," Buck said, giving his head a cautious pat. "Guess you don't like swimming in that lake any more than I do."

Joining him on the grass, Buck allowed the rain to assault his face and head. There he remained until Cyclone nudged him with his nose. Buck followed the dog to the shelter of a massive oak where they waited until the storm passed, Cyclone thinking doggy thoughts as Buck wondered why Humpback and Deacon John hadn't killed him.

CHAPTER TWENTY-ONE

Friday morning started out hot and grew steamier as the day progressed. By noon, as Pearl and Raymond busied themselves with final preparations for the barbecue, summer heat was turning mud holes to stucco. Wiley noticed the fresh scratches on Buck's arms and the dark bruise beneath his right eye when he joined him on the veranda.

"Now what happened to you? Wrestling alligators again?"

"Something like that. I had a run-in with a pit bull that tried to drown me."

Wiley poured himself a glass of lemonade from the pitcher on the table. Warm from unloading boats all morning, he slowly swiped the glass across his sweaty forehead. Buck's comment didn't nothing to cool him down.

"You had a what?"

"Just a little run-in while I was visiting Nation's construction site."

"Uninvited, I presume."

"There wasn't anyone there to let me in so I climbed through the fence."

"Man, you're lucky you're not under the jail, much less in it. One of these days your luck's going to run out."

"It came close last night."

"And just what did your illegal activity accomplish?"

Buck ignored Wiley's critical tone. "Seems the site is located on an old Indian village or burial ground and I'd guess Hogg Nation has himself a little problem."

"Now wait just a minute," Wiley said. "Just because you found a few pieces of broken pottery doesn't mean the site is on an Indian village or burial site."

"Did I say broken pottery?" After a pause, Buck said, "Someone trenched the site in places unrelated to the construction. I found a complete pot in one of the trenches."

A flock of cattle egrets landed in a flurry of wings near the marina. Wiley gave them a quick glance before returning his gaze to Buck.

"An Indian pot?"

"I'm no expert but that's what it looks like to me." Wiley took the little pot and fingered it gingerly. "Humpback and Deacon John caught me pawing around in the trench and took it away from me. They weren't looking for Indian relics because they threw the pot back in the hole."

"And just what the hell would that something else be?"

"I don't know."

Details of Buck's trip to the construction site had put Wiley him in an irritable mood. "You're talking nonsense, man. Did they follow you to the construction site?"

"I don't think so. They were looking for something at the site and I get the feeling they didn't want either Nation or Travis to know they were snooping around. I'm betting we just picked the same time to have a look around the place.

The rumble of a big inboard engine interrupted their conversation. It was Raymond motoring up to the marina in a covered barge. Startled by waves and engine noise, the egrets deserted their feast of weeds and insects and soared skyward. So intent in hearing Buck's tale, Wiley paid no attention to the explosion of wings in motion. Finally his old grin returned.

"You sure you didn't give them a call and tell them what was on your mind?"

"I think they were looking at the archeological excavations in hope of finding something. Something Bones Malone knew about."

"Maybe that's the reason Bones disappeared," Wiley said, glancing toward the marina for the first time as the barge thudded against the dock. "I don't suppose you called Sheriff Wright to tell him what happened?"

"To give him a good laugh?"

Wiley rubbed his nose. "I've got a phone call to make. Meet you at the marina in about thirty minutes. Daddy has the party barge ready to pick up our guests."

Tiger was asleep on his lap when Buck dumped him unceremoniously on the floor. The kitty didn't seem to mind. After a lazy stretch he wandered off to check his food bowl. Buck went upstairs and changed into a tee shirt and pair of shorts, trying to relax but feeling tenser than usual.

Wiley and Raymond were waiting on the party barge when he reached the marina. They'd decorated the big boat with balloons, brightly colored crepe streamers and a large banner that said Party Time. Buck joined them on deck.

"Great barge."

"Twenty-five by forty feet of pure fun," Wiley said. "Air-conditioned cabin with a party deck on the roof."

"I'm impressed but it looks hard to handle."

Raymond grinned and shook his head. "Makes for tight maneuvering through the cypress brakes but it's a pussy cat out in the big lake. You'll get your chance to find out."

Wooden planking groaned as Raymond stepped off the deck and untied the front line. "You're not coming with us?" Buck asked as Wiley cranked the engine and backed away from the dock.

"Got chicken and ribs to barbecue," Raymond said. "You and Wiley can handle it. I'm too old for all that fun, anyway."

"Yeah, right," Wiley said as he backed away from the dock and turned the boat toward Deception.

Wiley, disturbing a row of turtles sunning on a log as he pushed the throttle forward, stretched in the captain's chair. Abandoning their perches, the turtles sent mini-ripples arching toward the cypress brake as the barge moved toward open water. Buck took a deep breath and let go of the rail.

"Need some help?"

"You bet," Wiley said. "Grab us a couple of tall boys from the cooler in the cabin. We don't have to worry about getting a drunken driving charge out here on the lake."

He cracked a mile wide grin when Buck saluted smartly and stepped to attention. They had already cleared the cypress trees ringing the island and were planing through clear water to the middle of the lake.

"And make it snappy," he said. "I got a powerful thirst."

Buck stumbled down the ladder where he found Ray, his feet propped on the red ice cooler, sitting on the built-in sofa. Ray didn't bother with a greeting but Buck was beyond worrying about his sour expression.

"What's happening?" he said.

Ray shook his head slowly, unable to mask a beleaguered smile. Opening the cooler, he handed Buck two beers. Buck thanked him and left him alone with his thoughts.

Last night's storm, washing away all but wispy remnants of yesterday's clouds, had left the sky an azure blue. A warm breeze wafted hoary tassels of Spanish moss and sent gentle ripples whispering across the lake. Buck climbed the ladder to the party deck and rejoined Wiley.

"You didn't tell me Ray was on board," he said, tossing Wiley a beer.

"I asked him to come along but I didn't think he would take me up on the offer. Guess he wanted to see Lila."

"She told me they grew up together."

"That they did. Take the wheel and I'll give you a driving lesson," Wiley said, changing the subject.

Buck forgot about Ray and enjoyed piloting the barge for most of the pleasant trip across the lake. They found a happy group, Brice and Sally Culpepper, and Lila and Sara waiting at the dock. When the barge touched damp wood with a soft thud Buck jumped out, lashing the barge to a pier. He noticed how Ray looked at Lila and how she looked at him. Sara broke the spell.

"Well, looky here. Three handsome fellows to take us for a weekend of fun and frolic. Ain't we lucky, Miss Lila?"

Lila's neck and face glowed bright red, the color clashing with her khaki shorts and yellow halter top. Breaking her gaze from Ray, she stood on her tiptoes and kissed Buck's cheek. Ray tried not to notice as he began hauling luggage from the dock to the barge. Sally Culpepper nudged Lila aside and gave Buck a big hug. When she pulled away, Brice pumped Buck's hand.

"From that tan of yours I can see you still don't have a desk job," he said.

"You know me too well. Fluorescent lighting always disagreed with me."

Brice and Sally seemed even younger than Buck remembered. Brice's shorts matched Lila's and his own bronze tan made a bold statement beneath the open collar of his gaudy Hawaiian shirt. Sally, her long blonde tresses draping halfway down her back, was radiant in white short-shorts and pink tee shirt. She smelled faintly of lime and eucalyptus.

Sara had turned her attention to Wiley and he was reciprocating, leering at her well-turned figure draped in yellow canvas shorts and skimpy polka dot bra. Wiley was all grins and stares, his mouth open wide. Buck thought for a moment he might have to lend him a handkerchief to keep him from drooling.

"Did everyone get introduced?" Buck asked.

"We have and we've already exchanged notes on you," Sally said, grinning at Lila and Sara.

"Your reputation precedes you," Lila said.

"Surely you didn't tell them all my secrets?"

"Does anyone know all your secrets?" Brice asked.

Buck let the question go unanswered. "Where's Ezra?" he said, looking around for the old man.

"Waiting for you over there," Lila said, pointing to a giant oak tree on the bank of the lake. "He wants to explain to you why he's not coming."

Ezra Davis waved when he saw Buck staring in his direction. "I'm too old for partying. You young people go on without me and have a wonderful time."

"No way. Raymond's barbecuing an extra rack of baby backs, just for you. He'll skin me alive if I don't bring you."

Buck's exaggeration made Ezra chuckle. "You don't need an old man spoiling the party."

"All right," Buck said. "But I don't want to be around when Pearl finds out you passed up the blackberry cobbler she's been working on all day. Blackberries she picked especially for you."

Ezra chuckled again. "You really are Emma's kin, aren't you?"

"Come on, Ezra. Wiley and I will go with you to your house and pick up some clothes for the weekend."

"No need," he said, disappearing briefly around the giant oak and returning with a small suitcase. "I had a feeling you wouldn't take no for an answer."

As Buck helped Ezra with his bag, the group on the barge had an unexpected visitor. It was Hogg Nation. Buck quickly learned it wasn't him he was there to see. Sara broke away from Wiley and joined Nation on the dock. The couple walked up to the parking lot where they had a short but heated discussion behind Nation's Chevy Suburban. After returning to the barge alone, Sara's smile quickly reappeared.

CHAPTER TWENTY-TWO

Ray seemed more animated than Buck had ever noticed on the return trip to Fitzgerald Island and it seemed fairly obvious that Lila was the object of his attention. He wasn't the only animated person on the barge. Sara measured Ray's large biceps between her palms as she oohed and ahed about his muscles. Ray only had eyes for Lila and Sara soon turned her attention to Wiley. Good thing. Wiley was leaning against the railing with his arms tightly folded and appeared an inch from slugging his older brother. Sally Brice interrupted Buck's observations.

"You look great. Any new women in your life we need to know about?"

"Just my new pony, Esmerelda. She's the only female I ever met that really understands me."

"That's a fact," Brice said, slamming his beer and popping the top on another.

Sally wouldn't let the matter drop. "What about Susie? That little waitress at Junior's."

"Mendez. Married a mud salesman and now has two kids."

"Looks like we have a lot of catching up to do," she said, encircling Buck's waist with her willowy arm.

Ray, motoring slowly past many small islands Buck never knew existed, took the long way back to Fitzgerald Island. Lila kept him company while the others two-stepped on the party deck to country and western music. It was near dark, everyone in a festive mood, when they reached the dock at Fitzgerald Island.

Ray jumped from the bow of the barge, lashing it to a post as Wiley and Buck grabbed the coolers and followed him ashore. White smoke hung over Aunt Emma's garden and the aroma of barbecue greeted them when they approached the lodge. Raymond's deep laughter, along with Pearl's own shrill hysterics, rolled from behind the shrubbery. They were caught in an affectionate embrace as the group rounded the corner.

"Can't leave you two alone for a minute," Wiley said.

Pearl gave Raymond a knowing look and they both rolled with laughter. "Wiley, I swear. You haven't changed a bit. Raymond and I had to put a lock on our bedroom door to keep you out when you were little."

"Maybe that's the reason he don't have no little brothers and sisters," Raymond said.

Wiley had little time to blush. Lila stepped from behind Brice and Sally, hugging the large black woman. Pearl's laughter quickly turned to happy tears.

"Miss Lila, look how pretty you are. You're all grown up."

"Pearl, you haven't changed a bit. And Raymond, tall and handsome as I remember when I was a little girl."

Raymond joined in the hug and said, "Still a charmer, ain't she, Pearl?"

"This is Sara," Lila said, tugging at her friend's elbow and pulling her closer for introductions. "Pearl, you may want to keep an eye on Raymond when Sara's around."

"Girl, if she'll just take him off my hands she can have the old man," Pearl said, giving Raymond a playful elbow in the ribs. "He's just about worn out, anyway."

Pearl gave Raymond a sharper elbow when he said, "Yeah, well it wasn't me that yelled uncle last night."

"Time out, you two," Wiley said. "This is Brice and Sally. They're friends of Buck's from Shreveport."

Ever the perfect hostess, Pearl embraced the two young people as if she'd known them all her life. "Welcome to Fitzgerald Island."

"It's lovely here," Sally said. "Like a perfect little Garden of Eden far from the modern world."

"Oh it's that, all right," Raymond said, leading Brice to a row of red ice chests. "Let's get a cold beer and I'll show you some of my barbecue secrets."

Ray stood alone in the shadows by the gate. As Buck listened to the friendly banter he wondered what was going on in the young man's mind. The thought melted away, along with the drone of a far off cicada, when thunder sounded in the distance.

Japanese lanterns cast ghostly light, swaying in the evening breeze blowing in from the lake. A scratchy old LP featuring ragtime piano, and banjo music vibrated from speakers in the yard. The melodies melded with a chorus of bullfrogs and Aunt Emma's collection of assorted wind chimes. When Ray finally came out of the shadows, he was pushing Ezra in front of him.

"Mama, look who else is here."

"Why there you are, Ezra Davis. I told Ray to drag you over here if he had to."

Raymond joined Pearl in greeting Ezra and they commenced another round of hugs, quips and friendly back slaps. Buck excused himself and joined the others as they admired Aunt Emma's roses.

"They're lovely," Sally said. "And so fragrant."

"They're from cuttings grown in my mother's rose garden," Lila said. "She gave them to Miss Emma years ago."

Fragrance from the roses combined with hibiscus, wisteria, and crepe myrtle in bloom. The odor of sweet flowers mingled with the tangy aroma of Raymond's barbecue. Pearl heard them talking about the roses and pointed toward the back door of the lodge.

"Let's get you settled into rooms before it starts raining. Dinner will be ready after you've freshened up."

Armed with cold beers and luggage, the guests followed Pearl upstairs to their rooms. Buck waited outside in the garden, sampling Raymond's barbecue. Heat lightning flashed over the lake, the evening still warm from the day's deluge of sunshine. Brice finished freshening up before Sally and joined him in the garden, exchanging the bound legal document under his arm for a cold beer.

"Title opinion for the Emma Fitzgerald # 1."

"Did you have a look at it already?"

"You bet. Two acres of the royalties belong to the Johnson's. There's a copy of the assignment of the deed in the title opinion. The land is clearly theirs. What's it all mean?"

"It means someone deleted record of the transaction from the county records."

"Who?"

"I suspect a man named Hogg Nation," Buck said. "He owns one of the abstract offices in Deception and is also the town mayor. He's the only person I know with the motive and the power."

Lightning flashed over the lake as Sally, looking fresh in pink shorts and a clingy cotton blouse, appeared. "Why the serious expressions?"

"We were wondering if we had the will power to wait on Raymond's barbecue any longer," Buck said.

By now, everyone had returned downstairs and Raymond, as if on cue, said, "Ribs are up. Let's eat."

Raymond and Wiley had pulled two picnic tables together. Ribs, smoked sausage, potato salad, coleslaw, pickles, and baked beans rested on Pearl's red-checkered table cloths. Buck grabbed a beer and sat beside Lila.

"It's been years since I last visited the island," she said. "It hasn't changed a bit."

"Except for Aunt Emma not being here."

Lila put down her fork. Taking Buck's hand, she gave it a motherly pat. "I'm sorry you never met Emma. She was a wonderful woman."

Lila's big eyes made Buck uncomfortable. "Hearing people talk about her is a big help," he said.

The picnic tables were large enough to seat everyone but Ray and Ezra ate alone at a smaller table beneath a sprawling pecan tree. Ray was ignoring his food, seemingly rapt in his conversation with the old man. From time to time Lila would glance in their direction.

Conversation had all but ceased as everyone enjoyed the savory layers of food on their paper plates. They feasted on Raymond's ribs and chicken and Pearl's barbecue beans and potato salad, topping it all off with watermelon and cold beer. Soon Buck was stuffed and tipsy.

"I think I overdid it," Brice said.

Sally, unlike her husband, had satisfied her appetite with only a single helping of ribs and fixings. "Quit whining," she said. "I still have room for desert."

Brice, wishing he hadn't eaten that last plate of ribs, was eyeing Sally's strawberry shortcake when Ray came over to their table and gave his mother a hug. Ezra was with him.

"Everything is great but I have another section to finish before I can get some sleep."

"Ray, can't you work on that dissertation of yours some other time? We're having a party here and it's still early."

"Don't you won't me to graduate?"

"At least take some shortcake with you," Pearl said.

She gave him no chance to refuse. Cutting him a generous helping of shortcake, she ladled strawberries over the top of the dessert. Ray took the package without arguing as Ezra edged closer to the head of the table.

"I had a wonderful time, Ms. Pearl, but it's a wee bit past this old man's bedtime. I'm going to call it a night myself."

Ezra gave everyone a backwards wave as he sauntered off to his room in the lodge. Ray kissed his mother's forehead and strolled away without a word to anyone else. His omission seemed to distress Lila. After a quick glance at Buck to check for disapproval she untangled herself from the bench and left the table.

"Please excuse me," she said, following Ray without a word of explanation.

Buck watched over his shoulder until Lila disappeared beneath the grove of pecan trees. Lightning flashing over the lake signaling an abrupt end to the frog and cricket serenade. Pearl finally broke the silence.

"You young people go on up to the veranda. After Raymond and I clean up I'll make you all a pot of coffee."

Pearl's orders generated a wave of protest. "No way," Brice said.

"We'll clean up for you," Sally and Sara both offered.

As they argued about who would put up the food, something unexpected happened — an explosion down by the marina. Everyone stared at the horizon as flames curled skyward and smoke billowed up over the trees. Flames and smoke masked the stars and colored the sky crimson. Wiley was the first to react.

"Something's on fire," he said, pushing away from the table. "Over by the marina."

Not bothering to use the garden gate, he vaulted the shrubbery in a running gallop as Brice and Buck followed close behind. As Buck rounded the corner to the marina he saw what was burning — a cross, a racist statement as old as the South itself.

In the field beside the marina someone had piled brush around the cross after securing it in the dirt. They had doused the brush with gasoline and set it ablaze. Something was tied to the base of the cross and the creature was whimpering and struggling to get loose. Sally and Sara came running up behind. Sally was screaming. The brush pile had yet to fully ignite but the outcome was imminent as flames licked down the burning cross.

"Oh God! That poor dog will burn to death. Somebody do something."

Sally ran for the fire, not waiting for anyone to react to her plea, and Brice chased after her. He tackled her from behind before she reached the flaming mass, rolling her in the dirt.

"Stop it Sally! There's nothing we can do."

He was right. Without a knife or something to cut the rope, there was no way to free the terrified animal from the flames. Buck's brain understood but adrenaline rushing through his veins dictated that he try anyway. It didn't matter that the frightened animal was Cyclone, the pit bull dog from Hogg Nation's development.

As he sprinted toward the cross he heard Brice yell, "Buck, no!"

The ground around the cross was damp from the last rain. Slipping in the mud, Buck slid face first toward the fire, slamming into the dog and knocking him off his feet. Buck sensed the animal's palpable fear as it cowered against him. His only plan was to grab the rope and yank until either his strength or the flame parted the strands. He quickly got a big surprise. The rope was neither hemp nor sisal. Instead he tugged helplessly on an unbreakable strand of steel cable.

Lila screamed behind him as blisters began appearing on the backs of his hands. "Get out of there!"

Buck wanted to do just that but Cyclone's quivering body and racing heart prompted him to hold on. He yanked the cable again, further frightening the dog wedged against him. Sensing there was no hope of saving the wretched beast, he had almost resigned himself to letting go. It was a decision he didn't have to make. Someone chopped the steel cable with one swing of a double-bladed axe.

It was Ray. Without waiting for Buck to run from the flame he lifted him bodily off the ground and dragged him from the fire, dropping him into a mud hole forty feet from the burning cross. Cyclone, frightened but otherwise unharmed, was still clutched in Buck's arms.

CHAPTER TWENTY-THREE

When Lila piled into the mud puddle she unintentionally inflicted more damage on Cyclone and Buck than the two had received from the fire. Despite the mouthful of muddy water he swallowed, Buck was grateful for her concern and smiled when she said, "Are you okay?"

Ray waded into the puddle to take Cyclone while Wiley, Raymond and Brice doused the smoldering cross with buckets of water. Sally and Sara followed Ray and Lila into the mud hole, helping Buck to his feet as Pearl waited in the shadow of a giant oak. She was crying softly and wiping away tears with her red apron.

Lila's words were barely a whisper. "Who could have done this?"

"And why tie a helpless animal to a burning cross?" Ray said. "This dog's scared half to death."

Buck, sensing he knew the answer to both questions, watched Ray comfort the frightened pit bull. He kept his opinion to himself. Wiley touched his brother's shoulder and guided him toward the shadows of a nearby tree, pointing with his free hand as he told Ray about Buck's encounter with Humpback and Deacon John at Nation's development. Wiley returned alone.

"Ray will keep the dog for the night. Patch him up and calm him down. Mama, you and Daddy go on home. Nothing more to do until tomorrow. I'll call the sheriff from the lodge."

The barbecue and subsequent cross burning had taken their toll on Raymond and Pearl's nerves and Pearl continued dabbing at her eyes. Raymond looked almost as forlorn as she. Wiley turned them toward their house, nudging them in that direction.

Raymond's barbecue was over and most of the guests were muddy messes. Warm summer rain sprinkled their shoulders and soon turned to fat drops. Mud began washing out of Buck's hair and down his face. Nearby thunder signaled the beginning of another rainstorm that quickly extinguished the last smoldering sparks from the charred cross. Buck took one last look. When he reached the lodge he found Brice and Sally huddled together by the big stone fireplace.

Wiley seemed the least disturbed by the burning cross. With a grin firmly affixed to his face, he broke out towels and a bottle of Jack Daniels. "I think we could all use a drink," he said. "Something a little stiffer than Budweiser."

From Aunt Emma's liquor larder, the very one Buck had raided his first night on the island, Wiley selected six crystal tumblers and poured an imposing quantity of Black Jack into each. No one declined. Sara appeared shaken but not like Lila and Sally. As Wiley dispensed the whiskey, Buck offered an explanation to Brice and Sally. "I certainly didn't intend to subject you to anything like this."

"We'll be fine," Brice said.

Sally touched Buck's shoulder and said, "We're just glad you're okay."

"I just hope you weren't too frightened, Sal."

"I'm not a baby. I was worried about you and that poor animal."

Sally jumped when Lila unexpectedly walked up behind them. Her start gave Brice and Buck a chuckle, and caused a needed break in the perceptible tension. Lila was already working on her second tumbler of whiskey and her usual articulation had taken on the thick Southern drawl Buck had noted at her father's party. Tears formed in her hazel eyes as she leaned against his shoulder. "I'm so ashamed."

Brice pulled out his handkerchief, handing it to Lila. Patting her shoulder, Sally tried to comfort her. "What are you talking about?"

"Deception," Lila said, dabbing her eyes with Brice's handkerchief. "This place is not the Eden it seems. There's a cancer here."

"Nonsense," Brice said. "Even if there were, it wouldn't be your fault."

"Knowing about the cancer and doing nothing about it is my offense. I've known it since I was a little girl."

Sally squeezed Lila's hand. "Lila, it's all right."

Lila pulled away, cradling the tumbler against her breast. "No, it's not all right. I've kept the evil hidden deep in my heart, never lifting a finger to try and change things."

"But you live here," Brice said. "Everyone's —"

Realizing he was about to make a giant faux pas, Brice swallowed the last words of his intended sentence. It didn't matter. Lila caught his meaning anyway.

"Everyone's a racist?"

"Not what I meant to say."

"I know you don't believe me but most of the folks around here are law-abiding and respectful of all races and creeds," Lila said. "The handful of radicals spoil it for everyone."

Sally rocked Lila in her arms. "I'm from Ohio and Lord knows I witnessed plenty of racism when I was growing up but it doesn't mean everyone from Ohio is a racist."

"Same where I grew up," Brice added.

"Thanks," Lila said. "But it's far uglier here."

"Lighten up, girl," Wiley said, joining the conversation. "We ain't had a hanging or a castration in a month or more 'round these parts."

Wiley's words brought a smile to Lila. He followed his comment with a fresh drink, this one with a couple of ice cubes. Sara was giggling uncontrollably over some joke and Wiley led Lila back to the couch to join her.

"It's been a long day and I've enjoyed almost every minute of it," Sally said. "But I need a hot soak in that antique tub upstairs and the king size feather bed is sounding better every minute."

"I'll be right behind you," Brice said, patting her muddy bottom as she started up the stairs. When she was gone, he said, "Racism isn't all we're talking about here, is it?"

Buck sipped his whiskey before answering and Brice laughed when he said, "What makes you landmen so smart? What someone really wants is this island and they're apparently prepared to do almost anything to get it."

"Hogg Nation?"

"Most likely. I'm not sure if he had anything to do with what happened here tonight but I think I know who did."

Buck filled Brice in on everything that had happened since he'd arrived in Deception as the storm continued outside. A nearby clap of thunder caused the inside of the room to gasp like a depressed bellows, reminding them.

"Tell me more about this treasure," Brice said. "You think it's somewhere on the island?"

"Lila says there's no way but she can't explain the brass fitting I found on the backside of the island."

"Hogg Nation wants your island to save his development. His two thugs are looking for the *Mittie Stephens'* treasure and they think you know where it is. What's Judge Travis' angle?"

"Don't know."

Wiley interrupted their conversation. "Anybody up for a swim? The lodge has a wonderful indoor pool."

"Better pass," Brice said. "Sally will come looking for me if I don't join her." He waved and hurried up the stairs.

"What about you, Buck?" Wiley asked.

"Sure. Maybe it'll sober me up."

"Girls?" Wiley called. "Anyone for a swim?"

Wiley's toddies had caught up with Lila and Sara. Now both were giggling uncontrollably on the couch.

"What about it, Sara?" Lila said. "You know you're dying to show off your new bikini."

"And we're dying to see it," Wiley said.

Sara continued to giggle but Lila stumbled to her feet, her face awash in a silly grin. When she squeezed Buck's hand, an electric surge, momentarily clearing the cobwebs from his head, raced up his arm. Heat lightning flashed over the lake.

"You and Wiley go ahead," she said. "If Sara and I don't pass out before we get to our rooms, maybe we'll join you."

Lila grabbed Sara's hand, pulling her to her feet. Arm-in-arm they made their way upstairs, still giggling like two pre-teens on their way to a slumber party.

"That's the last we'll see of them tonight," Wiley said.

"Just as well," Buck said.

"Suit up and I'll meet you in the solarium," Wiley said. "It's on the other side of the dining room."

After changing into his bathing suit Buck joined Wiley in what turned out to be a magnificent solarium. Shadows danced on the walls of the dimly lit room as he eased down the short flight of stairs to the Mexican tiles. Two beams of light, melding with lightning flashes through the skylights, glimmered up from the bottom of the turquoise pool. Otherwise, the room was dark. Amid massive palms, hanging baskets and aromatic tropical flowers, Buck felt as if he'd entered the Garden of Eden. Wiley waited by the pool, his feet dangling in the water.

"Wow," Buck said, gawking around. "Why didn't you tell me about this place sooner?"

When Buck joined him by the pool Wiley handed him a tall glass of ice water. "Guess I forgot," he said.

Aunt Emma's solarium was like an indoor tropical rain forest. Dreamy music, piped in from hidden speakers, blended with the delicate scents of orchid, hibiscus and magnolia. Several slow moving ceiling fans generated a gentle breeze that dimpled the pool, creating the tropical feel of a south sea island.

Wiley grinned. "Miss Emma used to call this her own private Shangri-la."

"I see why," Buck said, glancing at the redwood hot tub in the corner.

Light from the submerged beam in the pool danced up through the water and gentle ripples further distorted the beam. Water trickled from a fountain. Soft light, lush vegetation and moving water slowly began to work on Buck's nerves. Diving in, he leisurely stroked to the opposite side.

"This is a dream," he said. "Let's swim a few laps, then sit in the hot tub and talk."

"Help yourself with the laps," Wiley said, dipping his fingers into the steaming water. "You can join me when you finish."

"How is it?"

"Perfect."

Wiley gingerly submerged his toe, then his whole foot into the tub. He slipped into hot water up to his neck, lounging in silence, a relaxed smile on his face. After completing ten fast laps Buck joined him. Steam, leaving him limp and relaxed, rose in moist clouds from the surface of the water.

"This is the ticket," Buck said.

Wiley's attention turned to the door and he held up his palm for silence.

"Someone's in the dining room. Maybe the cross burners back for more mischief."

Wiley slipped out of the water and followed the shadows toward the front door of the solarium. He grabbed a loose brick from the fountain along the way as Buck held his breath and watched. The handle turned and the door slowly opened. When the first person's head appeared through the crack, Wiley raised the brick to strike. The resultant female scream came from neither Humpback nor Deacon John. It was Lila and Sara and they were still giggling.

CHAPTER TWENTY-FOUR

Lila and Sara stood against the dining room wall staring at Wiley and Buck.

"Lila, Sara, are you okay?"

"I didn't hit you, did I," Wiley asked, dropping the brick and grabbing Sara's hand. "I thought you were the Klan coming back for more mischief."

Sara glanced at Lila and grinned. "Looky here, Miss Lila. These two brave boys were frightened to death of us little ol' girls. I wonder what we did to scare them so?"

"Lordy, Sara, I wish I knew. Maybe they're just a couple of girly men."

As Wiley and Buck watched with open mouths Sara and Lila rolled with laughter, holding each other to keep from falling down. It was obvious they were both still very inebriated. Lila strutted into the solarium giving Buck's rear a solicitous pat as she strolled past.

Her sleek black one-piece bathing suit rivaled Sara's skimpy bikini for pure sex appeal. Bringing a large jug of red wine with them, they spread their towels by the pool.

"Guilty," Wiley said when Buck gave him a dirty look. "I got them started with the whiskey but they found the wine all by themselves."

Buck and Wiley returned to the hot tub as Lila and Sara, the half-empty wine jug clearly the cause of their levity, dissolved into another giggling fit. They finally spotted the hot tub.

"Well, look here, Sara," Lila said in the brash voice of a drunken Southern belle. "I think we found ourselves a couple of hot tub bunnies."

Lila's garbled statement caused Sara to giggle even more inanely as she stumbled over to the tub, leaning against it for support. "We're out of luck," Sara said. They both have their suits on."

"Maybe we can persuade them to take them off," Lila said.

"Would you girls like to join us?" Wiley said, his invitation making Buck even more uncomfortable.

"Sara, lets take a plunge in the tub."

Grabbing the wine and her towel, Sara followed Lila up the stairs to the redwood tub. Lila squeezed between Wiley and Buck, implanting a sultry kiss fully on Buck's lips as she did. Savoring his stunned look, she said, "Um, Sara, look at these muscles."

Sara sat the jug and towel on the top of the redwood deck and slithered into Wiley's lap, wrapping her long arms around his neck. "You boys don't mind a little company do you?" she asked.

"Plenty of room for everybody," Wiley said.

"Good," Lila said, removing the cork from the wine bottle. She hefted the bottle over her right shoulder until wine poured from the spout, spilling out the side of her mouth. A mighty hiccup launched Sara into another fit of laughter. "It's warm in here," Lila said as she untied the straps of her suit.

Like a sultry stripteaser, Lila vamped as she slipped the top of her bathing suit down over her breasts. Wiley grinned and Buck watched in near shock. Wine, burgundy red in muted light, dripped down between her breasts and a single drop hung momentarily suspended from an erect nipple. When she hiccupped again, the motion shook the wine into the water and she grabbed her mouth to hide her foolish grin.

"Sara, you're not going to let me sit here half naked all by myself in front of these sex crazed men, are you?"

Sara untangled herself from Wiley's grip and stood up on the bench. Straddling him, she pulled the bikini straps slowly over her shoulders. After working the tiny bra loose of her breasts she slipped the bottoms down over her shapely legs.

Wiley and Buck stared as only Sara's dark tresses covered her coffee au lait shoulders. When Lila switched on the jets, Sara looked like Venus rising from the foam. To Wiley's embarrassment, she slid slowly back into his lap, her arms encircling his neck. Once in that recumbent position she closed her eyes, the gentle sound of her breathing soon signaling she had either passed out or fallen asleep. Lila wasn't far from doing the same.

Leaving the hot tub, Buck plunged into the swimming pool, the cool water barely calming his ignited ardor. Wiley was busy reviving Sara and Lila then helping them out of the tub. Once he had them standing, he draped their shoulders with large towels.

"These two have had enough for tonight," he said. "After I escort them to their rooms, I'm going home for a little shuteye."

"Good idea," Buck said.

Buck completed a slow lap of the pool before trudging upstairs where he undressed and sprawled on the bed's feather mattress. The swimming pool had revived him and he remained awake after turning off the lights and closing his eyes. A half hour had passed when he heard footsteps in the hall.

The outside storm continued, unabated. At first Buck thought the noise outside his door was the old lodge creaking in the wind. A turn of the doorknob belied his theory. Someone entered the room and tiptoed toward the bed as he flicked on the lamp.

"Lila, what the devil are you doing?"

"Something I need to tell you," she said.

Lila's pale blue nightgown, revealing every not-so-subtle curve, clung to her lithesome frame. Buck had maintained a healthy sexual interest in the lovely Miss Richardson since their first meeting. Now, her near nudity and unexpected appearance in his bedroom sent him into another paroxysm of lust.

"You're a surprise all right," he said.

Lila dimmed the light and sat beside him on the edge of the bed. "I hope you didn't get the wrong idea about what happened tonight in the hot tub. I'm afraid Sara and I had too much to drink and we're not really the loose women that you may think. I don't wish to lose your respect."

Respect wasn't what Buck had on his mind, his racing thoughts focused on something else. His memories momentarily returned him to a hot summer night in the back seat of an old Ford. Dressed in her revealing nightgown, he assumed Lila had similar desires in mind. He was wrong. It was, in fact, the farthest thing from her mind and Buck was about to find out.

She kissed Buck lightly and tried to back away but he pulled her toward him until she was draped across his chest. Lila's heart was pounding and warmth and softness emanated from beneath the sheer fabric of her negligee. Still, Buck sensed Lila's unexpected reluctance after a prolonged kiss.

"Wait," she said, breathing heavily and struggling to pull away. "Please stop. This isn't why I'm here." Buck still didn't get the message. When he reached for her again, she pushed him away and slapped his face. This time it was much sharper than a love tap. "Stop it," she said.

Free of Buck's grasp Lila slid off the bed. Her negligee had fallen to her waist during the short tussle and she pulled the silken garment up over her breasts.

"Lila, I'm sorry. I thought —"

"It's all right," Lila said, her frown disappearing. "I have to go now."

Lila backed out the door into to the hall as Buck remained on the bed, his skin moist from the frenetic moments of intense body heat. Realizing she wasn't returning to her room, his curiosity overcame his shame and he followed her into the hall.

Buck tiptoed to Lila's room just to make sure she wasn't there. He found her door ajar, the place dark and empty. Something moving downstairs caused him to glance over the railing. It was Lila hurrying toward the front door, still wearing her silken negligee.

Rain continued to fall but now in large, slow drops. Lila didn't seem to notice, the flowing fabric of her gown rippling in the dim light of distant lightning as she moved across the clearing. She made her way to Ray's room at the marina where light radiated from his window. When Ray opened the door he quickly embraced Lila. His ardor was immediately reciprocated, leaving Buck with little doubt of their intentions.

CHAPTER TWENTY-FIVE

Buck awoke the next morning feeling better than he'd expected. At least until he remembered accosting Lila in his bedroom. Padding downstairs, he hoped he'd dreamed the whole incident but knew in his heart he hadn't. Pearl was waiting for him at the kitchen door and the aroma of bacon and eggs wafting from the kitchen momentarily riveted his thoughts on other matters.

"The sheriff has come and gone. He and that skinny deputy took some pictures but told us not to hold our breath on catching anybody."

When she squeezed Buck's hand, he said, "Somehow I'm not surprised."

Pearl returned to the stove. Brice, sipping coffee from a large mug, stood by the sink. "I was thinking about the foreclosure. I'd like to take a look at the legal papers. I have a law degree, you know. That makes me a lawyer, even though I've never taken the bar exam."

"I'd almost forgotten," Buck said. "Five years of night school, right?"

"Six. I'm not F. Lee Bailey, but the price is right."

"Thanks, pal," Buck said. "Lets go to Aunt Emma's study. That's where I left the papers Randy Rummels gave me."

Buck and Brice followed the long antique hallway to Aunt Emma's study. Buck directed Brice to a large oak chair and placed the legal papers in front of him.

"Sally and I were up at six," Brice said as he thumbed through the documents. "We had breakfast and took a long walk around the island when we finished. I'll look these over while Sally's in the shower."

"It means a lot to me having friends like you and Sally," Buck said.

Brice gave him a thumbs up as he turned pages of the document. Buck left Brice to his task, feeling better knowing it was possible he'd finally turned the corner on his investigation. The elation disappeared when he spotted Lila on the veranda. Wiley and Sara, engrossed with each other, were with her. Buck waved, beckoning Lila to join him in the kitchen.

"My apologies," Buck said. "I feel terrible about last night. I wish I had an excuse, but I don't."

Buck braced himself for Lila's verbal reprimand. She responded instead with a smile. "It was no more your fault then mine. I came to your bedroom long after midnight in my sexiest nightie. You would have crushed my fragile ego if you hadn't made a pass."

"Fragile?" Buck said, rubbing his jaw.

Lila squeezed his hand and said, "You are a rogue, Buck McDivit. If someone else didn't already own my heart, you could easily smite it away from my little ol' body."

"Ray?"

Lila nodded and stared at the floor. "Until yesterday, I hadn't seen him in four years. I thought I was finished with him. I'm not."

"I noticed the way you looked at each other and I think it's wonderful. Thanks for not being mad at me."

"I could never be angry with you. And Buck, can I ask a favor?"

"Ask me anything."

Pots clattered in the kitchen as Pearl prepared lunch and a mockingbird, angry at a marauding crow, raised a ruckus down by the lake. Lila and Buck didn't seem to notice.

"Please don't tell anyone about Ray and me just yet," Lila said." My father wouldn't understand and I doubt if Raymond and Pearl would either."

"You'll have to tell them sooner or later."

"I know," she said. "I'm just not ready right now and neither is Ray."

"My mouth is shut," Buck said.

Satisfied with Buck's response, Lila dragged him out the door to the veranda where Sara and Wiley remained locked in a spirited conversation. Wiley's eyes and arms were animated, his voice raised an octave for effect.

"Sara girl, this lake is haunted. I'm not making it up. Buck saw the ghost, didn't you?"

"I saw something. I'm not sure what it was."

"The ghost of Bessie McKinney?" Lila said.

Sara posed with her hands on her hips, grinning, "You gotta be kidding me. That's just a legend. Right?"

Wiley flashed his own grin. "Oh she's a legend all right, but she existed as surely as you and I. She died mysteriously almost one hundred and forty years ago and her ghost still haunts the lake."

"Is she the ghost you saw?" Sara asked in a mocking tone.

"Maybe," Buck said. "Sounds like Wiley knows more than I do."

Sara glanced at Wiley for confirmation. "Is that true?"

"You mean Lila never told you about Bessie?"

Sara turned her gaze to Lila. "Don't keep me in suspense."

Lila drew the three of them closer and began speaking in a conspiratorial voice. It made Buck wonder how many times she'd recounted the story at slumber parties or on dark verandas after midnight.

"Bessie's mother preceded her in death," she said. "Also dying unexpectedly at the age of only forty-one. Francine, Bessie's sister, ran the household following her mother's untimely death. Larkin McKinney, their father, was a drunk and died of chronic alcoholism. Francine married late in life, wedding Alton Richardson after her father died."

"How much older was Francine than Bessie?" Buck asked.

Lila and Wiley exchanged glances as they considered my question. "Fourteen years older?" Wiley said.

"Fourteen or fifteen," Lila said. "Why?"

"Just curious. Their son was your great-grandfather?"

"Yes," Lila said, "Clayton Richardson the first."

Pearl interrupted the discussion as she began serving breakfast. Everyone, famished for reasons of their own, tore into pancakes and maple syrup. Breakfast and conversation about Bessie McKinney took Buck's mind off his troubles for the first time since arriving on the island.

"It's a shame we don't have a time capsule," he said. "We could go back and see what really happened to Bessie."

Wiley winked at Lila. "We could do the next best thing."

"I'll bite," Buck said. "What's the next best thing?"

"We could ask Mama Toukee," Wiley said.

"You're right," Lila said, clapping her hands. "Why didn't I think of that?"

"The same Mama Toukee I've heard about?" Buck asked.

"A voodoo priestess. Lives on the other side of Fitzgerald Island," Wiley said.

"Wiley Johnson, are you pulling our leg?" Sara said.

"He's not, I promise," Lila said. "There's always been a large cult following of voodoo in areas populated by descendants of black West Africans. You can still hear drums across the lake when the practitioners meet on certain ritual nights."

"Sister," Sara said. "You got that right."

Lila continued her tale. "Mama Toukee is the local high priestess."

With Sara smiling and nodding her head, Buck felt like the butt of a growing prank. "You actually believe this Mama Toukee of yours can look back into the past using voodoo?"

"You were skeptical about ghosts before you saw one," Wiley said.

"I still am. I just don't have an explanation for what I saw."

Lila said, "Then you admit the possibility that there might really be ghosts?"

"Anything is possible."

By now Sara was bouncing in her chair. "You've convinced me. Let's go see Mama Toukee."

"Wait just a minute!" Buck said. "We're all civilized here. How can you justify belief in witches?"

"Do you always base your decisions on preconceived ideas or do you research them first?" Lila asked.

Duly chastised Buck said, "Guess it wouldn't hurt to check it out. When do we go?"

Lila beamed. "Tonight. It's a witch's moon."

"A what?"

"A quarter moon," she said. "To prevent nonbelievers from observing their ceremonies, witches congregate on nights of the quarter moon. When the moon is full it's too bright. The new moon doesn't provide enough light. It'll be a quarter moon tonight — perfect time to consult a witch."

"Good scientific reasoning," Buck said, deciding to go along with the fun.

The discussion of voodoo and witchcraft had brought a sparkle to Lila's eyes and now she fairly emanated enthusiasm. "We only have one problem. We need Mama Toukee to channel a spirit from the past. In this case, Bessie McKinney. To channel a specific spirit, it generally takes either a family member or close friend."

"You're a distant relative, Lila," Wiley said.

"Maybe too distant. We'll just have to try."

"Will anything else work?" Sara asked.

"Yes," Lila said. "An object once owned by the deceased. But not just any object. It must be one of their most valued possessions."

Buck fished in his pocket, retrieving the cameo brooch he'd found the night he saw the apparition. Placing it on the table in front of them, he said, "What about this?"

CHAPTER TWENTY-SIX

Darkness draped the island with the muffled glow of a witch's moon as time approached to visit Mama Toukee's. Yet another storm, a progression of dark clouds racing across the sky, brewed in the distance. Buck finally broke the silence as he and Wiley watched from the veranda.

"How early did people marry when Bessie McKinney was alive?"

"Younger than now, I'd guess," Wiley said. "Why?"

"According to what you and Lila said this morning, Bessie McKinney's sister Francine was fourteen or fifteen years older than Bessie."

"So?"

"Bessie's mother was forty-one when Bessie died at fifteen. Francine would have been twenty-nine or thirty. Unless I'm botching some important calculation, it means Bessie's mother was only eleven or twelve when she conceived Francine."

Buck's conclusion seemed so obvious that it perplexed Wiley, having obviously never thought of it himself. "That is strange. What are you getting at?"

"Just that Bessie's mother wasn't likely to also be Francine's natural mother. Maybe she was adopted."

Wiley scratched his chin thoughtfully. "Could be, I guess. What difference does it make?"

"I don't know yet but remind me to ask Lila."

Pearl interrupted their musings with coffee and homemade apple pie. After finishing his last lip-smacking bite Wiley left the table, not waiting for a second cup of coffee. "Think I'll relax in the den until we're ready do leave."

"Better take a walk with me and work off some of your mom's good cooking."

"You go ahead. I need a quick nap."

"Suit yourself," Buck said as Wiley sauntered into the lodge.

Buck savored the last drop of coffee before taking the path to the marina. Walking at an aerobic clip, he quickly began to feel better about the empty but delicious calories he'd eaten. He found the marina dark and deserted but had the eerie feeling that he wasn't alone. Seeing nothing to fan his paranoia, he continued at a more leisurely pace around the lake's edge, finally retracing his steps to the lodge. Lila met him on the porch before he had a chance to catch his breath.

"Let's go, slowpoke. Everyone's waiting for us at the dock."

Grabbing Lila's arm, Buck wheeled her around. "Wait... One question before we go. Was Francine adopted?"

Lila didn't have to think before answering. "Of course not. What made you think she was?"

"Curiosity. You're sure that Elizabeth and Larkin McKinney were her natural parents?"

Lila stared at him. "I'll show you the family tree in our Bible next time you visit the house if you don't believe me."

Hearing the injured tone of her voice, Buck said, "Whoa, I'm not calling you a liar. I'm just curious about the sequence of events leading up to Bessie's death."

"That's why we're visiting Mama Toukee," she said, grabbing his arm. "Now let's hurry or the others will go without us."

Lila hurried toward the lake beneath the semi-darkness of a quarter moon. Buck followed her as lightning illuminated the clearing in momentary bursts of frenetic energy. He didn't need a barometer to know that another large storm was approaching the island.

"Hurry up," Wiley said, lifting Lila over the gunnel of the boat.

Wiley steadied the hull as Buck climbed in. The noisy engine cranked into life as he pointed the bow away from the island and followed a narrow channel through the corridor of cypress trees. They exited into open water after a hundred yards of arboreal maze, the lake already growing choppy. Summer lightning back-dropped the lodge behind them, reminding Buck of a lonely lighthouse overlooking a stormy sea.

Once they'd cleared the moat of cypress trees encircling the island Wiley followed the shoreline, maneuvering the boat through a hazy mist curling up from the lake's surface. Amid tangled brush and submerged debris, glowing eyes followed their progress.

"Are we almost there?" Sally asked.

Wiley laughed. "Nervous?"

Sara gave him a friendly punch in the ribs. "I think you're having too much fun, buster."

"Sorry," Wiley said, the return of his humor signaling an end to his former somber mood.

They soon reached an opening in the rows of cypress trees bordering the island and Wiley pointed the boat into it. Following a distinct path through a maze of roots and vines, they reached a small cove. In the distance, a tar paper shack occupied a small clearing overlooking the cove. Wiley let the boat drift ashore.

Mama Toukee's shanty was tiny, its weathered porch creaking with age. They found the old woman sitting in a wooden rocker, watching as the group approached along the path. A black cat moved beneath her feet, rubbing its arched back against her legs. Neither seemed surprised by the unannounced appearance.

"It's Wiley, Mama Toukee."

A crooked grin appeared on the old crone's lips and she answered in an accent straight from the swamps of south Louisiana. "You come back for more love potion on such a night?"

Wiley gave Sara an embarrassed glance before embracing the little woman. "Just had a craving for a big hug."

Mama Toukee encircled her bony arms around Wiley's neck and imparted a toothless kiss. She had only one eye. When she pulled away from Wiley's grasp the remnant of the other stared up at them from an empty socket. Her one eye seemed to have a life of its own and Buck had no doubt the old woman could see their every movement clear as day.

"Who you brung to see me?" she asked when Wiley stepped back from the rocker.

"Friends, Mama. I didn't think you'd mind."

Mama Toukee turned around slowly and glanced at Sara, her ensuing laugh sounding like a tubercular cackle. "Mama's potion work good, yeah?"

Wiley grinned. "Guess it did at that."

"What for you come tonight, *mon amie*?"

"To visit the dead, Mama," he said.

Mama Toukee's cackle became a coughing wheeze. "You brung the pretty girls to protect you?"

"Don't need no protection with you here, Mama," Wiley said.

The old hag's wrinkled skin was stretched across her face like a rubber mask pulled over a skull. Muted thunder rumbled in the distance.

"Maybe not, *mon amie*," she said.

The front of the shack was no more than an extension of the dirt pathway from the lake. A large cauldron occupied the clearing. Beside it sat a stack of hastily gathered firewood. Mama Toukee gazed at Sara with her one good eye.

"Cain summon no spirits when one doan belieb."

Sally and Brice were standing close together on the edge of the porch and the old woman's admonition made Sara fidget.

"Afraid you'll have to stay outside on the porch," Wiley said.

"No way," Sara said. "It's dark out here."

"Then you'll have to think more positive thoughts," Lila said.

"I'll do my best, Mama. Please don't make me stay out here all by myself," Sara said, edging closer to Wiley.

The old woman nodded her assent as Wiley helped her out of the chair and pointed her toward the door of the shack. Supporting herself with a gnarled cane she lead them into the shack where the reek of mold and burned oil immediately accosted their sense of smell. When Mama Toukee struck a match and lit a coal oil lantern on the table, its glow revealing a spartan interior.

Old newspaper and cardboard lined the walls for insulation and black patches of mildew caused by moisture dripping through the roof spotted the walls. Smoke, mingling with other sweet and rotting smells, snaked up from the lamp. It made the shack seem more like an animal's den than a house.

A musty bedspread hung from a wire stretched across the back wall and partially separated the tiny room from the cot behind it. Mama Toukee's bedroom. The room's only appliances consisted of an old two-burner stove and a white ice box jammed against the wall. Mama Toukee interrupted Buck's examination, pulling up a chair at an old kitchen table and beckoning Lila to join her.

Dim light from the coal oil lamp barely illuminated the table and created shadows that danced across the walls. When Mama Toukee's cat stationed itself between her legs, Buck saw it also had only one eye. A perceptible chill crept into the room as the old crone raised her head and stared at the ceiling. Buck felt the chill and Lila's folded arms suggested he wasn't the only one to notice it. He also felt the power of the old woman's penetrating stare when she pointed her bony finger at him.

"You brung somethin' for Mama Toukee?"

Buck assumed at first she was asking for money, but Wiley quickly interpreted her real meaning. "The brooch, Buck, give her the brooch."

Buck took the crusty old cameo from his pocket and handed it to Mama Toukee. Her hand shrank when she touched it. Her frail body began to shiver and the shiver quickly became a full-blown shake. In the throes of the ensuing convulsion, the old woman's fragile arms and head slammed against the table. Buck thought she had knocked herself out but Wiley shook his head and grabbed his arm when he moved to help.

Everyone sat transfixed as Mama Toukee's arms drummed against the table and a high-pitched drone began to emanate from deep within her lungs. It sounded like air escaping from a punctured tire and continued until Mama Toukee's gyrations became increasingly muted. When her extreme convulsions finally subsided and the high nasal sound of escaping air ceased, her bony old hand rose slowly up from the table top and spread into an open palm. As it did, the exposed chalcedony brooch emitted a dull but perceptible glow.

Now a different sound came from Mama Toukee's lips — a voice that seemed derived from another world. Though it spoke no more than a dozen words, Buck had no doubt he was hearing the voice of the long dead Bessie McKinney. It said, "Mother, sister, daughter, death? The answer lies in an icy grave."

A clap of distant thunder broke the ensuing silence.

The words spoken through the old woman echoed in Buck's brain long after Mama Toukee's trance had ended. When the old woman opened her good eye Lila grabbed her shoulders, shaking her gently until she regained her senses. Wiley brought a ladle of water from a bucket by the stove. Kneeling beside her, he held the ladle to her lips as she sipped the warm liquid.

"You all right, Mama?"

Cackling like a lunatic, the old crone said, "Mama fine. I tink you the one done seen the ghost."

The old woman was right. Buck glanced around the room, realizing he wasn't the only one with an open mouth. Brice and Sally were huddled against the far wall. Sara's eyes were wide, her mouth agape. Lila's mouth was also open, her hand partially covering it. Wiley was smiling and Buck had the feeling of déjà vu.

"Mama, we brought you something." Wiley said.

He carried in two grocery bags from the porch and retrieved a block of ice from one of the bag. He placed the block in the ice box then showed Mama Toukee a large ham, a dozen eggs and various other goodies. Buck helped him load the ice box and stack assorted canned goods in the cabinet.

"We gotta go now, Mama," Wiley said.

"Smoke with me first," she said, grabbing his wrist.

Mama Toukee removed something from beneath the table and Buck squinted to see the plastic baggy filled with what was probably marijuana. When she formed a joint in her hands and lit it he was sure of it. After taking a puff, she handed the joint to Wiley.

The old hag cackled when Wiley took a deep pull from the joint. When he handed it back to her, she fingered it a moment before handing it to Lila. Lila took a quick puff and passed the joint around until it was gone. Then Wiley began herding them toward the door.

"Thanks, Mama. It's late and we better go."

"Doan forget the brooch," Mama Toukee said, slipping the baggy of marijuana between her tattered blouse and flat chest for safe keeping.

When Buck took the brooch he noticed a lustrous glow not present before the old woman had touched it. Dizzy and lightheaded from the drug, he banged his head against a rafter on the porch. But even the drug's mind-altering properties could disguise the approaching storm.

Wind whistled through the pines and lightning played across the sky as they hurried down the dirt path to the boat. They quickly found it had drifted away from the bank, the storm already whipping a froth on the lake. Wiley didn't hesitate. Wading into the water, he grabbed the front of the boat and pulled it back to shore, steadying the bow until everyone had climbed aboard. Pointing the boat toward the lake, he gave it a push and jumped in behind. Engine noise melded with nearby thunder as Wiley maneuvered them through the cypress brake. Buck leaned back against the boat, still dizzy and disoriented by Mama Toukee's marijuana, the storm and drug combining to launch him into a giggling fit.

"Something funny?" Wiley said.

Wiley's voice caused him to laugh even harder. He continued to laugh uncontrollably until they were out of the narrow channel and into open water. There the wildly rocking boat finally quieted him and he sensed something in the air other than the storm — a reddish glow looking for all the world like a giant Lava Light pulsating above the trees. Buck sat up, suddenly sober, as

Wiley yelled above the wind.

"Something's on fire."

"The marina," Lila said.

Wiley throttled the engine, slicing the boat through choppy water, everyone holding on as they tore through the waves. Within minutes they rounded the last bend of the island and saw flames, whipped by gusty winds, licking the darkened sky. The marina was on fire and being consumed by flames. Docks, boats, and the marina of Fitzgerald Island were ablaze and burning out of control.

CHAPTER TWENTY-SEVEN

Mama Toukee's marijuana had affected Buck's senses. Now the shock of seeing flames licking the marina's roof prompted him to dive from the boat and start swimming toward the beach. His excursion into warm water sobered him quickly and he realized his mistake as the craft powered past him and nosed into shore. Wiley jumped out of the boat before its engine had died, the others following closely behind.

The marina, despite being surrounded by water, had only one water faucet from which to draw. Raymond had already hooked up a long hose to the lone faucet and stood as far out on the dock as he dared, spraying the flames. The fine shower of water was having little effect on the fire.

Pearl was hauling buckets of water from the minnow container to douse the fire but she was slow and Wiley grabbed the bucket from her. Despite being faster than Pearl, his extra effort did little to keep the marina from burning out of control. Pearl was frantic when Buck finally reached shore and dragged himself out of the water. Grabbing his arm, she pointed toward the flaming concession at the end of the dock.

"Oh, Mr. Buck, Ray's in there."

"In the fire?"

"Yes!"

Buck pulled away from Pearl's grasp and rushed headlong down the narrow dock. "I'll get him."

Raymond saw Buck coming and dropped his hose. "Man, are you crazy?" he said, seeing what Buck was about to do.

Buck sidestepped the larger man and lunged through the fire already lapping across the far end of the wooden walkway. He could hear Raymond screaming at him. "Don't do it, man!"

Paying no attention to Raymond's warning Buck high-stepped through the burning building, shielding his eyes as he covered the distance to the concession at the end of the walkway. Ray had already kicked in the door to gain entrance and Buck rushed through the opening as his water-soaked clothes began to scorch. The fire was not his only concern.

Thick smoke masked Buck's vision, sucking oxygen from his lungs. Ripping off his wet shirt he thrust it over his head and continued blindly through the burning store to Ray's room in back. He found Ray unconsciousness and lying on the floor beside his bed.

Flames engulfed the room as Buck grabbed Ray's arm and rolled him over. He was unconscious but still alive and had somehow maintained his grip on a large folder. It was clutched tightly in his hands, the veins in his wrists popping out from the strain. Buck struggled to lift Ray off the burning mattress but found him too chunky to accomplish the task. Blisters raised on his face and neck as he felt suddenly rejuvenated. More than rejuvenation, his new found strength exceeded reason.

Ignoring painful blisters, he yanked Ray off the bed and dragged his inert body across the floor. Fire chased them through the door and Buck clawed through dense smoke for another way out of the burning building. A lone window on the far wall seemed the only possible avenue of escape but Buck encountered another problem when they reached it.

Age and old paint had glued the wooden-framed window to its casement and Buck strained to budge it from its moorings. Knocking out one small pane was useless. He scanned the room for something heavy enough to knock out the whole window. Finding nothing he mustered his remaining strength, hoisted Ray off the floor and tossed him through the closed window, quickly following him through the opening as flames licked his back.

"They're in the water," Wiley yelled, sprinting into the lake.

Raymond and Pearl followed him into the water, pulling Buck and Ray to shore. They quickly began trying to revive their son. Thunder and a rainy torrent followed the last burning remnant of the dock and marina as it toppled into the lake. Wet drops relieved the pain of Buck's blisters but arrived too late to save the marina. Rain washed away the last vestige of the fire as he lay there, beside Lila and Pearl weeping for Ray. Raymond and the others looked relieved but a wave of nausea was already forming in Buck's stomach. Rolling over, he buried his face in the mud.

Rain continued throughout the night and Buck spent it tossing and turning, trying to decide what to do next. The marina had paid the salaries of Raymond, Ray, and Pearl. Without it he realized he couldn't support the island on his own meager resources. When the clock's alarm sounded the next morning, he crawled out of bed and stood beneath the shower head until the water ran cold. It was only then that he assessed his own damage.

Buck's skin was scorched, his ribs black and blue from clipping a railing on his way out the window. And several new sore spots became painfully apparent as he limped down the stairs. When Pearl saw him she burst into tears, almost breaking his good ribs when she rushed over and hugged him.

"Oh, Mr. Buck, you saved my baby."

Despite his discomfort, Pearl's reference to baby Ray made Buck smile. "He did the same for me the night before," he said, gently extricating himself from her grasp. "Is he okay?"

His question reduced her to an unexpected bawling fit and he had to pat her shoulder to calm her. "Ray's fine but what are we going to do now?"

"I'll think of something."

Buck's answer seemed to placate her and she dried her eyes with her apron, smiling weakly. "Thanks, Mr. Buck."

Pearl returned to the stove as Buck wondered if he really could take care of it. Brice was waiting on the veranda with a fresh pot of coffee and Buck joined him, leaning back in the chair and closing his eyes. He remained in that position until Brice's voice returned him to consciousness.

"You gonna make it, buddy boy?"

"I'm not worried about myself."

Brice had a legal document on the table and Buck recognized it as the foreclosure action. "I gave this a good look last night and I think it has a problem. I've never practiced law in Texas and my reading of their statutes may be faulty but —"

"But what?"

"You weren't accorded due process. You're a party-of-interest in the foreclosure and you should have had at least twenty days notice. They gave you ten."

"You think it'll save the island?"

"Don't know," Brice said. "From what you say about Judge Travis, he might just consider it harmless error and disregard it. Still, I think it's a chance of averting a sheriff's sale."

A motorboat passing on the lake sent a noisy flock of cattle egrets flying and a dozen sunning turtles into the water.

"Maybe I can prove the mortgage on the marina is a fake."

"You think it is?" Brice asked.

"Not really. It looked real to me but Pearl and Raymond aren't convinced."

"If it looked real to you then it probably is. Maybe we better just hammer away at the due process argument and hope we can get a stay until you can prove it. Whatever happens, I'll be right there with you."

"Thank's but after my visit to the good Judge's house, I don't have a lot of confidence in my chances."

Brice placed a brotherly hand on Buck's shoulder. "Nothing in the court system is ever a slam dunk. Travis doesn't like you and won't rule in our favor unless we back him into a corner. Leave him no other alternative. We'll insist on a court reporter and let him know we'll appeal any adverse decision in a heartbeat. Judges don't like having their decisions overturned."

Buck closed his eyes and rubbed his forehead. "Even if we win on appeal it'll be two years down the road. Where will that leave Raymond and Pearl?"

"We have to give it a shot. What else can we can do?" Brice said.

Brice left Buck alone on the veranda before he could answer the question, returning to the lodge to find Sally. Buck slumped back into the chair and groaned. The sun was high overhead, his face and neck warm and sweaty when he glanced up into Lila's hazel eyes.

"You looked so comfortable I didn't want to wake you but Sara and I are leaving now."

"Sorry. I didn't get much sleep last night."

Lila's cotton blouse and khaki shorts displayed her long legs to their best advantage. It didn't matter. Realizing the futility of his ardor, Buck averted his gaze. Lila's grin hinted that she understood his plight and even seemed to enjoy it.

"I'm sorry about what happened last night. Is there anything I can do?" she said.

"Maybe you can put me up a few days in case the Judge boots me off the island," Buck said, half in jest.

Lila wrapped her arms around his neck. "I'm so sorry. I hope Uncle Jeff doesn't take the island from you but if he does I'm expecting you to stay at our house. I'll even show you the family Bible."

Buck had none of Lila's faith in the fairness of her uncle's pending decision and barely remembered his request to see her family Bible. When Raymond called from the lake, Lila kissed him squarely on the lips.

"Gotta go. Good luck at your hearing."

"I'll walk you to the dock," Buck said, following her out the door.

Raymond and Wiley were waiting at the dock, along with Sara, Ezra, Brice and Sally. Ezra offered Buck his condolences over the marina fire.

"I just hope it didn't bring back too many bad memories for you."

"My memories will never leave me, nor my nightmares, but I'm okay with them. I just pray they catch the person that did this to you."

Everyone turned their attention to Buck when he said, "I think everyone knows Hogg Nation had a hand in it."

"Now wait a minute," Sara said. "What proof do you have of that? Hogg Nation is a good man. He had no part in the marina fire."

Taken aback by Sara's animation, Wiley asked, "How do you know that?"

"Because," she said.

Wiley pursued the question. "Cause why?"

"Because I've gone out with him. That's why. He doesn't have a mean bone in his body."

"You're dating Hogg Nation? What about me?" Wiley said, thumping his chest.

Wiley's jealous anger put Sara on the defensive. Everyone listened with interest when she said, "We had a quarrel. We broke up."

"You sure about that?"

"Sure I'm sure," she said.

"Sara, I'm sorry," Buck said as Wiley helped her onto the party barge. "I work at not jumping to conclusions. Maybe you're right about Nation."

Buck and Raymond watched from the bank of the lake as the barge disappeared in the direction of Deception. "You ain't wrong, Mr. Buck," Raymond said. "Hogg Nation burned down Aunt Emma's marina as sure as we're standing here."

Buck returned to the veranda to think about what Sara had said. After several more cups of coffee, he headed for the remains of the marina. What he found was far worse than he remembered. The docks and marina were a smoldering ruin of blackened toothpicks. A skeletal semblance of the marina's former shape protruded from the lake. Bits of charred lumber, floating reminders of the destroyed dock, lapped against the bank. The sight made him feel weak and helpless.

Sheriff Wright and Deputy Sam Goodlake were taking pictures of the marina's remains, the sheriff penning notes in his ever-present pad. Buck joined them.

"Find anything?"

The sheriff continued scribbling on the pad without looking up or answering Buck's question. "How many pictures do you want?" the deputy asked. "There ain't a bunch to see."

"You got enough," Wright said. He stopped writing and frowned at Buck. "Notice anything suspicious before the fire?"

Buck thought for a moment. "No."

Wright made a notation. "According to Raymond Johnson, he first observed the fire about one-fifteen this morning. The light coming through his window woke him up. Where were you at one fifteen, McDivit?"

"Returning from the other side of the island."

"And what were you doing there?"

"Visiting an old woman."

"At one in the morning?" Wright asked drily.

"Yes," Buck said, at a loss for a better explanation.

"Who was you with?"

"Lila, Wiley, Sara and some friends of mine, Brice and Sally."

"All visiting the old woman?" Wright said, sarcasm flavoring his words.

"Now look, Sheriff, I'm not the one under suspicion here." When the sheriff didn't reply, Buck asked, "Am I?"

"It's my job to check the alibi of anyone with a motive."

"What motive?" Buck asked.

"One hundred seventy-five thousand dollars. The value of the insurance policy on the marina."

Buck's mouth dropped. "I don't know anything about an insurance policy."

"That's not what your lawyer, Mr. Rummels, says."

"He's not my lawyer and if he says he is then he's a liar."

Sheriff Wright stopped writing and stared at Buck with cold, smoky-brown eyes. "You probably ought to watch who you call a liar around here, McDivit."

"I don't know anything about an insurance policy except what you just told me. If Rummels thinks I do, then he's mistaken."

Wright's expression gave Buck the impression of a coiled rattlesnake eyeing a rat. "It's a strong coincidence that your share of the money is the exact amount you need to pay off the bank mortgage."

"That's bullshit!"

Wright's eyes closed, almost imperceptibly. When he re-opened them his stare grew even colder, his calm facade hiding a temper that Buck realized was probably as violent and deadly as a Texas tornado. Wright's stare left

Buck visibly shaken.

"I didn't burn my own marina," he said.

"An arsonist started the fire. Burned it smack down to the water's edge. On purpose," Wright added, in case Buck didn't get the picture. "I can't think of anyone with more reason then you to do the crime."

"What about my alibi? I was with five other people when you say the fire started."

"We found a timing device. The arsonist set it at eleven to start burning at one. You were here at eleven and no one remembers seeing you at that time. Wiley Johnson says you took a walk."

Buck could only shake his head. "I didn't burn my own marina."

"We'll see about that," Wright said.

After making a final notation in his notebook, Sheriff Wright walked over to where the marina's walkway once stood and paced off some distances. Finally he motioned the deputy. Goodlake stopped taking pictures and Sheriff Wright glanced back at Buck as if considering something.

"One thing bothers me," he said. "Why did you go into the building after Johnson? Didn't want to add a murder rap to an arson sentence?"

"I didn't set the fire," Buck said.

Wright's continued stare made Buck feel guilty, even if he wasn't. "Let's get out of here Sam," Wright said, turning abruptly away. The tall deputy smiled dumbly, following along as Taylor Wright walked slowly to the boat. Before they had gone fifty feet the sheriff wheeled around and said, "You're under suspicion for arson and attempted manslaughter. Don't leave the area or I'll catch up with you and throw you in jail."

Buck could only nod dumbly. In a state of near shock, he watched the two men climb into the lake cruiser and back slowly away from the bank. When they exited the surrounding cypress trees a hundred feet from shore Goodlake gunned the engine, leaving two white fan tails spraying morning air.

Buck could see it clearly now. Someone had devised a complex plan calculated to cause him to lose the island. Set him up to go to prison for arson and attempted manslaughter. If he was lucky, he'd spend no more than the next ten years on a Texas road gang. He felt like the fifth ace in a stacked deck.

When Buck reached the lodge he went directly to his room and removed his clothes. Pulling down the covers, he crawled between the sheets and curled up into a comforting fetal position. Despite his aching mind and body, he nodded away in an instant.

CHAPTER TWENTY-EIGHT

Noise of saw and hammer coming from the direction of the destroyed marina attracted Buck's attention the following morning. He found Raymond, Ray, and Wiley building something from a large stack of wood.

"Morning," he said. "What's going on?"

"Well, good morning to you," Raymond answered in his deep baritone voice. He put his big hand on Buck's shoulder. "I just want to thank you for saving my boy's life. He ain't that special, but Pearl and I love him just the same."

Ray glanced up from his work and made a face when he heard his father's remark. "Glad I was able to help," Buck said. "What are you building?"

"Rebuilding the docks and marina," Raymond said.

Buck gave him a doubtful look. "Quite an undertaking, don't you think?"

"No hill for a stepper," Raymond said, grinning. "Wiley managed to cut most of the boats loose when the fire started. We rounded them up and tied them together in the cove over there. They all have motors. At least we don't have to worry about that."

"It's a start," Buck said. "Now all we need to do is rob a bank."

Wiley glanced up from his work. Raymond's good nature seemed dampened by Buck's remark and he returned to the board he was sawing. Buck walked over to the shirtless Ray who was nailing a sheet of plywood to a two-by-four frame. Cyclone, looking none the worse for wear, lay asleep near Ray's feet. He awoke at the sound of Buck's voice and wagged his tail.

"Hey, boy," Buck said, stroking Cyclone's head.

"You doing okay, Ray?"

"Look, McDivit, this doesn't change things between us. Why don't you just lay off?"

"You're welcome," Buck said, taking a backwards step. Cyclone followed him, hungry for attention.

Wiley got into the act, standing face-to-face with his older brother. "Ray, you're the one that needs to lay off. Buck saved your life last night. Can't you even say thanks?"

Their father stepped between them. "Wiley's right," he said. "Mr. Buck did save your hide."

"Quit calling him Mr. Buck," Ray said. "He's no better than you."

"You watch that mouth of yours," Raymond said. "You may be grown but I'm your father and I can still paddle your butt."

Buck threw his hands in the air. "It's all right. If Ray has a problem with me, I'm the one he should discuss it with. I don't have a problem with his attitude."

Wiley and Raymond exchanged shakes of the head as Ray returned to work. Raymond dusted his hands and walked away toward the lodge. A large fish broke the water's surface near the burned remains of the marina.

"Thanks," Buck said to Wiley.

Wiley's grin had returned. "My brother's a pistol, ain't he?"

"Don't worry about it. Something else is on my mind. Do you think Mama Toukee faked the seance?"

"No way," Wiley said. "I didn't tell her about the brooch."

"She impressed me, I'll admit. Assuming the voice we heard was Bessie McKinney's, what do you think the message meant?"

Wiley sat his hammer down and took a handkerchief from his back pocket to wipe his sweaty forehead. "Beats me, he said, tossing a stick into the lake. "I'm more worried about the marina right now."

Startled by the stick splashing in the water, three turtles abandoned their perch on a nearby log.

"Me too," Buck said. "And Sara seems pretty certain that Hogg Nation isn't involved."

Wiley frowned at the mention of Hogg Nation. "Yeah, well that girl has no taste in men. Present company excepted."

They both grinned. "I just wish we could find Bone's Malone. I think he has the answer to lots of questions."

"Forget about it," Wiley said. "No one's gonna find that man's hideout. Not from the lake, anyway. Maybe if you had a helicopter."

"How about a low-flying plane?"

Raymond seemed puzzled by the question as Buck started back to the lodge. "Keep at it," Buck said, pointing toward the marina. "I have an idea."

The day of the foreclosure hearing finally arrived and Brice met Buck on the courthouse steps dressed in an expensive three-piece suit. His dark hair was heavily moussed and his finery contrasted with Buck's utilitarian jeans, boots and western shirt.

"You okay, pal?" Brice asked.

"Except for the hole in my stomach from two pots of coffee."

Brice nodded knowingly. "I hear you. Don't worry. We're going to give them hell."

Buck touched the cuff of Brice's dark blue coat. "Hey, if looks can win a case, we're on our way."

Curious onlookers filled the courtroom and a buzz circulated through the crowd as Brice and Buck strolled down the aisle. Brice surveyed the courtroom but Buck stared at the impressive Judge's bench. Brice tapped his shoulder, breaking the spell. "There's Lila and her father," he said.

"Are Ezra and Sara here?"

"Judge Travis frowns on blacks in the courtroom."

"How does he get away with that?" Buck said.

"Don't ask."

The foreclosure hearing was scheduled to begin at one, just after lunch hour. Buck had skipped lunch and now his stomach growled in protest. At five after the hour the court clerk entered the courtroom through a door behind the judge's bench.

"All rise."

Everyone in the courtroom responded to the bald man's request and Judge Jefferson Travis entered to a swirl of starched black fabric.

"Be seated," was his terse command. Judge Travis adjusted his glasses and preceded to scan the file supplied to him by the court clerk. When he'd finished, he clasped his big hands on the desk, stared out at the crowded courtroom then glanced at the court clerk and said, "Call the docket."

"The First Bank of Deception versus Emma Louise Fitzgerald," The court clerk droned.

"Who's here to represent the plaintiff?" Travis asked.

"Randall Rummels, Your Honor."

Buck noticed Randy Rummels, sitting on the bench to his left, for the first time that day.

"And who's here to represent the interest of Emma Fitzgerald?"

"Brice Culpepper, Your Honor."

Judge Travis leaned forward on his elbows and adjusted his glasses, staring at Brice. "I haven't seen you in this court before, Mr. Culpepper. Are you from these parts?"

"Yes, Your Honor. I'm from Shreveport."

"Louisiana?" Judge Travis pronounced the state's name as if it were a particularly offensive piece of carrion.

"Yes, Your Honor," Brice said.

"You licensed to practice law in the state of Texas?"

"No, Your Honor, but —"

"No?"

"I can explain, Your Honor."

"Please do, Mr. Culpepper."

"Mr. McDivit is from Oklahoma and his attorney here in Deception is also the attorney for the plaintiff."

"So you just thought you'd help Mr. McDivit out yourself. Is that right?"

"Yes, Your Honor, I —"

"Hold it right there," Travis said, startling everyone in the courtroom when he slammed his gavel hard against the desk. "You told me you're not licensed to practice law in the State of Texas."

"That's right, but —"

"Sit down," Travis said, again hammering the gavel against the desk. "You won't break Texas law in my house."

Brice persisted. "But, Your Honor, Mr. McDivit—"

This time Travis almost broke his gavel. "Sit down. Would you like me to have you physically escorted from this courtroom?" Brice gave Buck an apologetic glance as he eased back into his seat. Travis'gravelly voice interrupted Buck's wildly racing thoughts."Now. Who's here to represent the interest of the defendant?"

Buck stood from his seat. "Me, Your Honor. James McDivit, Emma Fitzgerald's nephew."

Judge Travis surveyed Buck for what seemed a minute or two. Long enough to increase his apprehension level by several degrees. "Do you wish to deny your right to legal counsel, Mr. McDivit?"

Buck glanced at Brice's slight nod. "Yes, Your Honor."

"Fine," Travis said. "Take your seat. Mr. Rummels, what are we doing here?"

"Foreclosing on a debt, Your Honor. The defendant here owes the First

Bank of Deception one hundred and seventy-five thousand dollars. The debt is due and payable and the defendant has no funds to make good on the debt. The Bank, therefore, prays the court will order the defendant to surrender the collateral it pledged to satisfy the debt."

"So ordered," Judge Travis said, slamming the gavel against the desk.

Brice and Buck rose from their seats in unison. "But your honor, we—"

Judge Travis gave Brice no chance to finish his sentence, again banging the gavel. "Fitzgerald Island and all its buildings will be sold at sheriff's sale today at four o'clock on the courthouse steps. Bailiff, escort these two gentlemen out of the courtroom. I'll entertain no further outbursts while I'm on the bench."

A uniformed bailiff motioned to Buck and Brice. Realizing the futility of further protest, they followed him out the large swinging door.

"Buck, I'm sorry," Brice said.

"Not your fault," Buck said. "We never had a chance. The hearing was cooked. Let's get a drink."

Buck and Brice followed the sidewalk back to the rows of lakefront shops and restaurant. Remembering the bar where he'd met the old drunken pilot, Buck made a beeline directly to it. This time he and Brice found a dark booth in back.

"I let you down. I'm really sorry," Brice said after the flat-headed bartender had brought them two cans of Coors.

"We just got a little taste of East Texas home cooking. Travis had his mind made up before we ever walked into court, but thanks for being there for me."

As they talked, Lila came through the door and saw them at the booth. "Buck, I'm so sorry. I can't believe Uncle Jeff was so mean to you."

"Hey, I'm okay."

"What's going to happen to Pearl and Raymond?"

"I'll think of something," Buck said, not really believing his own words.

Lila scooted in beside Buck and gave him a comforting hug. "You come stay with Daddy and me until you do."

At this point Buck needed every ally he could muster and refrained from reminding her it was her daddy's bank that had repossessed Fitzgerald Island.

"We need a plan," Brice said. "You must have something in mind. I know you too well."

"I need to talk to Bones Malone. I think he's somehow responsible, or at least knows who is, for Aunt Emma's death. If I could just find his hideaway on the lake."

Before Buck could finish his thought, Otis Spangler, the old drunken pilot, stumbled through the door and his toothless grin ignited when he saw Buck.

"Lila and Brice, this is Otis Spangler, the best crop-duster in these parts." Otis edged in beside Brice as Buck motioned the bartender for another round. After watching Otis partake in the first long pull from his drink, Buck said, "Otis, I think I'm ready for that plane ride."

CHAPTER TWENTY-NINE

Two days passed before Buck braked to a stop in front of the Richardson Mansion. Unhappy about losing Fitzgerald Island, he had mixed feelings about staying with the bank president that had foreclosed on his island. Still, his curiosity about Bessie McKinney's former home and what he might find there intrigued him and his heart beat faster than normal when Lila met him at the front door.

"Thanks for putting me up in your beautiful home," he said when she hugged and kissed him.

"A touch of Southern splendor created by several generations of slave labor," Lila said.

Robert, the butler, waited behind Lila. When Buck reached for his bags, the man said, "Let me help with that."

Buck handed him one of the bags and strapped the other across his shoulder. Lila protested, "Please let Robert do his job. Daddy's waiting on the back porch."

Acquiescing to Lila's determined tone, he said, "How are you?"

"Happy as a peach sitting in a bowl of cream. Now let's hurry. We don't want to keep Daddy waiting."

They followed the flagstone path around the house to a side porch that provided a striking view of the beautifully manicured lawn and rose garden. The porch had its own back door to the mansion and it was there hey found Clayton Richardson, sipping a tumbler of bourbon. An old man and woman reclined in rocking chairs behind him.

"Sorry about the island, McDivit," he said. "I guess you heard that Hogg Nation bought it at sheriff's sale?"

"I heard."

"I did business with your aunt for years. I hope you don't think there was any manipulation on my part to cause her to lose her property."

The thought had crossed Buck's mind but it seemed likely that Hogg Nation had done the manipulating on his own.

"I understand, Colonel. I realize you had no other choice but to do what was best for your share holders. No hard feelings," Buck said, extending his hand.

"You're most gracious, Buck and I appreciate your understanding." Clayton quickly changed the subject, pointing toward the two old people sitting behind them. "This is my father and mother, Clayton Jr. and Dorothea Richardson," he said, his East Texas drawl returning.

Although the temperature was at least eighty in the shade, both old people had crocheted afghans draped across their laps. the old man's hair, goatee and mustache were snowy white and he wore a white suit, complete with an old style black bow tie and wide-brimmed white hat. His outfit conformed exactly to Buck's stereotypical image of a Southern plantation owner. The pasty faced old man's expression never changed as he stared with glaucomatous eyes at the manicured lawn. Clayton Richardson Jr., it seemed, was totally senile.

Lila's grandmother was different. She had a gold-flecked twinkle in her hazel eyes and a grin on her wrinkled lips. Buck could see immediately where Lila had inherited her extraordinary bone structure. Clayton returned to his chair and motioned Buck and Lila to join him.

"When people visit they expect me to drink mint juleps," he said, noticing Buck eyeing the bourbon. "My personal opinion is mint and sugar ruins the already perfect taste of sipping whiskey."

"I couldn't agree more," Buck said.

"A man after my own heart. Pansy," he called, clapping his hands loudly. "Get out here."

In a moment a harried black woman appeared from the house. "Yes, sir, Mr. Clayton," she said, out of breath.

Richardson didn't smile or immediately acknowledge her presence. Instead, he looked at Lila and asked, "What do you wish to drink, Daughta?"

"A glass of lemonade, please, Pansy," she said to the black woman barely older than herself.

"And you?"

"I'll have what you're having," Buck said.

When Clayton grinned Buck noticed the gap between his otherwise perfect front teeth. Sending Pansy back into the house with a frown and a flick of his head, he said, "Nigras!" His inflection read like an open encyclopedia of his apparent contempt for blacks.

Seeing Buck's discomfort at her father's bigoted remark, Lila tried to change the subject. "Did you get your things off the island?"

"Finally. At least Nation gave us an extra day."

"Maybe he's not all bad," she said.

Before Buck could reply Pansy returned with their tray of drinks. She smiled at Lila and sat her lemonade on the table. After freshening Clayton's drink, she caught her heel in a crack on the wood porch, lurched forward and spilled Buck's bourbon in his lap. The glass toppled to the floor, shattering into a thousand pieces.

"Damn it, Pansy!" Clayton said, jumping to his feet. "Can't you hold on to anything?"

Pansy dropped to her knees, trembling. Buck stooped to help as Lila rushed into the house. Buck gazed up into the glowering eyes of Clayton Richardson, for a moment fearing the angry man might kick the frightened woman.

"Let her do it," Richardson said. "It's her job."

Before Buck could reply, Lila returned with a broom and dust pan. Pulling Buck's chair out of the way, she began sweeping glass into the pan.

"Lila!" Richardson said.

Ignoring him, Lila cleared the spill quickly before taking Pansy's arm and helping her to her feet. Handing her the broom and dust pan, she pushed her gently toward the door then dabbed away the spilled liquid from Buck's chair with a napkin. She finished so quickly her father had little time to protest.

"Would you like to change clothes?" she said.

"I'm fine. Most of it spilled on the floor."

"Then sit back down. You too, Daddy." Grabbing his arm, she directed him to his chair.

"You are embarrassing me in front of Mr. McDivit, Daughta. You should let the help do the work."

Lila kissed his forehead and hugged him. Her gesture, along with a healthy sip of bourbon, seemed to calm Colonel Richardson but Buck could tell by Lila's suddenly ashen complexion that she was hiding more than a little anger of her own.

When Pansy returned with another drink, Lila raised her hand for the young woman to stop where she stood. Tears streamed down the black woman's face. Lila took the drink and put her arms around Pansy, comforting her momentarily before shoving her gently back toward the door.

Clayton continued staring at the lawn. When Lila flashed Buck a disturbed glance, her striking eyes explained the degree to which the incident had embarrassed her. Buck glanced around in time to see that Lila's grandmother had missed nothing.

"Sorry," Clayton said. "I'm afraid we lost our edge with these people when we quit using bull whips."

"Daddy, please."

Richardson's words angered Buck but he refrained from commenting in deference to Lila. He was Richardson's guest. Richardson, already half tanked, noticed nothing and grinned foolishly as he held up his glass.

"Cheers," he said.

After fifteen minutes of inane conversation a little girl, no older than eight, appeared at the table. Her smile was so infectious even Clayton seemed affected. "Mama told me to check on your drinks," she said.

The pretty little girl was clearly the daughter of the distraught Pansy. "What's your name, Sweetie?" Buck said.

With her hands behind her back, she said, "Bessie."

Her name stunned him. "You're very pretty, Bessie."

"Yes," she said. "Mama told me."

Lila smiled. "I know what the gentlemen want, Bessie. I'll help you."

As Lila exited the porch with the pretty black child, Buck noticed Richardson was smiling and acting almost as if the little girl was as white as he. Lila returned alone with the fresh drinks.

"Daddy, let's take Buck for a walk outside. We could all use a little fresh air."

"Good idea," Richardson said, his words slurred by alcohol.

Drinks in hand, they followed Lila into the rose garden. "My wife loved roses."

"Lila mentioned that," Buck said.

Lila walked ahead with Buck as they passed through the pecan grove. When they reached the gravel path beneath a group of very old oak trees, they followed it to the family cemetery guarded by an old iron fence. It lay perched on a knoll overlooking fields of cotton and corn. Fewer than twenty headstones occupied the cemetery, all large and elaborate.

"This is the Richardson family cemetery," Clayton said. "Three generations of Richardsons are buried here."

Two bourbons had dulled Buck's senses but Richardson's words excited him.

"Here's Bessie McKinney's grave," Lila said.

Buck knelt in front of the marble gravestone and read the inscription:

Bessie McKinney
the loving daughter of Elizabeth and Larkin,
taken too soon from the arms of those who loved her.
October 10, 1858
July 16, 1872

Transfixed, Buck studied the gravestone, rereading the inscription several times. Another gravestone, standing all alone beneath an ancient oak tree, caught his attention and he scraped away the lichen covering the inscription. The old marker, worn and dulled by time, resisted reading and he barely made out the inscription.

Elizabeth Donald McKinney,
my loving wife.
Born January 5, 1817
Died June 11, 1858.

Buck read it twice before realizing the importance of the two headstones. Elizabeth McKinney had died before Bessie was born. Clayton and Lila, noticing Buck's interest in the old gravestone, stopped chatting and joined him.

Clayton asked, "What have you discovered?"

"A slight discrepancy," Buck said.

Clayton seemed puzzled. "Discrepancy?"

"According to the dates on these headstones, Elizabeth McKinney died before Bessie McKinney was born. Four months before."

"No one worried about exact dates in those days," Clayton said. "Let's hurry now. We have more to see before dinner."

As they left the family cemetery Clayton continued to mimic a tour-guide, explaining points of interest as they passed. Buck didn't hear a word until Lila grabbed his elbow and shook him. "You still with us?"

Buck failed to immediately register a reply but her smile returned his thoughts to the present. "Sorry. Just thinking about the inscription on

Bessie's gravestone."

"Probably a mistake. I'm sure Elizabeth was Bessie's natural mother. We'll check the family Bible later."

The slave quarters, nestled in a grove of trees, seemed like a deserted, make-believe village. "The plantation had more than two hundred slaves before the Civil War," Clayton said. "They tended nearly three thousand acres of forest and bottom land — the largest plantation in East Texas. At the height of local activity nearly twenty different steamboats passed through every month. They brought with them famous actors and actresses, divas from the opera and prima ballerinas from all over the world. Ah, sadly, the war ended all that."

"That's not true, Daddy," Lila said. "The war was over and the slaves free long before the raft broke."

"The raft?" Buck said.

Clayton explained. "The Red River Raft. A mass of uprooted trees and other debris plugging the river years before the arrival of the white man into these parts. With time, the log jam became larger and formed an effective dam that backed up the river all the way to Oklahoma. The Raft caused water in Caddo Lake to reach a depth of more than a hundred feet in places."

"What happened to the raft?" Buck asked.

"The Corps of Engineers dismantled it," Clayton said. "Hoping to reclaim thousands of acres of swamp for farming."

Lila added, "Its destruction marked the end of Caddo Lake as a major seaway."

They soon reached the back door of the large house Buck had seen on his first visit to the plantation — the large out-building with no windows.

"McKinney's ice-house," Clayton said. "He stored huge blocks of ice in it. Walls three feet thick kept the ice from melting for months. Even through the hottest summer. We still use it for food storage and such, but now we cool it with electricity."

"Daddy used to threaten me when I was naughty," Lila said. "'I'll lock you in the ice-house if you don't act nicer,' he would tell me."

"You were a headstrong child, Daughta, but I would never have really locked you in the ice-house."

"Interesting," Buck said. "Mind if I have a look inside?"

"Not at all," Clayton said, reaching for his keys and unlocking the double padlocked door. "We have to keep it locked to keep some child from getting trapped in here and freezing to death."

The open room was cold as a meat locker. Exactly what Clayton used it for. Halves of beef and pork hung from rafter hooks. Buck took a quick look around and headed for the door.

"The grounds continue for forty acres," Lila said. "I suggest we go into the house and freshen up."

"I second the motion," Clayton said. "This talk of the heat has made me thirsty."

Lila led them through the back door where Robert handed Clayton a fresh bourbon. "If you'll excuse me," Clayton said. "I have some business to attend before dinner. Robert will show you to your room."

"We'll look at the Bible after dinner," Lila said.

"If you'll follow me, sir," Robert said

Robert showed Buck to his room at the end of the hall, leaving Buck alone in a setting that had changed little since the days of the Red River Raft. The oversized room was filled with antiques. Feeling like a visitor to a historical monument, Buck removed his shoes and shirt and lay on the giant canopy bed. He soon fell asleep, not waking until Robert tapped on his door several hours later.

"Dinner is served in half an hour."

Buck washed his face with cold water from an antique golden tap, still thinking about the two headstones in the family graveyard. It meant that Elizabeth McKinney's was neither Bessie's nor Francine's natural mother. He hoped the family Bible would shed light on the mystery.

Robert, waiting at the base of the stairs, directed him to the dining room where they dined in nothing less than regal splendor. Clayton excused himself after dinner and Lila and Buck convened to the study where they found the old Bible on a gilded lectern by the wall. Robert interrupted, bringing Buck a snifter of brandy. Buck thanked him, took a sip then touched the browning pages of the book. Sensing its age, he carefully thumbed to an elaborate hand-lettered family tree.

Larkin and Elizabeth McKinney were the first names. Below them, complete with Lila's name at the end, branched each of the succeeding generations. Each name had a date of birth and death, if appropriate, beside it. All except one. The ink proclaiming Elizabeth McKinney's death was smeared, the date illegible. Buck rubbed his finger across the smear.

"Have you ever noticed Francine's name?" he asked.

Francine's name, written in blue instead of black, was beside Bessie's. Lila seemed oblivious to the implication.

"I've neglected my business so long, I simply must work on my books tonight," she said. "I'll join you for breakfast tomorrow."

Buck found a comfortable chair and settled down to finish his brandy, wondering if someone had smeared the date of Elizabeth McKinney's death on purpose. Perhaps the same person had deleted Francine's original entry, reentering different information with a modern blue ballpoint.

Buck decided to go outside and watch the stars, following the long hallway to the back porch. As darkness flooded over him, he had the strange sensation he wasn't alone. He wasn't. Dorothea Richardson was behind him in her rocking chair, startling him when she spoke. "Didn't mean to scare you." she said, her face wrinkled into a wry grin.

"I didn't expect anyone to be up."

"Don't like spending too much time in bed. Time enough for that in eternity. Come and sit down," she said, patting the cushion of her husband's vacated rocker.

"Beautiful night," he said.

"You don't like Clayton, do you?"

Buck, taken aback by the old lady's bluntness, pivoted in the rocker and smiled at her. Her open mouth revealed not a single tooth. "Why do you say that?"

"I'm old, but I ain't blind. I saw the look on your face when he yelled at Pansy." Buck started to reply, but refrained when the old woman put a bony hand on his. "Don't matter," she said. "I don't like him much either and he's my only child."

"I never said anything about not liking your son."

The old woman ignored his reply. "He gets it honest. His daddy was the biggest hell-raiser in Marion County. Mean as a snake, he was. Never quit chasing women till the good Lord took his mind away. Had his own black mistress, he did."

"His own black mistress?"

"A tradition with Richardson men. Clayton keeps his right under everyone's nose."

Her words struck Buck like a blow to the head. "Are you saying that Pansy is your son's mistress?"

Dorothea Richardson laughed out loud, as if sharing the secret had given her great pleasure. "You got eyes don't you?"

"Then the little girl is—"

"Yep," she said with a nod.

"Does it bother you that your granddaughter is black?"

The back door opened before she could answer Buck's question. A large woman said, "I swear, Miz Dorothea. You gonna catch your death out here."

Helping the old woman out of the rocker, she herded her toward the door. Halfway there Dorothea Richardson glanced at Buck and said, "Might surprise you who's black and who's white around here."

CHAPTER THIRTY

Several days had passed since the bank foreclosure of Fitzgerald Island and Buck was chafing to do something about it. Waking long before breakfast, he drove the short distance to Deception and got directions to the local airstrip. He had an appointment to keep with Otis Spangler.

Buck found the country airport with little difficulty and eased his truck down the narrow dirt road to the single hanger, groaning as the vehicle bounced across a rain-formed pothole. The sky had lightened from dull gray to faded blue and five or six small planes stood tethered near the hanger. He found Otis Spangler sitting on an orange crate and drinking coffee from a plastic cup.

"Mornin'" Spangler said. "Cup of coffee?"

"Thanks," Buck said. "We're not going up while it's still dark, are we?"

"Hell no," Spangler said. "Be light soon."

Glowing crimson, with orange softened edges, streaked the eastern sky and low-lying clouds raced overhead. Buck asked, "Which one is yours?"

"Ol' Yeller there," Spangler said, pointing.

Ol' Yeller was a biplane, at least seventy years old Buck guessed. It was painted garish yellow, hence the name. Proudly emblazoned on its side, in contrasting red, white and blue, was the Union Jack.

"What's the flag for?"

"I was born in England. Came here when I was eight."

"You don't have an accent."

"Guess not. Least not British."

Spangler finished his coffee and grabbed a cotton gauze mask lying beside the pot on a rickety wood stand.

"Why the mask?"

"Gotta load the chemicals," Otis said. "Don't won't to inhale more than I have to."

"Chemicals?"

"To kill boll weevils and flat worms. And whatever else comes along, I guess."

"What kind of crop are you dusting?"

"Cotton. Texas here grows more cotton than any other state."

"Texas? You sure?"

"Course I'm sure. I do this for a livin' don't I?"

Buck had to agree. He watched Spangler roll a chemical drum from the hanger, tap into it and install a pump and nozzle. Inserting the nozzle into a tube in back of the plane, he pumped it until the drum was empty.

"Is it diluted?"

"Course it's diluted," Spangler said. "Don't want to kill everyone in the county, do we?"

"What about us?"

Spangler grinned, showing his black teeth. "Ain't no danger. Been workin' round this stuff for years and it ain't hurt me none."

Spangler's assurance provided Buck with little comfort. When he finished with the chemicals he tossed Buck a leather cap, just like the aces used in World War I.

"Let's do it," Spangler said. "Here comes the sun. Front cockpit," Spangler said. "Rear one's mine."

"You got it," Buck said, giving him a thumbs up as he crawled into the open cockpit.

Once situated in the plane Spangler tapped Buck's shoulder. "Put that headset on so we can talk once we're airborne."

Buck heard Spangler's tinny voice test the headset. "One, two, three."

Glancing around at the tiny airport, he asked, "You sure this runway is big enough?"

Spangler chuckled through the headset. "You're gonna find out, Mate."

Spangler switched on the engine and it roared to life like an awakening dragon. Buck's back stiffened as the plane creaked and groaned. They taxied away from the hanger and Buck quickly found the runway was little more than a wide dirt road, bounded on both sides by tall trees and phone lines.

"You sure this is long enough?" Buck asked again.

Spangler didn't answer. Instead he switched off the engine and crawled out, taking something with him.

"Needs a quart of oil," he said, pouring the contents of the can into the engine.

When he finished topping up the crankcase Spangler threw the empty can aside and crawled back into the cockpit. Restarting the engine, he let it idle. The plane shook, coughed and wheezed like a bronchial old man.

"Is everything okay?"

"Why hell yes," Spangler said. "This old girl's been around way longer than you have."

"That's what I'm afraid of," Buck said.

Spangler chuckled. Without a word of warning he gunned the engine and let it rip toward the far end of the short runway. With the plane vibrating like a broken windmill, Buck's tongue constricted as he watched the high lines approach. The plane picked up speed but continued to hug the bumpy runway. Buck clenched his jaw, grabbed a metal rail and braced himself for the impending crash. Within a few feet of the end of the runway, the old plane lifted straight up into the air like a kite catching an upward gust of wind.

Spangler jammed the rudder and Buck closed his eyes, not wishing to see the scant margin between the bottom of the plane, the high line and the trees. When he opened them again they were airborne, circling effortlessly over the tiny airstrip.

"Gonna dust a cotton crop over by Hosston," Spangler informed him over the tinny headset.

"Where?"

"Just this side of the Red River in Louisiana. 'Bout forty miles from here.

As the noisy old plane roared straight up into the sky, Buck's heart rate abated and he released his grip on the cockpit. He stared out of the plane as they floated high above massive greenery that looked like a living diorama he could reach out and touch. Soon, the forest opened up into miles of treeless farmland and Buck got his first glimpse of the Red River when it appeared on the horizon. Red clay, gouged from damp Louisiana earth, imparted the river's color and giving it its name. Within minutes rolling fields merged into rich Red River bottom lands and Buck saw something he'd remember forever—miles of endless cotton, looking for all the world like the aftermath of a massive summer snow storm.

Spangler began a slow, circular descent. "Let's get that cotton dusted before the weevils gets it."

"How do you keep the chemical from blowing away before it hits the ground?" Buck asked loudly, barely able to hear Spangler over the wind and engine noise.

Spangler laughed out loud, his hearty guffaws resonating in the tinny headset. Instead of answering, he pointed the nose of the plane downward, almost perpendicular to the ground. At the last possible moment, just before Buck thought they would burrow into the white field of cotton in a fiery crash, he pulled up the nose.

Instead of rising skyward immediately, they remained no more than five feet from the furrowed ground for what seemed an eternity, all the while the yellow monstrosity spewing a smoky plume of chemical out the back. Buck grasped the seat and held on as they approached the high line at the edge of the field. Again, Spangler waited for what seemed a millennium before pulling back the controls and gunning the throttle, the plane, miraculously, sailing up and over the electric line.

The fun wasn't over. Spangler banked the old plane steeply, turning and diving again toward the field, again barely missing the telephone line. Skimming the sprawling cotton plants, he sprayed out a billowing chemical plume, repeating the line jumping feat at the other end of the field. Spangler continued until every pearly foot of the cotton farm was dusted. Once again high in the air, Buck's heart dislodged from his throat and he loosened his grip on the seat.

"Have you ever crashed?" he asked, his voice shaky.

"A time or two," Spangler said with a chuckle.

"Why do you get so close to the trees and telephone lines?"

With plane wings shuddering, Spangler's tinny reply came as they ascended through lacy, low-lying clouds. "If I didn't, the farmers would hire someone else that would."

"Oh," Buck said, still trying to relax as they penetrated low-lying cumulus clouds.

Spangler turned away in a lazy roll from the cotton fields, following the natural path along the river that snaked its way lazily toward Shreveport. After ten minutes he banked hard right, Buck swallowing to dislodge the baseball-sized knot in his throat. When he opened his eyes he saw a small town at the edge of a large lake.

"That's Caddo," Spangler informed him. "It's more like a lake here on the Louisiana side and we call it Big Lake. Becomes more a swamp in Texas."

Spangler righted the plane and glided low over the open expanse of water filled with fishermen and water skiers. A highway bridge bisected it into two pearly settings. Banking steeply to the west, Spangler pointed the plane toward Texas. There, narrowing into a sinuous body of water separated by breaks of cane and cypress, the mysterious lake unfolded into a maze of channels and islands. Adjoining passageways stretched for miles through cypress trees hung with Spanish moss that draped the water's dark unmoving surface with waves of symbiotic growth.

"How do you know where you're going?" Buck asked, amazed at the tropical setting.

"Lived here all my life. That's the old boat channel right below us," Spangler said, pointing. "Kinda follows the county line."

Buck looked and could see the darker color of the water following a path down the middle of the lake. "Looks too narrow for a big boat," he said.

"Is now," Spangler said. "The lake used to be deeper and wider. The boats weren't ever as big as the Mississippi boats at any rate."

"Where are we heading?"

"We just passed over Little Green Break. That's Swanson's Landing to the left and Potter's Point to the right. After we pass Pine Island we'll go overland and circle Deception."

Diving low, Spangler followed the south shore, passing over the tiny town of Deception before heading back to the center of the lake. As they flew over a landmark, he would point and call out its exotic name. Names like Red Belly, Hogwallow and Stumpy Slough.

"That's the Government Ditch," Spangler said, tipping the wing so Buck could see.

Below them massive cypress trees bounded a long, straight channel. Buck asked, "What is it?"

"Rebels and slaves cut it by hand during the Civil War to hide ammo and supplies from the Yankees," Spangler said.

"Are you kidding?"

"Not hardly. Good many drowned, were snake bit, or died of yellow fever."

Spangler turned the plane north, following the path of the old river boat channel. Soaring above such exotic sounding places as Alligator Slough, Judd Hole and Blind Slough, they soon crossed Alligator Thicket to the clear water of Back Lake. From there they circled the Big Hole at Carter's Lake, passing over Hell's Half Acre and then doubling back to Horse Island. Below them the terrain was wild and beautiful with little evidence of human inhabitation. The unexpected size and complexity of the lake, and the scope of his enigma began to make itself apparent to Buck.

"I think we're wasting our time, Otis. We'll never find Bone's hideout in this jungle."

"Don't give up too quick," Spangler said. "If I wanted my privacy I'd look for a place straight north from the Big Thicket where there was islands and lots of cypress brakes for cover."

"You have an idea?"

"Whangdoodle Pass," he said.

As they turned abruptly overland, Buck held on to the sissy bar. Spangler followed Clinton's Chute, banking the plane at Devil's Elbow and crossing the lake to Whangdoodle Pass. Flying at a dangerously low altitude, he followed the narrow ditch bordered by shoreline on one side and a massive cypress break on the other. A small island appeared beneath them when they reached the mouth of the pass It looked like an emerald resting in a basket of obsidian. Spangler buzzed the tree tops and Buck spotted several small structures nearly hidden by the vegetation. Twice Spangler circled the tiny clearing.

"I'll bet that's it," Buck said. "There's even a boat dock down there. How far is it to Fitzgerald Island?"

"I'll take you there and show you," Spangler said as he banked away.

Malone's island, if it really was Malone's island, was well hidden and approachable only by air or through a winding maze of cypress trees. Still, it was no more than five miles from Fitzgerald Island. They reached it in minutes.

"Can you circle the lodge?"

"You bet," Spangler said.

As Otis Spangler banked the plane and glided over the island, Buck got a big surprise. Fitzgerald Island was anything but deserted. Dressed in camouflage fatigues, platoons of soldiers were doing close order drill while others practiced marksmanship on newly created rifle ranges. Fitzgerald Island, it seemed, had been converted into a skinhead training camp.

CHAPTER THIRTY-ONE

Buck sat alone in the rocker, watching the moon ascend to its zenith in the clear summer sky. It was very late and the voice behind him shook his already jangled nerves. It was Dorothea Richardson, Lila's grandmother.

"Didn't mean to scare you. Couldn't sleep for that damn air conditioner rattling every time it comes on. Need a drink?" The old woman held up a full bottle of Old Crow for him to see and grinned when she noticed him looking for a glass. "Don't need a glass. Real men drink straight from the bottle."

To show him, she opened the bottle and tipped it to her lips. After taking a healthy pull, she handed the bottle to Buck and he mimicked her demonstration.

"Thanks," he said.

The old woman took another drink from the bottle and handed it back to Buck. "Something troubling you?"

"Your grandson, Judge Jefferson Travis," he said, his lips loosened by hundred-proof alcohol.

Dorothea Richardson cackled. "That bag of hot air's no grandson of mine. Clayton's daddy took him in as a youngster. Two peas in a pod, those two. Both mean as cottonmouths. That boy was more trouble then a bag of tom cats. Cost us plenty when he raped that nigrah gal."

"He raped someone?"

"Probably more than one," she said. "The last one, though, almost got him sent to prison. She called the po-lice and pitched a fit. Wouldn't let it die. Clayton's daddy had to pay off half the county."

"What happened to the girl?"

"She was mad but there weren't a lot she could do about it. When she got pregnant she refused to give it up. She had the baby."

"Travis' baby?"

Dorothea Richardson swigged from the bottle and cackled as she handed it back to Buck. "Crazy, ain't it? The good Judge Jefferson Travis has a black son and no one around here even knows who it is. 'Cept me, that is."

Light-headed from the bourbon and riveted by the old woman's pronouncement, Buck asked, "Who?"

"Pearl Johnson was the girl J. Travis raped. His son is Pearl's boy Ray."

Buck was dumbfounded. "You have to be kidding me. Ray Johnson is the illegitimate son of Judge Jefferson Travis?"

"If I'm lying, I'm dying," the old woman said.

"Does Ray know?"

"If I know Pearl Johnson, she's leveled with him by now. Never known that woman to lie."

Buck took another drink from the bottle before returning it to Dorothea Richardson. "No wonder he hates white people."

"What's the story on Elizabeth and Larkin McKinney?" he asked, changing the subject.

"Larkin McKinney was another hateful ol' drunk," she said. "Worried his wife into an early grave. He'd get so mean when he drank that he'd bullwhip anyone he could catch. Used to lock his own pretty little daughter in the icehouse just for the meanness of it."

Buck's senses were reeling from the effects of the whiskey. So, apparently, were Dorothea Richardson's, her lips loosened to the point she'd told him several family secrets. It didn't seem to matter. His condition was such he probably wouldn't remember anything come morning.

The old woman faded long before the bottle was empty, leaving Buck alone on the porch. Not liking the silence he jumped the railing, Dorothea Richardson's bottle of bourbon in his hand. What he'd seen on his flight over Fitzgerald Island lingered in his thoughts and now he knew why Ray Johnson was so militant. Something else also troubled him.

In their haste to vacate Fitzgerald Island, he had forgotten Tiger. Buck could only blame his heightened stress level for the mental error. A tap on the shoulder startled him and interrupted his musings. It was Lila Richardson.

"It's so late, Buck. What are you doing out here?"

"I could ask you the same question."

Lila smiled. "When I have trouble sleeping, I sit in Mother's rose garden and take in its warm summer fragrance."

Lila was dressed in the same nightgown as the fateful night on Fitzgerald

Island. In deference to the weather she hadn't even bothered slipping a robe over her shoulders.

"I left Tiger on the island," he said. "I've got to get him."

"You've had too much to drink. You can get Tiger tomorrow. I'm sure he's okay."

Buck checked himself before blurting out about the paramilitary operations on Fitzgerald Island. When Lila grabbed his hand, he kissed her then pulled away. "Gotta go," he said, his words a drunken slur.

Buck hurried to the front of the mansion, not giving Lila a chance to protest. He could hear her calling, "Come back here, Buck McDivit," as he crawled behind the wheel of the Ram Charger.

Had he heeded his own usual advice, he would never have contemplated driving in the condition he now found himself in, but his last trace of good sense had trickled down the trunk of a nearby pecan tree long before Lila's appearance. With a frenzied laugh, he started the engine and headed for Deception.

Buck passed the massive front gate with deliberate motivation. Somewhere between the graveyard and the whiskey bottle the consummate connection between the island and the brooch exploded within his brain. The riddle's solution waited somewhere on the island. This he knew without a doubt, although he had no idea how or why. Given this absolute awareness, his only course of action was to return to the island. This unspoken necessity loomed immediate and absolutely urgent. And there was also the matter of Tiger.

Buck was drunk but drove with caution and deliberation,

like an alcoholic trying desperately to make it home without wrecking his car. Passing through the dark streets of Deception, he watched for marauding policemen on patrol. Leaving caution to the winds after crossing the bridge out of town, he gunned the throaty engine, not slowing until he reached Caddo Lake.

A feathery mist wafted up from the blacktop between the pines bordering the road and reminded Buck of a dream sequence in a horror movie. This, despite his advanced state of inebriation, left him in a state of confused unease. A moored boat from Fitzgerald Island, barely visible by the light of the moon, lay cloaked in shadows. Still clutching Dorothea Richardson's bourbon, he stepped into the boat.

Buck rocked the gunnel in the shallow water and windmilled his arms to retain his balance. Head spinning, he gazed across the water. Gone was the soup-like fog of his first solo crossing, replaced now by a jungle of moss-draped cypress trees, night-blooming hyacinths and a plethora of aquatic flora and fauna. An almost mystical glow of dim moonlight reflected off the lake's ebony surface and a night bird called from somewhere in the distance.

A frog splashing in the water and the buzz of a mosquito around his head punctuated the silence as Buck cranked the engine. When it roared to life, its steady hum joined the lake's chorus. Pointing the bow toward the center of the lake he twisted the throttle, grinning as the boat speeded forward.

The boat's bow parted the water making it seen like the rippling muscles of a snake's back. Buck remembered his first impression of the lake — a Mesozoic, backwater slough. A living bowl of soup teeming with life, both plant and animal. Seeing, smelling, and hearing it now, he knew it was more than that. It was, without a doubt, an ancient omnipotent womb.

Buck navigated the boat across open water and through the winding cypress maze. An alligator, floating in the lake, flashed red reptilian eyes at him. After passing beneath dense overhanging vegetation, he finally exited the brake, immediately encountering a shallow lily pond. He slowed the boat to prevent fouling the motor.

Moonlight reflected off shoreline shadows when he cleared the last cypress brake. It also revealed the weather-beaten shack of the witch, Mama Toukee. Pulling the boat from the water, he followed the path up the slope. When he reached Mama Toukee's shack he heard the creak of long dried wood. A voice spoke from the shadows.

"You come."

When Buck's eyes adjusted, he saw the old woman rocking in her chair on the porch. "Mama, it's me, Buck."

"Been spectin' you," she said. "Come."

Buck approached the porch as the one-eyed black cat wove an easy path beneath the rockers of the chair.

"I brought you something, Mama," he said, holding up the bottle of bourbon.

Cackling, the old woman slapped her bony right hand on the arm of the rocking chair. "Sit wi' me," she said.

Buck sat beside her on the porch and held up the bottle. "I didn't bring a glass."

His statement sounded ridiculous, even to himself, but Mama Toukee only cackled. "Doan nee' no glass," she said, taking the bottle.

Hiking the container upwards, she tilted back her head and let amber liquid pour into her mouth until it spilled down the sides of her withered face. For the second time that night an old woman shared spirits with him from the same bottle. Even in his advanced state of inebriation the irony didn't escape him. Dorothea Richardson, though anything but young, seemed like a girl compared to Mama Toukee. The old witch was a living metaphor of the word ancient but her timbre of voice and vibrancy of thought suggested a young genius trapped in a long-ruined body.

Buck reached for the bottle when she finished. "No," she said, jerking it away. "You have other business tonight. You need this instead."

As if by magic, a match appeared in her free hand, along with a crooked joint. Deftly she placed the joint between her lips and lit it in a single motion, drawing its smoke deep into her lungs. The acrid smoke mingled with moist night air supercharged by traces of recent rain and the pungent odor of rotting vegetation. Mama Toukee handed him the joint and he put it between his lips and inhaled deeply.

Descending into Buck's lungs, the harsh smoke created a sensation like nothing he'd ever felt. Searing heat began at the base of his neck, continuing in a slow spiral until it engulfed his entire body. Like heated plastic, he felt his mind expand and begin to pulsate. Whatever was in the cigarette, it was not marijuana.

As the smoke took effect, every cell, every muscle, every tissue in his body slowly escaped its former rigid being and flowed into a natural, unconfined state. Buck smiled at Mama Toukee, her strange cat's eye glowing in the dark.

Buck had never experienced such a drug, the smoke dissolving his inebriation. Mama Toukee took the joint and it disappeared in her hand quickly as it had appeared. When she spoke, a deeper, educated voice replaced her slow south Louisiana drawl.

"Now," she said. "You have secrets to learn and little time to spend. Are you strong?"

"Yes, Mama."

"Good. You mus' go now. Doan let Mama down," she cackled, her accent returning.

Buck shook like a leaf as he took the old woman's hand. "Thank you Mama. I won't."

Backing away from the porch, he made his way through rampant darkness guided by some instinct he hadn't known he possessed. Moving like a cat on the prowl, silently and with deadly intent, he hurried toward the far side of the island to inspect the camouflaged buildings he and Spangler had spotted from the plane.

Not a single specter of light penetrated the thick cover of overhead vegetation. Still, Buck had no problem sensing everything around him clearly as if it were illuminated by a hundred-watt bulb. He navigated the undergrowth using the long hidden compass of his ancestral being.

When he neared the lake's edge, undergrowth grew thinner and heat lightning streaked the sky followed quickly by thunder. A gentle downpour in the form of fat drops rolling off his bare back began to fall. His toes dug into soft earth as the ground became saturated. Some unspoken urge caused him to emit a primal snarl.

Silently, unperturbed by falling water, Buck reached the edge of the pine forest. Directly before him, in a crescent-shaped clearing fronted by a hundred yards of shoreline, stood two earth-toned rectangular buildings. A cypress brake cloaked from the main body of the lake. Camouflage netting covered the flat-roofed buildings. Two make-shift shelters, situated near the lake's edge, guarded the path from the lake and two men armed with machine guns waited beneath their canvas roofs.

Buck stood at the edge of the clearing, not attempting to hide from the guards in any way. He not only felt strangely invincible but also invisible. Then it dawned on him. This side of Fitzgerald Island was almost inaccessible, Only a single narrow boat channel wound a circuitous path through the maze of cypress and cane. It was a path easily guarded. The front of the island had a clear view of the lake. With Aunt Emma's lodge as his base, someone could effectively control the island, restricting ingress and egress with a handful of men, his nefarious business totally hidden from prying eyes. Lightning flashing against the horizon revealed the shadows of the two guards.

"Damn weather!" one man said. "Wish I was back in Nashville."

"Quit bitching and light the lantern," his partner said.

"Maybe we better leave it off."

"How we gonna see what we're doing if we leave it off?"

"Don't know," the other said. "But I sure wouldn't want Sarge to show up and catch us."

When the man lit the lantern, he and his partner saw Buck standing ten feet from them. It took them a moment to react. All the time Buck needed.

Rushing forward, he pushed the surprised man into the arms of his cohort and sprinted back into the forest. As the guards recovered their senses, sending a hail of gunfire over his head, Buck dived toward muddy ground. When the hail of gunfire abated, he jumped up and ran for the thicket, the two men close behind him. A single round nicked his shoulder but he continued forward, hurdling brush and fallen trees like a deer in flight.

Stopping at the edge of the clearing and grabbing his partner's arm, one of the guards said, "Wait, Jim. We ain't gonna catch that fool. We better call the big house."

They hurried back along the sloshy trail to one of the canvas shelters and immediately got on the radio. "Big Cat, this is OP one," the guard said, static crackling from the receiver in the wake of the impending storm. "We have an interloper coming your way."

They listened to amplified noise on the military radio until someone answered. "OP one, this is Big Cat," the distant voice answered. "You think it's FBI?"

"No way, Big Cat."

"How do you know?"

"Cause he was butt naked and drunk as a skunk."

CHAPTER THIRTY-TWO

Mama Toukee had given Buck a psychedelic drug that had enhanced his senses, including his night vision. It had also radically changed his personality. At least temporarily. Shortly after leaving the old woman's shack Buck had doffed all his clothes, even ditching his shoes and socks. Not only did he not know why he did this, he didn't even realize that he had. Now he moved through the forest like a wild animal.

Buck was a hundred yards from the guard post before slowing to a walk. Rain dripped through the trees and damp leaves beneath his bare feet sent spongy, tactile messages to his response-altered brain. Wiping hair from his eyes, he shook away water trickling down his face.

He listened to the dim rumble of distant thunder as another sound invaded his heightened senses. It was the persistent whop, whop, whop of a helicopter. Bolting silently and effortlessly through the forest, he reached the small bluff overlooking the lodge in minutes. There he crouched in the darkness and stared at the clearing.

Descending through haze and pouring rain, the chopper landed in front of the lodge. When two men jumped out, stooping to avoid the rotating prop, Buck recognized them as Humpback and Deacon John. The helicopter hovered momentarily above the lodge, then disappeared in a flurry of blowing leaves and debris.

Buck studied the new additions to the front of the lodge. Beside the chopper pad, several fluorescent lamps cast an eerie blue light on the surroundings. Buck counted three men patrolling the clearing, each carrying weapons similar to those he'd seen on the opposite end of the island.

The barrels of automatic weapons protruded from three canvas-covered foxholes and two large cigarette boats lay moored in the cove. Nearby, another helicopter was anchored on a newly constructed landing pad. As he watched, a strong gust of wind flattened shrubs near one of the canvas coverings. Buck had seen enough and started down the hill to the rear of the lodge.

The lodge abutted a hill that elevated steadily from that point to the center of the island. There were no lights shining on the second floor of the building, every window dark and presumably locked tight. All except one. Someone had failed to close an upper window and its white curtain flapped in the damp breeze.

Buck shinnied up a convenient tree and crawled out on an overhanging limb, his weight lowering him to the window sill where he almost lost his footing on slippery shingles. Grabbing the eave of the roof, he pulled himself into the room. Once satisfied he was alone, he opened the door and peeked into the hall. Only the steady thump of his own heart and the rainy soliloquy on the lodge's wood roof disturbed the solitude of the hallway.

Pulling the door shut behind him, he tiptoed down the hall to his room. He found it empty, just as he'd left it. Except for one thing. On the night stand beside the bed was Bessie McKinney's cameo brooch. Until that moment he hadn't realized he'd forgotten to take it with him. And something else about the brooch was strange. Someone had attached it to a silver necklace.

Buck put the necklace around his neck, letting the brooch dangle against his bare chest. Then he returned to the hallway where he hoped to find Tiger before someone found him. The lodge was dark as he crept down the stairs to the rustic den. He made a quick sweep of the large room, softly calling Tiger's name. Not finding the kitten, he checked the dining room and behind the bar. Still no Tiger. His search led him to the kitchen and that's where he found the errant feline.

"Tiger, you little rascal. I've looked all over for you."

Tiger came out from behind the kitchen table and rubbed against Buck's bare leg. Buck picked him up and stroked his head. They didn't have long to commiserate. Someone entered the room behind them, turning on the lights.

"What the—" the surprised man in uniform said when he saw Buck.

Startled, Tiger leaped out of Buck's grasp and bounded behind the stove. Tiger was frightened and Buck took the hint. Before the surprised skinhead could react, Buck shoved him against the wall and ran out the kitchen door, upstairs to the open window. He shinnied back down the tree and hid in the bushes, assessing his next course of action.

The guard had alerted the troops and howls of tracking dogs and shouts of men searching the hill behind the lodge blended with the storm's cacophony and occasional gunfire. Lazy rain drops fell on Buck's bare shoulders. He waited several minutes before poking his head around the building and gazing across the illuminated front yard.

Reasoning that many of the guards would be in the woods searching for him, he decided the best place to hide was in the undergrowth near the lake's edge. When Travis' men finished searching the lodge and realized he wasn't there, he would return for Tiger. With no better plan in mind, he started for the water.

Buck spotted an armed man crossing the yard with a dog on a leash. Buck recognized the slender beast as a German shepherd. Considering the armaments he had already witnessed it wouldn't have surprised him if he saw the barrel of a 105 millimeter Howitzer protruding from a shoreline emplacement.

Torrential rain masked his path to the lake but he reached it undetected about a hundred yards from the site of the old marina. A newly completed walkway jutted far out into the water, its buoyant foam supports rocking in storm-raised waves. Giant cypress trees at the water's edge blocked most of the falling rain, shielding him from the brunt of the storm as he skipped lightly over fallen brush, mud oozing between his bare toes.

Darkness and thick undergrowth would have left him uneasy except for Mama Toukee's magic smoke. Under its influence he hurried confidently, not flinching when his foot brushed a large water moccasin. An alligator in his path slipped noiselessly into the murky depths of the lake. It didn't matter to Buck as he pushed through hanging undergrowth.

Buck neared his objective, wondering why security seemed to fall apart on this side of the island. He decided it was because there was no place for a boat to come ashore, cypress trees, quicksand and dense underbrush forming an effective barrier. He quickly discovered another reason. This part of the island was also booby-trapped.

The trap he'd sprung was humane, meant only to capture and not to maim or kill. He'd stepped into a camouflaged loop of rope, the sprung trap yanking him high into the air. He struggled, waiting for soldiers to arrive. They soon did.

Howls of hounds coming in his direction through the woods, alerted him to two men exiting the undergrowth. Seeing Buck hanging from his ankle, three hounds stood on their hind paws, baying at him as he swayed in an arc above them. One of the men kicked a hound, frightening it and causing it to yelp with surprise.

"Shut up, dammit! We know he's up there."

Shining a powerful beam up the tree, the other man focused on Buck's face. "Well, lookit what we done found. A nekkid night crawler. Cut him down," he said.

Before Buck could brace himself for the fall, the man cut the rope with a single slash of his machete. He landed on his shoulder with a thud, soft earth cushioning his fall. The headlong plunge from the tree stunned him and he rubbed his aching shoulder as the man surveyed him with the light.

Still influenced by Mama Toukee's magic smoke, Buck covered his eyes as the hounds howled and strained against their leashes. Despite his sore shoulder, his mind continued working smoothly and he assessed the situation. His only chance was a fast reaction. In one smooth motion he grabbed the leash of the nearest hound, giving it a hard pull. In doing so, he yanked the man with the machete toward him. Unprepared for the assault, the soldier lost his balance, sprawling in damp grass.

Buck grabbed the man's wrist and punched him hard in the face. With strength he didn't know he possessed he lifted the man and pitched him into the surprised arms of his partner. Then he sprinted along the shallow muddy bank of the lake, hurdling fallen limbs and cypress knees while remaining in a low crouch to avoid the hail of bullets above his head. A narrow opening appeared in the brake. Running faster, he lifted his knees higher as the lake deepened. When he reached the breach in the trees, he dived into black water of the lake.

Buck glided beneath murky water until his lungs threatened to explode from the pressure. Surfacing, he swam frantically toward the center of the lake. When he reached open water he stopped and glanced behind him, confident the two men hadn't followed.

Exhausted from his frenzied escape, he flipped over and floated on his back, trying to catch his breath and let warm water relax the stiff muscles in his back and neck. By now the storm had passed and all that remained were scattered drops falling lazily into the lake.

A spectral glow emerged between the clouds frayed edges. Buck was out of breath, his solitude invaded by the drone of a tiny electric engine. A fishing boat, powered by an electric trolling motor, appeared from behind the cypress trees and moved slowly toward him.

Buck couldn't tell how far away it was so he slipped beneath the water, only his head above the surface, and dragged his toes in the ooze. A powerful beam was mounted on the front of the boat and the two men inside it spotted Buck, turning the small craft in his direction. Again Buck took a deep breath, managing but one powerful stroke before feeling a searing pain in his back.

Buck fought the searing agony but whatever had him in its grasp wouldn't let go. Relentlessly it pulled him toward the boat. One of the men had nabbed him with the vice-like pincers of a frog gig. After dragging him to the side of the boat, the man knocked Buck senseless with the butt of a shotgun.

A strangely shaped cloud, floating silently above the lake, was the last thing Buck remembered seeing before slipping into unconsciousness.

CHAPTER THIRTY-THREE

When Buck regained consciousness he found himself hanging by his ankles again. This time from a rope extended over a metal rafter above the lodge's swimming pool. His vision had to clear considerably before he recognized the grinning face of Deacon John.

"Why in hell is a grown man running around butt naked on a night like this?" Deacon John asked. His words brought a peal of laughter from the room's occupants. "What do you think, Hump?"

"Beats me, Deak," Humpback said.

Deacon John returned his attention to Buck. "When I ask you a question, I expect an answer."

A hard slap in the face surprised Buck, but did little damage. Not having a ready answer he remained silent, this time earning himself a damaging kick in the head.

"Dip him," Deacon John said.

Humpback untied the rope and pulled it along the rafter until Buck was suspended directly over the center of the pool.

He had little time to draw a breath before Humpback dropped him into the deep end of the pool. The first dunk lasted only a few moments and was just a warning. The next three dunks lasted longer and Buck was seeing double and hacking up pool water when Humpback finally hoisted him out of the water. Buck twirled from the rafter, coughing and blowing pool water from his nose as Deacon John and several paramilitary types looked on. After what seemed an eternity, Deacon John pointed to the side of the pool.

"Come on, Deak. Let me dip him again," Humpback said.

"He's done. Put him in the basement and do it now."

Humpback and two skinheads lowered Buck to the tile floor. "Move it," one said, prodding him with the barrel of a large pistol.

They dragged Buck to the basement door and pushed him in, a blow from the weapon hastening his arrival. Rolling on the flagstone floor he tried to massage away the ache in his head when the stark reality of his situation struck him. Judge Travis' skinheads weren't interested in letting him leave the island alive and the basement was cold, almost like a grave.

The cellar was illuminated by a single fluorescent bulb, the temperature near freezing. Buck shivered, arms folded tightly against his chest, the temperature severely uncomfortable to his bare skin. He shouted for someone to let him out, or at least bring him some clothes. His captors did neither. Taking a bottle of wine from the rack, he found a corkscrew hanging from a hook on the wall. With cold hands, he removed the cork from the bottle.

Buck, shivering as icy liquid dribbled down his throat, drank from the cold bottle. He couldn't remember if an elevated blood-alcohol level impeded or encouraged freezing but decided it didn't matter. Chugging half the contents of the bottle, he hoped it would at least dull the cold. Time melded with the dull drone of the outside cooling unit, gently vibrating the dim cellar's concrete floor. The wine did little more than provide numbness to his face and base of his spine. Pacing the floor and running in place to increase his metabolism, he sank deeper into lethargy as time passed.

When he could no longer feel the cold, Buck sat on a bench, arms folded, his senses detached from his body and floating above him like an ephemeral cloud. How long he had sat there, unmoving, he didn't know or care. His resolution and will to live had disappeared like the last few drops of wine trickling from the second empty bottle. He'd ceased to think or care and found himself looking down from the ceiling at his own frozen body. His detachment included mindless euphoria — a pleasant, painless ascent to another level of consciousness.

Mesmerized by his image and the variations of shadows on the wall, his detached being moved between the ceiling and his unfeeling body. He'd become an interested voyeur to his own impending demise. When the door opened a crack, he drifted down from the ceiling.

Through frozen eyes Buck watched a beautiful young girl descend the stairs and enter the room. Suspended six inches above the flagstone she floated toward him, kissing him with cold lips icier than his own. Then, with the palm of her hand she touched the cameo brooch still hanging from his neck.

A warm glow emanated from the spot and extended outward in a circular pattern from Buck's neck and face. As the heat spread throughout his body, his skin began to throb from the effect of prolonged contraction. His lungs prickled when he took a deep breath but he was alive. The beautiful girl touched his shoulders and kissed him again before disappearing like star dust at dawn.

Buck wondered if he was still hallucinating from Mama Toukee's drug. Even if he were, he realized that someone had left the heavy metal door wide open. He was free to leave and he crept up the stairs, out of the basement. When he reached the hall he heard the ticking of the grandfather clock in the den. Still cold, he made his way to Malone's room for something to wear. Footsteps down the hall interrupted him.

"Search every room. He's here someplace."

Deacon John's men had already discovered his escape. Worse, from the sound of the creaking floor someone was heading directly for Malone's room. Grabbing a pair of pants, Buck opened the window and crawled out on the ledge that encircled the lodge.

"Take the place apart. Don't let him escape."

Buck stood outside the window on the ledge, his back to the wall of the house, as two men searched the room. "I'll take care of this floor," One of the men said. "Check behind the house."

Buck knew they would soon spot the open window so he crept along the steep overhang, halting when he reached the front of the lodge. There he learned why the house was empty when he'd escaped the cellar. Twenty armed men were milling around in the clearing near the helicopter pad. Hiding behind a gable, still clutching the pants he'd taken, he heard an approaching helicopter.

Flying low over the tree tops, its rotor whipping their branches, the chopper appeared through the darkness. Someone exited and when the man reached the light at the front door of the lodge Buck recognized him. The tall man, dressed conspicuously in a Nazi officer's uniform, was Judge Jefferson Travis.

High-powered spotlights illuminated the front of the lodge. When a wandering beam focused on the roof near Buck's perch, he slipped and dropped the pants, hoping no one would glance up toward the roof. Helicopter noise masked the sound but spooked Buck enough that he inched back around to the rear of the building, taking a chance the inside search was done. He never found out. Slipping on the slick ledge, he tumbled into the shrubbery at the back of the lodge.

Buck opened his eyes to someone slapping his cheek. He took a roundhouse swing as his attacker but his assailant grabbed his wrist and quickly wrestled him to the ground.

"Whoa, boy," the man said. "It' me. I'm on your side."

It was Ray Johnson. When Buck stopped struggling, Ray released his grip and allowed him to rise up into a sitting position.

"What the hell are you doing here?"

"Looking for you," Ray said.

"Didn't you forget something?"

"Like what?" Ray asked.

"You hate my guts."

Ray grinned and said, "I think you're the one that forgot something. What happened to your clothes?"

"Long story," Buck said. "How'd you know I was on the island?"

"Lila called. Said you were drunk and that you'd left the mansion. I found your truck down by the lake. Personally I don't care much for your worthless hide. I'm doing this for Lila."

"Thanks," Buck said.

"Besides," Ray added. "You may be white and stupid but it doesn't take a fool to see you're not part of Travis' army."

Buck wondered if Ray knew that Travis was his father but decided not to broach the subject. "Now that you found me how do you intend to get us out of here, Mr. Super intelligent, never made a mistake black man?"

Ray ignored Buck's sarcasm. "There's a canebrake on the north side of the island. It's fairly inaccessible and I have a boat hidden there."

"I came for Tiger and I'm not leaving without him," Buck said.

"What?"

"I saw him in the kitchen."

"You still drunk? There's probably fifty armed men in there by now." It was Buck's turn to be stubborn and the frown on Ray's face expressed his feelings. "You wait here. I'll get your damn cat."

"No," Buck said. "I'll go. Lila would kill me if I let you get hurt."

Ray rubbed his forehead and closed his eyes. "I'm the one Lila's going to kill if I don't get you off this island in one piece. Now, I've lived here all my life and I know every inch of the lodge. You wait here like I said and I'll get the cat. If not, I'm going to kick your ass and get him anyway."

Buck was still half crocked and in no mood to argue. Ten minutes passed before Ray returned from the lodge with the sleeping kitten in the pocket of his jacket. He also had a shirt and a pair of pants.

"Put these on and lets get the hell out of here," he said.

Mama Toukee's magic smoke had long since dissipated. After donning clothes for the first time in several hours Buck followed Ray through the island's undergrowth. This time with human difficulty. They reached a canebrake on the north side of the island and Ray led them through a narrow opening, the ensuing maze ending at the lake. A small boat awaited their arrival.

"What now?" Buck asked.

"Home," Ray said, pushing away from shore.

The storm had passed, the sky clear, and a crimson halo just above the trees signaled the coming of dawn. Ray's tiny motor barely made a ripple, and nothing more than the slight rustle of a muskrat slipping into the water made any other sound. Buck finally broke the silence.

"I'm confused. Hogg Nation bought the island at sheriff's sale but Travis and his skinheads are occupying it. What's going on?"

Buck didn't really expect an answer, mostly bouncing the question off Ray so he could reflect on it as he heard himself ask it. He was surprised by Ray's candid reply.

"Despite what Daddy says, I think Nation's getting a bad rap around here. He bought the island for Travis. You saw what they're using it for."

"Yeah," Buck said. "It's perfect for Travis. I should have guessed."

"Travis must have had Emma killed to get her island," Ray said.

"And he coerced Hogg Nation, Clayton Richardson and Bones Malone to help," Buck said. "Otis Spangler and I spotted Malone's hideout from the air but I could never find it by boat in a million years. We need to get to him. He's our key to breaking Travis' stranglehold."

"If what you say is true, Malone is a dead man if he talks."

"It's the only chance we have," Buck said.

Ray reflected on Buck's pronouncement, then said, "I know where he is. I'll take you there but we need Wiley's help. Bones is slippery and it'll take all three of us to corner him. We have to hurry. When I saw him yesterday he was packing to leave town."

CHAPTER THIRTY-FOUR

Since their eviction from Fitzgerald Island, Raymond, Pearl, and Wiley had stayed with Ezra Davis. When Buck and Ray reached Deception they avoided the throngs of ever present tourists, slipping unnoticed into Ezra's hidden alleyway. Ray moved at a full sprint and Buck, though in excellent physical condition, had trouble keeping up with him. They were both out of breath when they reached the back door to Ezra's house.

"My, oh my," Raymond said when he first saw the unlikely duo. "Get the Bible, Pearl. I think the end is near."

Pearl and Ezra stuck their heads in from the kitchen. "Ray?" Pearl said.

"It's really me, Mama," he said. "Where's Wiley?"

"Someone looking for me?" Wiley said, buttoning his pants as he came out of the bathroom. When he saw Ray and Buck together, he said, "You have a stroke out there in the heat, big bro?"

Ray didn't bother answering. "Get your pants on. We need your help."

Wiley finished tucking his shirt into his pants. "Don't go just yet," Pearl said. "Breakfast is almost on the table."

"No time, Mama. We got business on the lake."

"Mr. Buck," Pearl said. "Please tell me what's going on."

Ray shook his head. "We'll tell you everything when we get back. Right now we're in a hurry."

Raymond put on his shoes and stood up from the couch. "Sounds like I better go along and supervise."

"No way," Ray and Wiley said in unison.

"Wait a minute," Buck said. "If Bones is as slippery as you say he is, we might need Raymond's help."

Ray was in a hurry and didn't take long to decide. "All right," he said. "But

I'm the boss on this trip. You in or out? And don't take all day to make up your mind."

"In," Raymond said. "We'll talk about your attitude when we get home."

Ray clenched his fist and nodded. "Good. You and Wiley give us a head start then take the bass boat and meet us at the Whangdoodle Pass duck blind in an hour. Don't go directly there and don't let anyone know where you're going." Raymond grabbed Buck's arm and opened the back door. Before exiting, he said, "And take your twelve gauge. We may need it."

"Wait up," Ezra said.

"We have enough warm bodies," Ray said. "You and Mama hold down the fort while we're gone."

"Then at least take my cart. There's a path that leads down to the lake and you'll get there twice as fast."

Already tired, Buck felt relieved when Ray accepted Ezra's offer. Mounting the leg-powered cart, they started toward the lake.

"You know for sure Bones is leaving town?" Buck asked as they pedaled toward the lake.

"I saw him yesterday. That's what he told me."

"Why didn't you tell us? He may have killed Aunt Emma."

"Bones never killed anyone," Ray said.

"Then why's he running?"

"We'll both find out soon enough, now want we?"

Ray's answer duly chastised Buck. Remaining silent, he concentrated on helping pedal Ezra's contraption. They made it to the lake in less than half the time it took them to reach Ezra's house. Leaving the cart in the alleyway behind a convenient clump of bushes, they ran along the edge of the lake to the boat.

They reached the duck blind at Whangdoodle Pass in less than an hour. Ray pulled the boat beneath the blind and they crawled up on its elevated floor. The blind was equipped with stools for sitting, several magazines and an ice chest. Ray fished in the chest and handed Buck a warm beer.

"It's better than nothing."

"You don't hear me complaining," Buck said.

They waited in silence, sipping their beer, listening to the revving of distant motorboats and squawks of various lake birds. When Raymond and Wiley arrived, Ray told them what he and Buck were up to and explained his plan.

"There's only two ways out of the brake surrounding Bones' island and he has all sorts of warning devices to tell him when someone is coming. Buck and I will go up the main pathway. You and Wiley wait for Bones here. When he comes out, stop him with the shotgun. Shoot him if you have too, then bring him back to his island."

"How will we find it?" Wiley asked.

Ray had to rearrange some vegetation to reveal the back entrance to Bones' island. "Bones doesn't know I know where his back door is. Once you nab him, just follow this path into the brake. It only goes one way."

Buck and Ray motored around the brake, about a half mile from the duck blind, to the main entrance of Bones' island.

"Bones isn't expecting me but he may figure out who it is and wait until we get there. I'll bet he tries to get out the back way. He's half Caddo Indian and twice as sneaky."

Only a person with a paranoid personality could have created the maze through the cane brake, but Ray knew all the markers. They soon exited the brake and immediately saw Malone's island. A boat, partially hidden by bulrushes, proclaimed their discovery. Ray had silenced the engine before entering the brake, paddling through the maze to the island. Still, there was no sign of Malone. Ray put his finger to his lips as he and Buck stepped from the boat. They proceeded on foot to the center of the tiny island where they found a camouflaged shack. Ray stuck his head into the shack, circling it when he found no one inside.

"Bones has a tree house," he said, pointing.

Buck gazed up into the trees at the covered platform. A filled tow sack hung from the railing. Ray ascended the ladder, up to the tree house, motioning Buck after he'd checked inside.

"He's gone," Ray said, no longer attempting to maintain silence. "Let's hope he didn't leave earlier this morning."

Finding a cooler, they helped themselves to a couple of Bones' beers and waited for Wiley and Raymond. They weren't disappointed. Soon, the sound of an approaching motor broke the silence and five minutes later the motor stopped and Wiley and Raymond appeared in the clearing. They were leading Bones Malone at the point of the shotgun. Malone looked nothing like Buck had imagined. Except for his snowy white hair he was tall, slender and dark. He didn't look very happy as Raymond nudged him with the point of the shotgun.

"This is Buck McDivit," Raymond said. "Emma's nephew. You got something to say?"

"You look like Emma," he said. "She talked a lot about you and I'm sorry she never had a chance to meet you."

"You sure you didn't have something to do with that?" Buck said.

"I loved Emma," Bones said. "I'd never have hurt a hair on her head." Glancing at the beer in Ray's hand, he said, "Mind if I have a drink?"

"If you tell us what you know about Miss Emma's death, you can have anything you want," Ray said.

"I didn't kill her, if that's what you think."

"Then who did?" Wiley asked. When Bones didn't immediately answer, Wiley said, "Give him a beer."

Ray complied with his younger brother's order. As Bones sipped the beer he looked at Wiley, Buck and Raymond. His demeanor was contrite.

Buck finally said, "If you didn't kill Aunt Emma, why did she kick you off the island?"

"Long story."

"We got all day," Raymond said, nudging him with the shotgun.

Bones pointed to a fallen tree. "Mind if I sit down?"

"Take a load off," Wiley said.

After a lengthy pause, he began to talk. "I was AWOL during Korea and hid out here on the lake until after the war. All the locals knew I was here and a few of them kept me supplied with clothes and things. Hell, I'd even run into town on occasion. No one seemed to give a damn."

Bones finished his beer and tossed the can into a pile of brush. Wiley handed him another and said, "Go on."

"I grew up with Jeff Travis. On opposite sides of the track you might say, but he paid me to take him hunting and fishing."

"That asshole is a friend of yours?" Raymond said, backing up a step.

Bones laughed. "Travis is a certified asshole all right but I needed the money. I don't know a soul that really likes the lying cottonmouth." Bones laughed again. "Guess he has all the traits of a good judge."

"Cut to the meat," Wiley said.

"I kept doing things for him after the war and he kept on paying me. Pretty soon I was doing more than just taking him hunting."

"Like what?" Wiley asked.

"Helping him get reelected when he didn't have enough votes. Fabricating evidence against people he didn't like. Things like that."

"You're pretty low, Bones." Raymond said.

"It wasn't just the money. I knew he'd turn me over to Army authorities if I didn't do what he said."

"And when Hogg Nation came along Judge Travis had you appointed state regional archaeologist," Buck said.

"He needed me to cook the required reports."

"But why?" Wiley said. "Buck found a few shards of pottery at the development but there's pottery and arrowheads almost everywhere you look."

"There's more than just a few pottery shards and arrowheads at Nation's development. When his men started digging, they found an entire Caddo Indian village. It's historically significant and there's no way the state of Texas would let the development proceed if they knew about it."

"So what's the deal with Hogg Nation?" Wiley asked.

A gentle breeze swayed the tall cypress trees growing on the island. "In case you haven't noticed, Judge Travis is a control freak. He had Nation by the nuts and he used this advantage to get something he wanted badly."

"Such as," Wiley said.

"Fitzgerald Island. Travis coveted it above any place in the area. He wanted it to train inductees into his Nazi bullshit organization and needed me and Nation to manipulate the plan. He knew Clayton would never go along with throwing Emma out."

"What happened that night on the island?" Buck said.

Bones killed his beer, tossing the empty into the trees. "You know about the Confederate gold ship, the *Mittie Stephens*? Trying to find it has been my passion for years. Earlier this year I did just that."

"That's pure bunk," Raymond said. "And what's it got to do with Miss Emma's death, anyway?"

"Humpback and Deacon knew I'd found it. I had a few too many drinks with them one night and showed them some coins I'd found. I've regretted it ever since."

"Go on," Wiley said.

"They tried to intimidate me into telling them where it is, but stopped short of hurting me because they were afraid Judge Travis would have them shipped back to prison. They followed me, broke into my office and even my room on Fitzgerald Island. I didn't want Travis to know what I was doing either so I dug some holes on the island and planted some artifacts to try and throw them off the trail."

When Malone paused and licked his lips, Wiley popped the top on another beer and handed it to him. After letting him take a drink, Buck said, "You still haven't told us why Aunt Emma kicked you off the island?"

"The mortgage payments," Malone answered. "She gave them to me every month to take to the bank. Thanks to me and the judge, they never got there. When Emma got the foreclosure notice, she realized who was to blame."

"So why did you return to the island that night?" Buck asked.

"My plan worked too well. I had Hump and Deak convinced that the *Mittie* was somewhere on Fitzgerald Island and they decided to throw caution to the wind and make me show them where. They bushwhacked me on the edge of Deception, threatening to kill me if I didn't take them to the wreck. Their plan was to kill me, dump my body in the lake and take the gold."

A gator slid into the nearby ooze, disturbing a crow pecking out the eyes of a dead fish on the bank. When the crow's noisy tantrum finally subsided, Bones continued his story. "There was a storm that night. I planned to escape, knowing they'd never find me if I could make it into the brakes."

"How did Aunt Emma get involved?" Buck asked.

"She shouldn't have been," Malone said. "I was digging a hole, trying to buy a little time, when she appeared in the clearing. She must have followed the light of our lantern until she found us. When she saw me, she went ballistic."

"And you killed her?" Raymond said.

"No way. Deacon John and Humpback were watching me dig from the shadows. When Emma showed up, they hit her on the head with a shovel," he said, tears forming in his eyes. "I felt her pulse and knew she was dead. There was nothing I could do so while they were trying to decide what to do with the body, I made a run for it."

"You may not have slung the shovel but in my way of thinking, you're as responsible as they are," Raymond said, nailing him across the face with the barrel of the shotgun.

CHAPTER THIRTY-FIVE

Wiley reacted immediately, grabbing his father's shoulders and shoving him against a pine tree. "Now wait a minute, Daddy. Deacon John and Humpback killed Miss Emma, not Bones. Give me that shotgun and you back off. Now!"

Raymond lowered his head as Wiley took the gun away from him. Buck and Ray squatted beside Malone's inert body, shaking him and patting his face. "He okay?" Wiley said.

Ray nodded. "Except for a few loose teeth."

With his handkerchief, he wiped blood from Bones Malone's mouth. "You gonna make it?" Wiley asked. Malone's eyes blinked. "Will you tell your story to the proper authorities, just like you told us?"

"No way. The judge would have me castrated and hung up by the thumbs," Bones said.

"I promise that won't happen," Wiley said. "With your testimony, we'll have enough to put Travis away for twenty years to life." Everyone's eyes grew large when Wiley pulled a badge from his shirt pocket. "U.S. Bureau of Alcohol, Tobacco and Firearms. Undercover. The ATF has had this group staked out for almost a year now. You cooperate and I'll personally guarantee we'll go easy on you. Including the AWOL."

Wiley took Bones' slight nod as a yes. Producing a cell phone from his pocket, he dialed a number. "Riley. We got what we need. Arrest Travis and start shutting down his operations on the island. I'll explain when I get back to town."

Bones took a long breath. Then he exhaled, seeming to deflate from loss of stress.

"What about the *Mittie Stephens*?" Buck asked. "You said you found it.

Where is it if not at Nation's development or on Fitzgerald Island?"

Talk of the *Mittie Stephens* brought a spark to Malone's eyes. "You're practically standing on it so I might as well show you," he said.

Buck waited until Wiley nodded his approval before giving Malone a hand off the ground. "This way," Malone said.

They followed Bones along a path through the canebrake. It was obvious he had chopped it with a machete as the cut marks on the cane were still visible. Within five minutes they reached the edge of the lake and what they found was like something out of a treasure-hunter's fantasy. Buck could hardly believe what he saw.

It was the *Mittie Stephens*. Not just a wooden remnant. The entire old sidewheeler lay before them, complete as the day it left port in New Orleans. Part of the boat was charred from the fire that caused the passengers and crew to scuttle it that fateful night. Many of the original timbers had loosened with age, but it was complete in every way. There was but a single difference.

Cypress trees had grown up through cracks in the boat. Now the giant trees skewered the entire frame, covering it from the sky with their towering limbs. Two smoke stacks, just in front of the tiny building from which the pilot steered the craft, remained in place atop the boat. A lifeboat remained behind one of the side wheels. The name, *Mittie Stephens*, was still visible on the outside wall of the side wheel. Sight of the ghost ship left Buck with the creepy sensation that he was viewing a maritime graveyard.

"How did you ever find it?" Ray asked.

"I found a few parts and pieces after the war when I was hiding out. I came on the actual wreckage about a year ago by accident when I was duck hunting. The bird I'd shot dropped into the brake and I cut my way in from the lake trying."

"And you found the *Mittie*?" Buck said.

"Yes. I don't usually drink a lot, but that night I had cause to celebrate. I got drunk as a skunk and shot my mouth off to Humpback and Deacon John."

"And the gold?" Buck asked.

"Not there, except for a few scattered coins. Either someone found the *Mittie* long before me and took the gold, or else there was never any in the first place. It's a significant find, but valuable only in its historic sense."

Long past midday, Wiley, Raymond, and Ray herded Bones Malone into the boat. Cuffed and curtailed, the tall man with snow-white hair seemed resigned to his fate.

"Mind if I ride with Wiley and Malone?" Bucked asked Ray. "I have a few more questions I need answered."

"No problem," Ray said. "Daddy and I will return Ezra's cart and we'll see you at his house after you take care of your business."

When they'd cleared the maze and entered open water of the lake, Buck said, "I wondered what you were doing out the night you rescued me from Humpback and Deacon John. One thing still puzzles me."

"Such as?" Wiley asked.

"Why didn't you arrest them then? You knew they were trying to kill me."

"They're bit players in a bigger show. I couldn't jeopardize the whole operation and I knew you could take care of yourself."

"Thanks," Buck said.

"Oh, and because of the diskette you copied at the coroner's office we know that he was in on the collusion. Like Bones said, Miss Emma didn't commit suicide. She had no water in her lungs and she sustained a critical blow to the head from a blunt instrument. The information on the diskette will corroborate his testimony. The coroner changed his report to reflect suicide rather than murder. Nation and Travis had to do some scrambling and pull some strings when Deacon John and Humpback killed Miss Emma. Otherwise you'd have collected the insurance money and paid off the mortgage.

"And that's why I was the prime suspect in the burning of the marina," Buck said.

"Exactly. We're fairly sure that Humpback and Deacon John set the fire, under Travis' orders of course. I would have told you sooner but I couldn't take the risk and there wasn't a lot we could do with information you obtained illegally. Now we have reason to obtain a search warrant."

"And the money Nation used to buy the island?"

"Funneled straight to him from the New Southern Right. He never intended it as part of his development. Deacon John and Humpback were really working for the judge all the time."

Wiley slowed the boat to traverse a patch of lily pads. A large frog, green as the pads, contrasted with the towering white blossoms topping the tiny floating islands. "What'll happen to Fitzgerald Island?" Buck asked.

"Since it was being used for terrorist activities, the government will confiscate it. The record will show the bank had no part in the scam so when you get your insurance money the government will allow you to reverse the error and pay off the mortgage." Wiley added, "If you want to, that is."

"Of course I do," Buck said. "What about Aunt Emma's will? Randy Rummels must be in on this up to his neck."

"We'll get a search warrant for his files too. I bet we'll find the will there, along with enough info to imprison him or at least get him disbarred."

They soon reached Deception, the throng of summer tourists oblivious of the ensuing government sting. The sheriff's squad car was waiting at the dock, Deputy Sam Goodlake behind the wheel and Sheriff Taylor Wright alongside, Hogg Nation cuffed in the back seat.

"The sheriff isn't in on the conspiracy?"

Wiley shook his head and grinned. "Travis thought so but Sheriff Wright was cooperating with us the whole time. He's the one that came to Austin and tipped us off in the first place. He's a good guy."

Wiley laughed when Buck grunted and said, "You could have fooled me. What'll happen to everyone involved?"

"We're about to break the reign of terror that's plagued this part of Texas since Reconstruction. We'll link Travis to a couple of specific lynchings and church bombings. One thing is certain. He's a goner."

"You okay, McDivit?" Sheriff Wright asked as Deputy Goodlake cuffed Bones Malone and led him to the squad car.

The sheriff came as close to smiling as Buck had seen when he answered, "The best I've felt since arriving in Deception."

As Wiley accompanied the sheriff and his prisoners to the jail, Buck walked away through the throng of milling tourists on the sidewalk, up the bank of the lake toward Lila's shop. He was worried how she would take the news of her Uncle's arrest.

"Buck," she said, grabbing his hand as he walked through the door.

"I'm fine. I guess you've heard about Judge Travis?"

"Ray just left. He told us what happened."

"I'm sorry, Lila. I know he's part of your family."

"He's not blood," she said. "Tell you the truth, he always frightened the hell out of me. Our family won't miss him."

Sara was behind the counter. Her arms were folded and a cold frown replaced her usually ebullient smile. "I'm sorry about Hogg Nation," Buck said. "You were right about him not being a racist."

"Not your fault," Sara said. "It's just a shame to see his dream for Deception die on the vine."

"Maybe it won't," Buck said. "According to Wiley, Nation isn't really part of the conspiracy. The government will likely go easy on him in exchange for his testimony. He'll be back."

Sara's mood lightened considerably after hearing Buck's pronouncement. "Doesn't matter anyway. I got a new boyfriend now and Mr. Hogg Nation can take care of himself."

CHAPTER THIRTY-SIX

Things moved quickly following the arrest of Judge Travis and his two henchmen. The ATF and FBI wasted no time clearing the island of skinheads and collecting pertinent evidence. When they finished, the Government took an assignment of Aunt Emma's life insurance claim and returned the island to Buck. After receiving the insurance claim for the burned marina, he continued his aunt's dream in earnest.

Several days after returning to the island, Brice and Buck sat on the veranda of the lodge at Fitzgerald Island. Brice had taken a short vacation and he and Sally were spending it on the island. The old lodge hummed with activity, five carpenters and painters having arrived at five, two remodeling the lodge and three rebuilding the marina with the help of Ray and Raymond. As Brice and Buck chatted, Pearl appeared from the kitchen.

"Lordy, it's like a beehive in there," she said, glancing over her shoulder. "How long will we have to put up with this, Mr. Buck?"

"Two weeks or more, I imagine."

"Two weeks? I think I may take a vacation."

Pearl gave Brice and Buck a fresh carafe of coffee and returned to the kitchen. Tiger lay sleeping between Buck's legs and Cyclone was curled in the corner, gnawing a bone.

"Thanks for all your help," Buck said. "I appreciate everything you did."

Brice shrugged. "You had it under control all along. You accomplished everything you set out to do except solve the mystery of Bessie McKinney." When he saw Buck's smug smile, he said, "Is there something you haven't told me?"

Buck nodded. "I know what happened to Bessie."

Brice cocked his head, looking for a sign that Buck was pulling his leg. He saw none. "Oh yeah? How's that?"

"Deduction, induction, and the metaphysical."

"Okay, I'll bite" Brice said. "Tell your story."

Buck grinned. "We've had all the pieces of the puzzle since we've been here. I just needed a little prodding, so to speak, to put them together."

"I'm going to prod your head with a baseball bat unless you tell me right now what you think happened to Bessie McKinney. Who killed her?"

"No one killed her," Buck said. "Her death was an accident but the person responsible was her father, Larkin McKinney, and not the young man hung for the deed."

"What accident?" Brice said. "There were no marks to suggest an accident. You told me yourself."

"There was something strange about her body. The searchers used the word petrified to describe the condition of her body. They found her sitting on a fallen tree, her hands in her lap, staring out across the lake as if alive. There were no marks of violence, but her skin was cold and clammy."

"And what does all that mean?"

"She died in the summer of 1872. July, the same month as now. Have you been cold even once since you arrived here?"

Brice shook his head. "What are you getting at?"

"No one killed Bessie. She froze to death."

"Froze to death! Even if her skin was cold and clammy when they found her it doesn't mean she froze to death. Where did you get that idea?"

"Bessie told me," Buck said.

"Bessie!" Brice's face turned red.

Buck held up his palm. "Hear me out. Bessie did speak to us the night we visited Mama Toukee's. The message didn't make sense then. Now it does."

Brice's head bobbed slowly up and down. "Refresh my memory."

"She said 'Mother, father, daughter, death. The answer lies in an icy grave.'"

Sarcasm laced Brice's reply. "And what do you presume that gobbledegook means?"

"I learned from the respective dates on Bessie and Elizabeth McKinney's graves that Elizabeth McKinney wasn't Bessie's birth mother. Elizabeth died in 1858, four months before Bessie was born. Elizabeth wasn't Bessie's mother, nor was Francine Bessie's sister."

"And how do you know that?" Brice asked.

Buck fished in his pocket, removed the brooch he still carried and handed it to Brice. Brice took the antique cameo and studied it carefully, turning it in his hand.

"Read the inscription," Buck said.

"To my loving daughter, E.M.M., 1872."

"Elizabeth McKinney died in 1858, fourteen years before her real mother gave her this brooch. Elizabeth wasn't Bessie's real mother and Bessie knew it."

"Then who was?" Brice asked, still eyeing the brooch.

"Francine," Buck said. "I found Francine's name scratched in the family Bible in blue ink. I believe it's the reason Elizabeth McKinney killed herself and Larkin McKinney drank himself into an early grave."

"How do you know all this?" Brice said.

"The story started making sense when I found out how Bessie died. I spent the night on Fitzgerald Island locked in the basement. The temperature was below forty degrees. I walked, jumped up and down and even drank a couple bottles of wine to keep warm. I never really gave up, but I lapsed into a semi-conscious state. I know this sounds crazy but I had an out-of-body experience. I saw myself sitting on the bench, my hands in my lap, staring at the wall. That's when it occurred to me that Bessie froze to death. When I left the island I realized that even though Bessie had no marks of violence on her body, Darius, the young man hung for her murder, did."

"What marks?" Brice asked.

"According to Wiley, the doctor that examined Darius' body after he was cut down from the tree reported burns on his face and arms. They weren't burns from a flame, but ice burns from carrying Bessie's frozen body from Larkin McKinney's ice-house."

Brice's mouth dropped and he leaned back in his chair. "How did she get trapped in the ice-house?"

"Not trapped, locked in intentionally by her own father, Larkin McKinney."

"But why?"

"Lila mentioned once that her father always threatened to lock her in the ice-house whenever she was bad. He never did, of course, but according to Dorothea Richardson, Lila's grandmother, the threat was a carry-over from Larkin McKinney. He actually used the ice-house to punish his slaves, his servants, and even his daughter."

"I can believe McKinney locked his daughter in the ice-house to punish her but why didn't he let her out before she froze to death?"

"Because he was an alcoholic. He was also, by all accounts, a very cruel man, often using his bullwhip to discipline both servants and family. After his wife's death his alcoholism became chronic and he became a self-destructive recluse. The only respite from his increasing brutality was when he passed out from the alcohol. His condition when Bessie died of hypothermia."

"How do you know that Elizabeth killed herself and Francine was Bessie's mother?" Brice asked.

"Dorothea Richardson, Lila's grandmother, told me about Elizabeth's demise. It's a family secret, a skeleton in the closet, so to speak."

"Then why did she tell you?"

Buck grinned. "Just like her son, the old lady likes an occasional nip of bourbon. We shared a bottle before I went to the island. It loosened her tongue and she told me that Elizabeth, distraught over Larkin's continuing affair with Francine, poisoned herself with a fairly potent mixture of arsenic laced moonshine."

"Where did Francine come from? If she wasn't Larkin's daughter, then who was she?"

Buck grinned again. "Unfortunately, I didn't get the old lady drunk enough to tell me that, although I'm sure she knows very well. I checked the court house, hoping to answer that question for myself."

"And?" Brice said.

"There's no record of Francine being a member of the McKinney family in any of the detailed records of the white community from that period."

"The white community?"

"That's right," Buck said. "No record exists because Francine wasn't white."

"How do you know if Lila's grandmother didn't tell you?"

"Because I found Francine's name on a slave manifest."

Buck took a piece of paper from his wallet and handed it to Brice. "It's a photo-copy of the manifest for a shipment of slaves from New Orleans. The fourth name on the list tells the story. The date on the manifest is 1856, two years before Bessie's birth. The fourth name on the manifest is 'Francine. Late twenties. Mulatto'."

Brice's head continued to bob. "There's no record of Francine in the family or historical records because she was a slave."

"Absolutely," Buck said. "Larkin McKinney bought her right off a river boat from New Orleans at the slave market in Jefferson. She was a mulatto, a person of mixed ancestry. He became immediately enamored with her and took her as his mistress."

"Wasn't that common then? Do you think it was enough to cause Elizabeth McKinney to kill herself?"

"Francine was white as we are. Larkin fell in love with her and wasn't content to visit her only at night. She lived in the mansion with them. He even told visitors and townspeople that she was his daughter and she propagated the story after his death. Larkin's aberrant mental state was prevalent even then. Maybe he thought Francine really was his daughter. Whatever, it eventually caused Elizabeth to take her own life."

Brice was silent, considering the ramifications of what Buck had told him. "So," he finally said, "Larkin McKinney, feeling guilt and despair after his wife's early demise, drank himself into an early grave."

"Yes, but not before creating a hell on earth for those around him. He locked Bessie in the ice-house during a drunken rage for some real or imagined transgression and must have collapsed into a stupor, forgetting what he had done.

"Darius, Bessie's friend, looked for her. When he found her in the ice-house he carried her to the lake in hopes of reviving her in the warm water. Finally, realizing the futility of his plight, he sat her on the fallen tree and waited in a state of shock until the searchers found them."

"And hung him," Brice said.

Buck nodded. "Larkin was a monster but he loved Bessie. He died soon after. He had few, if any, friends. After his death Francine continued running the plantation as she had the last years of his life. The townspeople accepted her, without question, as his daughter. She married Alton Richardson, the returning Civil War hero, and the rest is history."

"I wonder who added Francine's name to the family Bible?" Brice said.

"We may never know," Buck said. "It could have been Clayton or his mother, or anyone in the family before that time."

"Simply amazing," Brice said after hearing the rest of the story.

"And ironic," Buck said. "Clayton Richardson is a bigot, yet he is part black himself. He has a black mistress and a black daughter. And Ray, a young black man with a Ph.D. in black history is the son of the most notorious white racist in recent times in East Texas."

"And he's engaged to marry Clayton's daughter," Buck said. "Like Dorothea Richardson said, there's black and white in all of us."

Later that night Buck paced the veranda, staring at the moon-illuminated lake. Brice had long since gone to bed and Buck was alone as he listened to the frogs and crickets. In the distance an outboard motor melded with the sounds of night. As he peered out the screen door a wide grin quickly replaced his worried frown.

Opening the door he trotted down the wooden steps and walked briskly to the water's edge, stopping a hundred feet from the bank. Outboard motor sounds grew louder as he waited, the front of a small boat finally disappearing around the cypress brake.

When it was gone, bullfrogs took up a throaty chorus across the lake. Above Buck, a single diaphanous cloud passed in front of the moon, momentarily blocking its golden aura. Then, like the last dying embers of a Roman candle the cloud evaporated into a multicolored prism of reflected light and disappeared forever.

THE END

Printed in the United States
29284LVS00003B/70-204

9 781413 759365